DEATH COMES
TO THE
RECTORY

Books by Catherine Lloyd

DEATH COMES TO THE VILLAGE

DEATH COMES TO LONDON

DEATH COMES TO KURLAND HALL

DEATH COMES TO THE FAIR

DEATH COMES TO THE SCHOOL

DEATH COMES TO BATH

DEATH COMES TO THE NURSERY

DEATH COMES TO THE RECTORY

Published by Kensington Publishing Corp.

DEATH COMES TO THE RECTORY

CATHERINE LLOYD

KENSINGTON
PUBLISHING CORP.

www.kensingtonbooks.com

KENSINGTON BOOKS are published by

Kensington Publishing Corp.
119 West 40th Street
New York, NY 10018

All Kensington titles, imprints, and distributed lines are available at special quantity discounts for bulk purchases for sales promotion, premiums, fund-raising, educational, or institutional use. Special book excerpts or customized printings can also be created to fit specific needs. For details, write or phone the office of the Kensington Special Sales Manager: Attn. Special Sales Department. Kensington Publishing Corp, 119 West 40th Street, New York, NY 10018. Phone: 1-800-221-2647.

Library of Congress Card Catalogue Number: 2020944029

The K logo is a trademark of Kensington Publishing Corp.

ISBN-13: 978-1-4967-2325-3
ISBN-10: 1-4967-2325-2
First Kensington Hardcover Edition: February 2021

ISBN-13: 978-1-4967-2327-7 (ebook)
ISBN-10: 1-4967-2327-9 (ebook)

10 9 8 7 6 5 4 3 2 1

Printed in the United States of America

Thank you, Sandra Marine, and Ruth Long for reading this manuscript and offering me your amazing feedback.

As this is the last book in the series, I'd like to thank everyone at Kensington Publishing for giving me the opportunity to write the Kurland St. Mary mysteries. I also offer my gratitude to all the readers who have enjoyed the books over the years.

DEATH COMES
TO THE
RECTORY

Chapter 1

Kurland Hall,
Kurland St. Mary, England, 1826

"Robert, I just had a rather odd letter from my aunt Jane."

Lucy, Lady Kurland, came into her husband's study, the closely cross-written letter still in her hand. It was a cold day in Kurland St. Mary, with sullen gray skies holding the promise of snow. No one had yet ventured out for very good reason.

"Odd?" Robert looked up at her from his position behind his desk, where his two dogs slept quietly at his booted feet. "Your aunt Jane is one of the most upright and starchy people I have ever met. I doubt she even knows the meaning of the word."

"Well, that's just it." Lucy returned her attention to the letter. "She says that Julia will no longer accompany her to Elizabeth's christening and that Julia's engagement to Lord Penzey is at an end."

"Your aunt Jane is going to be Elizabeth's godmother, so why does it matter whether Julia comes or not?" Robert asked. "If Julia ended her engagement, she might not feel like attending a party in the countryside with a bunch of curious relatives."

"But we have already received our invitation to the wedding. Aunt Jane doesn't say whether Julia called it off or whether it was Penzey." Lucy frowned as she turned the letter sideways to read her aunt's crossed scrawl.

"Why does it matter?"

"Because if Julia did it, that will damage her chances of attracting another suitor because she will be considered flighty, and if *he* did it, then I suspect my uncle will be inquiring as to why."

"And taking Penzey to court to air the family dirty linen?" Robert shrugged. "I can't see that happening, can you?"

"It depends how far the marriage contract has progressed, and whether any money has changed hands." Lucy sighed. "Whatever the outcome, I cannot help but worry about my cousin."

Robert rose to his feet and came around the side of his desk to wrap a comforting arm around his wife's shoulders. "My dear girl, you have enough to worry about organizing this christening without taking on a problem that I am fairly certain the Earl and Countess of Harrington can deal with perfectly well by themselves."

"You're probably right," Lucy admitted as she briefly rested her head against her husband's shoulder. "Aunt Jane says Max will be joining them instead."

"Max?" Robert raised an eyebrow. "Now, why on earth would a young man about town allow himself to be roped into a family christening?"

"Because he's in disgrace again?" Lucy consulted the letter. "Apparently, Max is in debt. My uncle is refusing to even discuss settling his obligations and has insisted that Max accompany them to the christening."

Robert sighed. "I'm glad our children are still young."

"I can assure you that neither Ned nor Elizabeth will *ever* behave like this," Lucy said tartly.

Robert chuckled and flicked her cheek with his fingertip. "Don't be so sure, my dear. As you well know, I was quite wild in my younger years. Now, are you ready to accompany me to the rectory? I need to speak to your father about the new pony for Ned, and, I'm fairly certain you will enjoy a comfortable chat with my aunt about all the arrangements for the christening."

"She has offered to put some of our guests up in the rectory, which is very kind of her considering the twins have just come home for the school holidays," Lucy said as she tucked her hand into his elbow and headed toward the stairs. "I can't believe how much Luke and Michael have grown!"

"They are certainly going to be as tall and broad as your father," Robert agreed. "I can't imagine how much food they consume, can you?"

"Having been my father's housekeeper for years before my marriage, and responsible for ordering supplies for all my brothers, I can tell you that Cook will be kept very busy," Lucy replied.

Robert paused at the top of the stairs and looked up toward the nursery above. "Shall we take Elizabeth with us?"

His obvious adoration and devotion to their newly born daughter had taken Lucy somewhat by surprise. She never mentioned it directly, because it was such a pleasure to watch her rather stern husband leap to satisfy Elizabeth's every whim.

She glanced out the window. "As I suspect it is about to snow, I'd rather she stayed in the nursery in case she catches a cold before her christening."

"You are probably right." Robert resumed walking. "It would be a shame to ruin her big day—especially when her godmother is going to be a *countess*."

As Elizabeth had been born earlier than expected and was rather small, Lucy was aware that she was a little overprotective of her daughter. She had delayed the christening until her father had begun to ask some rather pointed questions about his granddaughter remaining a heathen. At three months old, Elizabeth had gained weight and was a charming, sunny child whom everyone said greatly resembled her mother.

It was unusual for Aunt Jane to confide family business to Lucy, and this made her wonder just how difficult things had become in the titled branch of her father's family for her formidable aunt to stoop to explanations and excuses. Max would not enjoy the christening, which would irritate his parents and probably make matters between him and his father even worse.

As Lucy put on her bonnet, stout boots, and warmest coat, she promised herself that whatever happened at the ceremony she would find a way to deal with it. She was known as a remarkably resourceful woman who had faced down murderers and thieves. A mere christening should not trouble her at all.

After greeting his aunt Rose, whose marriage to his wife's father had somewhat complicated their family relationships, Robert retired to the rector's study. His father-in-law was an avid horseman, rider to hounds, and dog breeder, and thus the perfect person to choose a horse for Ned, who at the age of four was itching to ride by himself. It was a skill Robert was unable to teach him without resurrecting too many memories of his horse rolling on top of him at Waterloo.

He'd taught himself to drive a gig again, and could tolerate being in the stables, but the ability to watch over his son while he learned to ride with all its terrifying implications was beyond him. It was a bitter pill to swallow, but he'd had to accept it. Luckily, his staff and his horse-mad father-in-law were more than willing to teach Ned all he needed to know.

The choice of a suitable pony had diverted the rector's attention from his three congregations for at least a month, and Robert was heartily sick of the matter. As a child, he'd scrambled onto the back of any horse he'd been allowed to mount without concern for the horse's disposition, height, or breed. He'd been thrown off a few times, which was entirely his own fault, and perhaps, on reflection, not something he would wish for his son.

"I've found the perfect pony for Ned."

Robert redirected his wandering attention to his father-in-law.

"Ah, finally! I mean, that is excellent news. Is the pony close by?"

"Yes, indeed! In Kurland St. Anne of all places. A retired groom of mine bred him, and I couldn't wish for a better animal." The rector cleared his throat. "As to the matter of payment, I instructed Albert Lawrence to send the bill directly to you. I did not have the necessary funds on me to pay for the transaction when I met with him yesterday."

"That's quite all right." Robert said. "Will the pony be brought over to Kurland Hall, or do we need to fetch it?"

"Albert will bring him over. We thought we should wait until after the christening, then surprise Ned for Christmas."

"An excellent suggestion." Robert nodded. "He's not been happy about Elizabeth's arrival and has been making his feelings known rather too loudly. I suspect rewarding him with a pony right now is the last thing he needs. In fact, I'll keep the little blighter away from Ned for good if his behavior doesn't improve."

The rector chuckled. "I remember Tom being most indignant when his younger brothers and sisters arrived. He kicked the cradle and insisted that it was still his and that no one else should be allowed in there." His smile disappeared. "Alas, poor Tom didn't live long enough to experience the joys and travails of being a father himself, God rest his soul."

"Indeed." Robert allowed a moment of silence to develop between them. Tom, the rector's oldest child, had died in the wars Robert had barely survived. "I know that Lucy still misses him very much."

The rector busied himself pushing a pile of papers to one side on his desk. "The first Mrs. Harrington and I lost two children shortly after their births, but somehow it is far worse to lose an adult son." He looked up at Robert, his gaze clear. "Please do excuse my reminisces. I do not normally choose to dwell on the negative, but this year has been rather trying."

"It must gladden your heart to have the twins home for Christmas, then, sir?" Uncomfortable with his father-in-law's unusual display of emotion, Robert attempted to redirect the conversation into a more positive vein. "They are growing into fine young men."

"Yes, they are." The rector glanced at the stack of papers again. "But, goodness me, their school fees are enormous."

"Perhaps you could find a school closer to home so they don't have to board?" Robert suggested.

"Oh, no, that wouldn't do at all," the rector said firmly. "The Harrington family has *always* gone to Harrow and Eton."

Even though Robert had attended a lesser public school and suffered no harm from it, he declined to get into an argument. His father-in-law was the second son of an earl and held himself and his family to very high standards. Robert doubted the twins would care where they went to school, but it was not his place to interfere. He would leave that to his wife.

Robert bowed. "Well, I am glad that you have found a suitable pony for Ned, and I offer you my thanks. Tell Albert Lawrence to send the bill directly to Mr. Fletcher up at the hall."

"It was a pleasure." The rector stood and gestured to the door. "Shall we go and join the ladies? I'm sure Lucy will want to discuss the final details for the christening. Like most women, she does tend to fuss somewhat."

Robert made no reply to that and instead followed his father-in-law through to the back parlor, where his aunt and wife were ensconced. The twins were nowhere to be seen, as they had gone out to visit their old village friends and would probably not return until dinnertime.

Rose looked up and smiled as they entered the charming parlor.

"Ambrose! Robert! How lovely of you to join us. Would you care for some tea?"

"That would be most welcome." Robert came to sit beside his wife. "And, although I am quite certain Lucy has already offered her thanks for your offer to accommodate some of our guests for the christening, I'd like to add mine."

"Oh, it's no bother." Rose waved away his concerns. "You know I love having guests—the more the merrier."

The rector cleared his throat and directed such a searching gaze at his wife that even Robert noticed. "Are you quite certain, my dear?"

"I am." Rose smiled up at her husband. "And I promise that you won't be put out at all, Ambrose. I have everything in hand."

Robert studied his aunt carefully. She did look a little tired, but with everything that was going on in the rectory—with the twins returning, the preparations for the christening, and the yuletide celebrations—he wasn't surprised. If Lucy had any concerns for his aunt's welfare, he was fairly certain she would share them with him later.

A tap at the door announced the arrival of the kitchen maid with a fresh pot of tea. Robert couldn't help but notice that the rector helped himself to a brandy from the decanter on the sideboard instead. It was unusual for his father-in-law to start drinking so early in the day, and he wondered if his sharp-eyed wife would comment on it.

As the maid left the room, there was a small commotion in the hallway, and a man raised his voice.

"If you please, Maddy, I just want to speak to the rector. I won't take but a moment of his time."

Robert instinctively rose to his feet as the man entered the room and then relaxed as he recognized a familiar face.

"Good morning, Mr. Harper."

The owner of the local mill took off his hat and stared down at his boots.

"Morning, Sir Robert. I don't want to intrude, but I need to have a word with the rector, here."

"What about?" Robert glanced from Mr. Harper to the rector, whose color was rising alarmingly and who appeared to have been struck dumb.

"It's his bills, Sir Robert," Mr. Harper blurted out. "He owes me almost a year's worth. I wouldn't normally ask, but my wife has just given birth to a new baby, and I need the money something rotten."

Robert put a hand on the younger man's shoulder and drew him back toward the door.

"Come with me, Sid, and let's see if we can straighten this out."

After sending Sid Harper up to the hall with a note for Dermot Fletcher, Robert returned to the parlor to find his father-in-law pacing the rug in front of the fire, his hands joined behind his back.

"The cheek of the fellow! How dare he come into my wife's parlor demanding money?"

Robert leaned back against the door and regarded the rector steadily.

"Perhaps he needs to feed his family?"

"I meant to pay him! It's a paltry sum, and it just slipped my mind. He could've waited until the next bill was due and written me a letter, but no, he had to turn up here and insult me."

"He was hardly insulting, sir," Robert said quietly. "In

truth, he was mortally embarrassed to have to raise the matter with you at all."

"Well, so he should be," the rector sniffed. "As I will no longer be a customer of his, I can tell you that."

"But, Father, you have always told me that he is the best miller around," Lucy interjected, her worried gaze going between Robert, Rose, and her father. "And—"

"I did not ask for your opinion on this matter, Daughter." Lucy's father cut across her. "May I suggest you concentrate on managing your own household and leave mine alone?"

He stormed out of the parlor, slamming the door behind him.

Lucy's mouth snapped shut, and Robert instinctively moved toward her.

"Perhaps it is time for us to leave as well, Lucy."

Rose put her hand on his arm. "There is no need for that, my dears. When Ambrose calms down he will realize that no one is holding him at fault here. We all realize that he has many obligations both pastoral and spiritual to occupy his time and can be forgiven for forgetting a tradesman's bill." She paused to resume her seat. "Maybe I should have made sure that the bill was paid on time."

Lucy sniffed, her chin held high. "It is good of you to take the blame for my father, ma'am, but as I know all too well, he has always insisted on controlling the family finances himself."

"I'm sure your father and Rose will sort this matter out in their own way, my love." Robert took hold of Lucy's elbow and gently squeezed. "Perhaps we should be on our way."

He smiled at his aunt. "Thank you for the tea."

Keeping a firm grip on his wife's arm, he headed for the door, only to stop again when it was flung open and another unexpected visitor marched into the parlor.

"There you are, Mama!"

Lucy's fingernails dug into the nap of his coat as Henrietta, Lady Northam, Rose's eldest daughter from her first marriage, swept into the room and gave them all a haughty stare. She was a handsome woman whose expression was often marred by a scowl. She wore a bonnet with such tall feathers that she looked six feet tall, and an elaborate embroidered pelisse that was most unsuitable for the countryside.

"What on earth are you doing here?" Rose asked.

"Am I not welcome?" Henrietta's smile turned glacial. "In my own mother's house?"

"Of course you are," Rose hastened to say. "But one usually writes a letter to let one's mother know of one's intention to visit."

"I did write. Did you not receive it?" Henrietta asked, which was such an obvious falsehood that even Robert noticed. "Perhaps the letter went astray?"

"If you had written to me, I would've told you that this is not a good time to visit." Rose raised her voice slightly. She was generally an even-tempered woman but not one to be bullied in her own home. "We are having a christening for Robert and Lucy's newest child, and the house is full to bursting."

"And you didn't think to invite *me*?" Henrietta pressed a hand to her bosom. "I am quite distraught, Mama."

Lucy cleared her throat. "I *did* send you an invitation, Henrietta, but as I received no reply, I assumed you had a prior engagement."

Henrietta turned her attention toward Lucy. "I didn't receive an invitation, and to be perfectly honest, I doubt you considered sending me one."

As Lucy bristled, it was Robert's turn to speak up. "I can assure you that one was sent, Henrietta. My wife is extremely efficient in such matters. One has to wonder whether your own secretary is half as competent?"

Rose stood, her color heightened. "This is all neither here nor there. We don't have room to accommodate you, Henrietta. If you wish to remain in Kurland St. Mary, then you can stay at the Queen's Head, or return to London and pay me a proper visit in a week or so when we will have more time together."

"I am aghast at your unfeeling nature, Mama. Living here with these people has changed you, and not for the better!" Henrietta produced a lace handkerchief and dabbed extravagantly at her eyes. "I cannot believe you are speaking to me in such a dismissive way after all I've done for you."

Robert raised his eyebrows and glanced at his aunt, who looked stricken. Henrietta had married an awful man and had merrily used her mother as a bank for her expenses and his debts for years.

He dropped Lucy's arm and stepped in between the mother and daughter.

"If you wish to stay the night at Kurland Hall, Cousin, you are most welcome. Then we can send you on your way back to London in the morning, refreshed."

He didn't need to look at his wife to guess she was glaring at him. Lucy had no love for Henrietta and was very protective of Rose. But what else could he do? He couldn't allow his cousin to stay at the Queen's Head, which, although an excellent hostelry, was hardly fit for a female member of the peerage traveling alone.

"Well, thank you for that at least, Robert!" Henrietta appeared to have forgotten she was supposed to be weeping. "It's nice to know that the Kurland family has some standards, unlike my own mother."

"Please, stop . . ." Rose passed an unsteady hand over her face and crumpled to the floor in an apparent swoon.

Henrietta screamed as Lucy and Robert ran forward to help.

"Her smelling salts are in her work basket," Lucy told Robert as she propped her patient up against the chair. "Can you find them?"

Even as Robert delved beneath her embroidery, found the crystal container, and handed it to Lucy, Rose was already coming out of her swoon. She reached out an impulsive hand.

"My goodness! I do apologize. I must have risen too quickly."

"It's all right. Just stay still for a moment before we help you back onto your chair. Robert? Can you call for Rose's maid?" Lucy uncapped the bottle and waved it under Rose's nose until she shuddered. She shot a furious glance back toward Henrietta, who had not moved from the same spot. "Please don't worry, Rose. Sometimes people can say the most upsetting things."

"What's going on?" The rector came back into the parlor, his gaze immediately going to his wife. "Are you well, my dear?"

Robert's attention was diverted from his father-in-law to the man who strolled in behind him. Leaving his wife to deal with Rose and her father, he walked over to Basil, now Lord Northam, who had recently inherited his father's title. He was a dark-haired man with light hazel eyes and a charming smile that belied his truly avaricious nature.

"I didn't realize your husband had accompanied you, Henrietta," Robert said. "I'm sure he is perfectly capable of escorting you back to London without the necessity of you staying the night at Kurland Hall."

Northam smiled at him and murmured. "Kurland, how delightful. I understand you have a new daughter. No wonder you were seeking the charms of London earlier this year while your wife was busy with her home and increasing family."

Robert didn't deign to reply to that deliberately provocative comment. He already knew Northam was the kind of man who thought adultery was common to all men simply because he practiced it so frequently. He'd also been privy to the generous marriage settlement Rose had given Henrietta, which had all been spent. He had no love for those who leeched off people he cared about.

The rector conferred briefly with Rose, who was re-established in her chair, before placing his hand on her shoulder as she faced the room.

"This is not quite how I envisioned sharing my news, but perhaps it is time," Rose began. "Ambrose and I are somewhat surprised, but delighted to announce that I am pregnant."

"What?" Henrietta shrieked loud enough to make Robert wince. "How can that be so? You're both old, and that's . . . *disgusting*, and wrong, and—"

She stopped speaking with a gasp as Northam grabbed her arm. Her husband regarded the rector, his expression icy.

"I do hope you don't expect us to congratulate you on your obvious attempt to control your wife's fortune."

"I, I beg your pardon?" the rector stuttered. "This is God's will, not mine, and we are both thrilled." He patted Rose's shoulder, and she looked up at him. "Aren't we, my dear?"

"Yes," Rose said clearly, her chin held high. "We are."

With a blistering curse, Northam urged his wife toward the door and walked out.

Rose stood with the aid of her husband, and they, too, exited the room, leaving Robert staring at his wife, who was uncharacteristically silent.

"Well, that was somewhat unexpected, wasn't it?" Robert commented.

"I want to go home," Lucy said, her voice trembling.

"As you wish, my dear." Robert was quick to open the door and usher her through it. "I suspect there is much you wish to say to me."

Lucy paced her bedchamber at Kurland Hall, her arms wrapped around her waist. She'd decided not to go straight to the nursery in case her current demeanor unsettled her children, but a quarter of an hour of quiet reflection hadn't helped much. She glanced up as Robert entered the room and sat down at her dressing table.

"You might as well spit it out, my dear," Robert said. "You'll feel so much better."

"I . . . don't exactly know what I want to say," Lucy confessed.

He shrugged. "You can say anything you like. I won't be offended, you know that."

"It never occurred to me that my father and your aunt would . . ." She waved her hand. "*Procreate*."

"I agree. Rose is much younger than my mother, but I thought her childbearing days were over." He frowned. "She was only seventeen when she had her first child, so I suppose it *is* possible."

"Obviously," Lucy said shortly. "No wonder my father is so pleased with himself."

"Your father is definitely acting rather oddly."

Lucy paused her pacing. "Probably because he was afraid to tell me what was going on."

"I don't think it's that," Robert said thoughtfully. "He's not paying his bills, and he was complaining about how much the twins were costing him."

"As he knows he is about to be a father again, then perhaps he is concerned about how he is going to pay for that child." Lucy refused to allow her husband to change the subject. "He'll probably pray for a girl, who will not require expensive schooling."

"Why are you so agitated, Lucy?" Robert regarded her keenly. "It hardly impacts you, or your life."

"I'm not, it's just that . . ." She sighed. "It was something of a shock. I knew they cared about each other, but it never occurred to me that they would be sharing a bed."

"I hope we'll still be doing that when we're in our dotage." Robert's slow smile was almost enough to lighten her mood. "In truth, I'd be devastated if we weren't." He stood up and came toward her. "Come now, I've never taken you for a prude, my dear."

She halfheartedly punched his arm as he gathered her and kissed her soundly until she relaxed against him. Eventually, she looked up into his dark blue eyes.

"Now that you have talked me out of my bad mood, I can go and see the children."

He hesitated. "Ah, perhaps you might care to deal with our guests first?"

"What guests?" Lucy tensed. "Has someone arrived early for the christening?"

"No, it's the Northams." He grimaced. "They turned up at the hall just before we did and told James we had given our permission for them to stay here. I only found out because I encountered Henrietta in your morning room attempting to order tea."

"*What*?" Lucy eased free of his embrace. "Why on earth would they think they would be welcome here after the way they behaved toward Rose and my father?"

"I did make the mistake of inviting Henrietta," Robert reminded her.

"That was before we knew that her odious husband had accompanied her, and before she was shockingly rude to her own mother!" Lucy headed for the door. "Do you want me to tell them to leave? I am more than happy to do so."

"I'm not a coward." He regarded her steadily. "If I'd wanted them gone, I would've attended to the matter myself. But I had a note from my aunt asking me to accommodate them for the night. She has some mistaken belief that when Henrietta calms down they will be able to have a proper conversation."

"But—"

He grimaced and held up his hand. "I know what you're going to say, but as my aunt is in a somewhat delicate condition, I am reluctant to argue with her at this moment."

Lucy regarded him for a frustrated moment and then sighed. "I suppose you are right, but I can assure you that I will not hold my tongue if they say a single bad word about my father or Rose."

"I wouldn't expect anything less from you, my dear." Robert followed her to the door. "Now, I'd better get downstairs before Northam makes himself comfortable in my study with my best brandy."

"The Stanfords are arriving tomorrow for the christening, as are the Harringtons," Lucy reminded him. "Do you think we can persuade the Northams to leave before then?"

"We can only do our best. Andrew dislikes Northam as much as I do, which isn't saying much, as he is persona non grata in many polite circles."

"Aunt Jane won't receive Henrietta in her house," Lucy added as they progressed down the corridor. She'd have to put off her visit to the nursery until she spoke to her housekeeper to arrange to open up another room for the unwelcome guests. "Perhaps we should allow them to stay until Aunt Jane arrives, and let her deal with them."

"That would be something to see." When they reached the landing at the top of the stairs, Robert took Lucy's hand. "Please don't worry. We will be rid of them well before the christening."

"I sincerely hope so," Lucy said. "The last thing Elizabeth needs is an ill-wisher like Northam at the celebration of her baptism."

Chapter 2

Two evenings later, much to Lucy's chagrin, the Northams were still ensconced in her house. Rose hadn't been well and had asked them to allow Henrietta to stay until she was able to speak to her—a request Robert had found impossible to refuse. Lucy had invited Captain Joshua Coles, an old military friend of Robert's who was going to be Elizabeth's godfather to join them for dinner with the Harringtons, the Stanfords, and the Fletchers.

Northam, at least, had decided to excuse himself, but his wife sat there, either oblivious to or unperturbed at the undercurrent of distaste circling her. In truth, having married Northam and constantly defended him from censure, Lucy had come to believe that Henrietta was impervious to such criticism.

Robert said Henrietta had been a self-centered child with her gaze set firmly on marrying into the peerage regardless of the cost. Well, she'd achieved her aim, and Lucy hoped it had been worth it. Sometimes it was hard to believe Rose had produced such an unpleasant, self-centered daughter.

As James and the other footmen removed the last course, Robert caught her eye, and she rose to her feet.

"Shall we leave the gentlemen to their port?" Lucy inquired to the ladies. "There is tea awaiting us, and a warm fire in the drawing room."

She led her friend Sophia Stanford, who was going to be Elizabeth's second godmother; her aunt Jane; Penelope Fletcher; and Henrietta into the drawing room, where the curtains had been closed against the freezing winds. Despite her efforts, in such an old house, it was impossible to keep the draughts from whistling down the chimney or under the cracks of the doors, but her staff did their best.

She settled her aunt in the seat closest to the fire and sat next to Sophia, leaving Henrietta and Penelope to jostle over the remaining couch.

"The house looks very well, Lucy," Aunt Jane said graciously as she poured out the tea. "You are an excellent manager."

"Thank you." Lucy passed the cup to Sophia. "I have a very competent staff."

Penelope gave an audible sniff. She hadn't been up to the hall for at least a week but, as she was usually in alt about something, Lucy hadn't minded the lack of her somewhat critical company.

"It is easy for Lucy to maintain high standards, my lady, when she has such a large staff at her disposal," Penelope said.

Henrietta turned to regard Penelope, who had come out at the same time as her. With her blond beauty, Penelope had been expected to have her pick of her aspiring suitors but had set her cap at Robert and then lost interest in him after his injuries.

"As you chose to marry a country doctor, Penelope, you can hardly expect to have *staff*," Henrietta said, her tone condescending.

"Penelope runs her household very well," Lucy interjected, aware that it was unusual for her to be defending her somewhat prickly friend. "Dr. Fletcher says he doesn't know what he would do without her support."

Aunt Jane nodded. "A fine recommendation from your husband, Mrs. Fletcher."

"Thank you, my lady." Even Penelope was cowed by the haughty stare of Lucy's aunt. She shot a glare at Henrietta instead. "Most couples can only aspire to the respect and devotion Dr. Fletcher has for me."

"Well, if that's all you care about, then you have changed a great deal," Henrietta said tartly. "When I first knew you, all you wanted was a man with a title and the fortune you did not have yourself."

"As did you," Penelope snapped back.

"You mistake your deficiencies for my own." Henrietta smirked. "I had an excellent dowry."

"People do change," Lucy intervened again as the two women stiffened like fighting cocks. "And I, for one, appreciate Penelope's friendship and her support for the concerns of our villagers."

Now Penelope was staring at Lucy as if she were speaking gibberish, but at least she wasn't launching into a full-scale war with Henrietta, who really was the most obnoxious person.

"Thank you, Lucy." Penelope inclined her head a regal inch. "As I let Robert down so badly by not marrying him, I feel it is my duty to help you aspire to my level of competence. I am glad that you both acknowledge and appreciate my efforts."

Lucy tried not to choke on her tea as Penelope smiled serenely at her. Perhaps she should stop trying to defend her companion and let her face Henrietta alone. The two women obviously deserved each other.

She glanced over at her aunt, who looked remarkably tired. Under the guise of returning her cup, Lucy went to speak to her.

"Would you like to retire, ma'am? You have had a very long day of traveling."

"Indeed I have," Aunt Jane agreed. "Perhaps you might accompany me upstairs?"

"Of course." Lucy turned to her friend Sophia, who was obviously enjoying the spectacle of Henrietta and Penelope trying to outdo each other. "I'll return shortly, Sophia. My aunt is ready for bed."

Sophia offered the countess a charming smile. "Good night, my lady."

Aunt Jane paused to speak briefly to Penelope while still managing to completely ignore Henrietta, a skill Lucy could only admire. Sophia leaned in and spoke in her ear. "Don't worry. I'll make sure these two don't start fighting in earnest."

"Thank you," Lucy said fervently.

She escorted her aunt out into the wide hallway, which had once been part of the medieval hall, and up the shallow oak steps to the best guest bedchamber overlooking the rear of the house and the parkland beyond.

Her aunt immediately took a seat and looked out of the diamond-paned window, her expression contemplative.

"Would you like some warm milk or a cup of chamomile tea?" Lucy asked as she took a quick survey of the room to make sure everything was as it should be. Her aunt's maid had already built up the fire and laid the countess's night things out to warm on a chair.

Aunt Jane pressed her fingers to her temple. "The tea would be most welcome."

Lucy nodded, then hesitated. "Is everything all right, Aunt?"

"Apart from Julia ending her betrothal and Max constantly getting himself into debt?" Aunt Jane sighed. "One always hopes one's children will be a credit to the family, but I cannot say that either of mine deserve such an accolade right now."

"I'm certain things will get better," Lucy said cautiously. It was so unlike her aunt to confide in her that Lucy was anxious not to spoil the moment of intimacy. "Max will eventually settle down, as most men do, and Julia will find a man worthy of her."

"Julia will—" Aunt Jane abruptly stopped speaking. "Julia will be going abroad with my cousin Eliza for a few months. She is somewhat low in spirits. We decided that a complete break from society and a new adventure might help her recover in peace."

Lucy sat on the chair opposite her aunt. "It will certainly help her avoid any unkind gossip or misunderstanding of her decision. By the time she returns, society will have moved on to the next scandal, and she will have her pick of all the new men."

"Indeed." Aunt Jane's answering smile was not reassuring. "One can only hope."

"Was it Julia's decision to end the engagement?" Lucy asked daringly.

"It was mutual." Aunt Jane raised her chin. "Now, I have wasted enough of your time. Perhaps you should be getting back to your other guests. Please tell your uncle that I have retired to bed."

Lucy rose hastily to her feet. "I will do so. And I'll ask your maid to bring you up the tea."

She headed for the door, aware that she had perhaps overstepped her bounds and eager not to push the matter any further. All families had secrets, and the Harringtons were obviously no different.

"Lucy?"

She looked over her shoulder. "Yes?"

"Thank you for inviting us to Kurland Hall and for the opportunity to be Elizabeth's godmother."

"I couldn't think of anyone better to guide her than you," Lucy said.

"That is . . . most kind of you."

"Good night, Aunt."

Lucy closed the door and paused on the landing to admire the clearness of the night sky and the hint of a crescent moon visible through the large window. Julia had always been a sensitive child, and Lucy could only imagine how she must be feeling at the very public ending of her betrothal. Having met Lord Penzey on their recent visit to London, Lucy had liked him and thought him very well suited to her soft-spoken cousin.

But as she knew to her own cost, relationships were rarely straightforward, and a public face could conceal the darkest of secrets. She made her way down the stairs to the drawing room and discovered that Henrietta had disappeared, leaving Penelope sitting tall and flushed with victory.

Sophia raised her eyebrows at Lucy. "Henrietta stormed off in something of a huff."

"Only because I bested her," Penelope added. "She loves to criticize others but cannot stand it when confronted with her own failures."

Lucy resumed her seat by the fire. "I can't say I miss her company, so perhaps I should be grateful to you, Penelope."

"Why on earth did you invite her?" Sophia asked.

"After ignoring my invitation to the christening, Henrietta came to ask her mother for something—probably money—and was most put out to discover that Rose wasn't prepared to ignore her responsibilities and give in to her." Lucy poured herself some more tea, grimaced at the lukewarm taste, and got up to ring the bell. "Unfortunately, she and Northam are refusing to leave until they can speak to Rose, which means they will be here for the foreseeable future."

"I'm surprised you didn't ask *her* to be a godmother, Lucy," Penelope said tartly. "Your choices do seem rather random." She stared pointedly at Sophia and then stood and shook out her skirts. "I need to get home. My son much prefers it if I am there to wish him good night."

"How lovely," Sophia said.

Penelope sniffed. "We don't have the money for a full-time nursery staff, which means that with Dr. Fletcher being called out at all hours, I am the only person responsible for my son's care at night."

"As Lady Harrington noted, you are obviously the perfect choice for a doctor's wife," Sophia added, which made Penelope smile for the first time that evening.

"Thank you, Mrs. Stanford, and good night, Lucy." Penelope headed for the door. "Don't get up. I'll find Dr. Fletcher myself."

Sophia stared after Penelope before returning her attention to Lucy.

"Goodness me, is Penelope's nose out of joint because you didn't pick her as a godmother?"

"Yes," Lucy replied baldly. "And, being Penelope, she has made her feelings very clear on the matter." She sighed. "I almost feel as if I am under an obligation to have a third child just to keep her happy."

Sophia chuckled, which was just what Lucy needed and confirmed her decision to include her friend in Elizabeth's life.

"I don't visit Kurland St. Mary as often as I should, because the boys take up so much of my attention and Andrew is often working," Sophia confided. "But I do miss you all."

"But you are happy in London?" Lucy asked.

"Oh, yes." Sophia smiled. "I have the best life I could ever have imagined." She reached out a hand to Lucy. "Aren't we the lucky ones?"

"Indeed," Lucy agreed, and looked up as the men entered the drawing room. Her gaze settled on Robert, and she offered him a welcoming smile.

"Shall I call for more tea?"

"That would be much appreciated." Robert came toward her. He wore his favorite blue coat and brown waistcoat, and his dogs were at his heels. "Where is Henrietta?"

"I was just about to ask the same question."

Both Robert and Lucy turned to find Basil Northam propping up the door frame. His hair was damp, and his boots had tracked mud all through the hall.

Robert and Lucy converged upon him, blocking his view of the rest of the room and its occupants.

"Where is my lovely wife?" Northam drawled, his breath so laced with brandy that Lucy almost recoiled.

"I believe she retired to bed, sir."

Northam continued to stare at her. "If I might venture a comment, you're not making me feel very welcome in your house, dear cousin."

"She has been perfectly polite, considering you were foisted on her during a family celebration," Robert said quietly. "Perhaps you might follow your wife's example and have an early night so that you can leave in the morning."

"You'd like that, wouldn't you?" Northam stuck a wavering finger in Robert's face. "Leaving my wife's mother with all that money and a predatory husband just waiting to fleece her."

"My father doesn't need Rose's money," Lucy said.

"Are you sure about that?" Northam grinned at her. "I've heard differently. Why do you think we came down here? It certainly wasn't for the pleasure of your company, I can assure you of that."

Robert stepped forward, blocking Lucy's view of their obnoxious guest, and shoved him back into the hall.

"You're drunk, and if you say one more word about my wife or my family, I will have you thrown out of my house. Do you understand me?"

Northam staggered backward and held up his hands. "No offense, Kurland. Only having a little joke at my own expense. Good night, my lady."

He turned and headed for the stairs, stumbling over the first step, leaving Lucy and Robert staring after him.

Lucy checked over her shoulder to see that her remaining guests were still unaware of the contretemps and shivered.

"He's such a horrible man. I don't know how Henrietta puts up with him."

"Maybe because she is just as unpleasant?" Robert answered, his watchful gaze still on the figure retreating up the stairs. "I can't wait to be rid of them."

"Neither can I," Lucy agreed. "But I have a terrible suspicion that we are going to be stuck with them for the christening."

And, so it proved, although the Northams at least had the decency to stay out of the church while the ceremony took place. It had started to snow quite heavily, and even though it was a short distance from Kurland Hall to St. Mary's, Robert decided to ferry his guests in the carriage rather than expect them to stumble through two feet of snow in their Sunday best.

Ned was kept well in hand by Aunt Rose, who looked far better than she had for days, and by Dermot Fletcher, who was from a family of ten and well used to dealing with rambunctious boys. The Earl of Harrington was his usual jovial self, but his son, Max, made no effort to be pleasant, which made Robert want to march over and snap at him to smarten up and be respectful.

Alas, Max wasn't under his command, so Robert consoled himself by taking covert glances at his wife, who was dressed in bronze silk, and his daughter, who was almost invisible inside the rather large Kurland christening gown. His friend Joshua, resplendent in his Hussar uniform, strolled over to Robert's side as they awaited the rector who was late.

"Nice crowd you've drawn here, Kurland. Peers of the Realm, even. You did punch above your weight marrying Lady Kurland, didn't you?"

Robert smiled. "Indeed, I did. Thank you for coming down to see me so soon after your return from your regimental duties, and for agreeing to be Elizabeth's godfather."

"I don't think she'll need much protecting while her godmother is a countess," Joshua said. "But I'll do my best." He lowered his voice. "I didn't know you were acquainted with Northam."

"It is not a connection I have ever sought," Robert replied. "Unfortunately, he is married to my cousin, which makes my aunt his mother-in-law."

"Ah, that's a tricky one." Joshua cleared his throat. "You can't pick your family."

"He wasn't invited to the christening, but he turned up anyway." Robert sighed. "I hope he will be on his way tomorrow."

"I should imagine he might want to rusticate for a while longer than that," Joshua murmured. "I understand that Northam's debts have become insurmountable and that he's involved with some rather unscrupulous money lenders who don't take kindly to not being paid."

"Which is exactly why he is here to bother my aunt." Robert stopped speaking, as the door into the vestry opened. The rector emerged looking rather flustered at his lateness but ready to start the ceremony.

Robert glanced up to find his wife beckoning imperiously to him. He and Joshua walked over to stand by her side as the rector began to speak.

"Dearly beloved . . ."

His daughter behaved perfectly. Not even crying when the icy cold water from the ancient font was dribbled on her forehead and she was named Elizabeth Jane Sarah for her deceased grandmothers and her great-aunt. Even though it was very cold outside, sunlight streamed through the stained-glass windows of the church, bathing everything in a waterfall of rich color.

Robert had gained so much in the past ten years that minor annoyances such as the Northams were not worth worrying about. He had a wife he loved, two children, and with the robust help of his doctor much better health than he had ever imagined possible. He was indeed blessed.

As the ceremony ended, some of the more energetic guests, including Lucy's twin brothers Luke and Michael, decided to walk back to the hall, leaving the carriages to the ladies and the elderly. Robert accompanied Lucy so that he could take charge of Ned, who had begun to wriggle like a worm on a hook during the ceremony.

When they reached the hall, Mrs. Bloomfield was waiting for them along with James and the rest of the staff to coo over the baby and welcome the incoming guests. Foley, the retired butler who now lived in a cottage on the estate, was established in a chair close to the fire in the grand hall. Robert paused to speak to him, and Lucy set the baby on his lap.

"You can go up to the nursery, now, Ned." Robert let go of his son's collar. "Nurse Agnes will bring you down to see everyone after you've eaten."

Ned pointed over toward the fireplace. "What about her?"

Robert frowned. "Are you referring to your sister?"

"Yes, why does *she* get to stay?"

"Because it is her christening." Robert took his son's hand and marched him over to the bottom of the stairs. "Now off you go before I decide to come up there with you and tell Nurse not to give you any pudding."

Ned scampered away with alacrity as Robert fought a smile. His son had a similar forthright nature to his own. It was sometimes hard not to laugh at this miniature version of himself and discipline Ned's excesses as Lucy expected.

"Has he gone up?" Lucy had Elizabeth back in her arms.

"Yes, after I threatened him with no pudding." Robert gently stroked his sleeping daughter's cheek with the tip of his finger. "Are you going to take her out of that vast christening gown?"

"Yes. Can you cope with the guests until I come down again?"

"I think I can manage." He winked at her. "Although if the Northams show up I'm sure I have your permission to have them forcibly removed if they attempt to disrupt our happy occasion."

Lucy glanced around the rapidly filling hall. "I haven't seen them today. Mayhap they have already left?"

Robert doubted that, but, aware of his wife's concerns and not willing to disturb her on such a special day, he waved her away with a gruff instruction to not be too long.

He scanned the arriving guests, noting that Max and the earl were arguing quietly under their breaths, that Joshua was making himself known to everyone, and that the rector and Aunt Rose still hadn't arrived. He spotted Dermot Fletcher and beckoned to him.

"Any sign of the Northams?"

"Not to my knowledge, Sir Robert," Dermot said. "They are probably still in bed."

"Typical," Robert snorted. "I will be asking them to leave tomorrow morning, regardless of my aunt Rose's wishes." He nodded at Dermot. "Keep an eye out for them, won't you? I don't want anything spoiling my daughter's special day."

"Yes, sir."

Robert went to speak to Dr. Fletcher and accepted a glass of warm punch from his footman to stave off the chill caused by the constant opening of the front door. A flash of a silk skirt on the landing at the top of the stairs made him look up to see Lucy descending the stairs with Elizabeth in her arms.

When she reached his side, he cleared his throat and announced loudly, "Please join us for a buffet in the dining room to toast our daughter's future happiness."

He led the way with Lucy into the long formal dining room where the staff had set up a feast fit for a king. After seating Lucy at the top table, he returned to fetch her some food and, while she ate, then happily took the sleeping Elizabeth onto his lap. The Northams would be gone tomorrow, his life would go on with his family around him, and at some point his aunt Rose would deliver a new child—a playmate for Elizabeth—into the world.

He glanced around the room again. But where were his aunt and the rector? It was not like them to miss a family occasion. He hoped his aunt was feeling well. As soon as he delivered his short speech, he would ask Dermot to send a note down to the rectory.

"My lady?"

Lucy turned her head to find Betty, her maid, standing behind her chair. The christening guests had started to depart, and only those staying at Kurland Hall or the rectory remained.

"What is it?"

"Lady Northam is asking to speak to you."

Lucy frowned. "Now?"

"She is quite . . . frantic, my lady. It took James and the housekeeper to restrain her from bursting in here and making a scene."

"Then I'll come right away." Lucy glanced over at Robert, who was deep in conversation with her uncle, and decided not to disturb him. She'd taken Elizabeth back to the nursery earlier for her nap. "What on earth is the matter with Lady Northam now?"

She hurried up the stairs behind Betty, aware even as she approached the guest room that Henrietta was still shrieking loud enough to be heard through the door James was guarding.

"We locked her in, my lady." James held up the key. "Thought it was for the best when she shouted at Mrs. Bloomfield."

"Thank you." Lucy took the key and inserted it in the lock. "Stay here, please."

She went in and found her husband's cousin still in her petticoats pacing the room, her hair down her back and her arms crossed around her waist. Her gown and stockings were carelessly flung over the back of a chair close to the fire.

Henrietta spun around as Lucy approached.

"Where is he?"

Lucy pretended to look around the room. "Are you speaking of your husband?"

"Yes!" Henrietta shouted. "I woke up and he was gone! What have you done with him?"

"I have done nothing," Lucy replied in her calmest tone. "Maybe he went out for a ride without telling anyone, or stayed in one of the villages when the storm came on?"

"He would not leave me here without saying where he was going," Henrietta insisted.

"Then I'm sure he'll be back presently." Lucy half turned. "I'll check with the stables to see if they are missing a mount."

"I'll come with you."

Lucy allowed her gaze to take in Henrietta's bedraggled state. "I am more than happy for you to accompany me, but you might give some thought to your appearance before you appear in public."

Henrietta glanced down at herself. "Then ring the bell!"

"I will if you promise not to threaten or abuse any of my household." Lucy held her gaze. "You owe Mrs. Bloomfield an apology."

"One doesn't apologize to staff," Henrietta sneered. "She was impertinent." She glanced around the room. "Where is my coat? And what happened to my boots?"

"I'll speak to Mrs. Bloomfield." Lucy again turned for the door. "Please let James know when you are ready to depart, and he will accompany you downstairs."

Lucy was almost at the bottom of the stairs when the front door opened and her father and Rose came in looking distraught. Robert was exiting the drawing room with Dermot and met Lucy in the hall as the couple approached.

"Is something wrong?" Lucy asked.

"Yes, something terrible has happened." Aunt Rose shuddered. "Lord Northam . . ." She paused, and Lucy's father continued, his face pale.

"Lord Northam is dead. We found him in my study after we returned from the church."

Chapter 3

Robert's first instinct was to reach for his wife's hand. *"Dead?"* he repeated.

"Indeed." The rector nodded. "I went into my study to collect the present I had intended for Elizabeth, and there he was—slumped over my desk. It was quite terrible to see."

"Ambrose came to find me, and I was able to ascertain that Basil really was dead," Rose continued. "At which point we locked the study door and came up here to tell you."

"Which was exactly the right thing to do," Robert nodded. "I am the local magistrate, and I will need to investigate this matter." He turned to Lucy. "Will you excuse me while I accompany your father back to the rectory?"

Lucy glanced up the stairs. "I'd rather come with you before Henrietta appears."

"She is here?"

"Yes, and she's demanding to know where her husband is," Lucy said ominously.

"Then perhaps you can deal with her while I go down to the rectory?" Robert suggested, earning himself a glare.

"Before I knew about this, I offered to walk down to the stables with her to see if Northam had borrowed one of our horses."

"Then why don't you do that, and when I've confirmed what has befallen her husband, I'll send for you both."

Lucy sighed. "As you wish." She checked the stairs again. "Although if you want to avoid meeting her, you really should leave as quickly as possible."

"My gig is still outside." The rector, who had been listening to their conversation, cut in. "Perhaps Rose might stay here, too?"

"I'd be happy to," Rose said. "My daughter might need my support in this time of sorrow."

Robert drew Lucy close and whispered in her ear. "Send Dr. Fletcher down to the rectory as soon as possible. Try to keep the news from the rest of our guests if you can."

"Naturally." Lucy patted his shoulder. "Now go and do your duty, and don't forget to let us know when we can come to the rectory."

He swiftly kissed her cheek, took his hat and driving coat from the footman, and followed his father-in-law out to the gig. It had begun to snow again, and in the first brush of afternoon darkness it was hard to tell the sky from the land. Robert wished he'd had time to change into his warmest clothes, but the matter was too urgent.

It was a short drive back to the rectory, which stood opposite the parish church of St. Mary's that bordered Robert's land. They went in through the kitchen, where the maid was washing pots. The rest of the staff had taken the afternoon off, as the Harringtons were supposed to be at Kurland Hall and there was no need to prepare an evening meal.

"Here we are, Kurland."

The rector produced his key and unlocked the study door. The faint but unmistakable smell of death hit Robert squarely in the face, and he almost balked on the threshold. He'd fought in too many wars to mistake Northam for anything but a corpse. Northam was collapsed over the large mahogany desk. A glass of the rector's best brandy knocked over by his flailing outstretched hand only added to the pungency of the room.

Robert made himself walk over to the desk to observe the body more closely. There was no sign of a weapon, but the hint of blood was unmistakable.

"It appears that he was writing a note." Robert gestured to the quill pen still clasped in Northam's lax right hand.

"I wonder if he came to speak to me, grew impatient when I didn't return from the church, and decided to write to me instead?"

Robert glanced over at his father-in-law, who was still pale, his voice unsteady. He often forgot that most people hadn't experienced violent death in their lives and that they tended to be shocked by it.

"Perhaps it would help if we could sit him up?" Robert suggested.

"Yes, of course." The rector approached the desk and stood ready on the other side of the chair.

As Northam was a heavyset man, it took some effort to ease him back against the chair.

"Ah." Robert examined the ornate dagger sticking out at an obscene angle from Northam's chest. "That would be what killed him."

"That's my letter opener," the rector said shakily. "It was a gift from my brother when he returned from his Grand Tour."

"We'll leave it where it is until Dr. Fletcher gets here. He'll be able to tell us exactly how Northam died."

"Must we?" the rector murmured. "It is quite upsetting." He sat down heavily on one of the chairs, removed his spectacles, and dabbed at his face with his handkerchief. "I cannot imagine what has happened! I thought—when I saw he had collapsed like that—that his heart had failed, or that he'd had a seizure, not that someone had deliberately *stabbed* him. Who would do such a thing?"

There was a knock on the door, and the rector visibly flinched as Robert went to open it.

"Dr. Fletcher, thank you for coming so promptly." Robert pointed at the desk. "It appears that Lord Northam has been murdered."

"Yes, my lady. Lord Northam did come in early this morning to take a horse out."

Lucy turned to Henrietta, who had accompanied her to the stables. It was proving quite difficult to deal with Henrietta when all of Lucy's thoughts were with Robert at the rectory. She almost wished she could blurt out what had happened, but she didn't wish to enrage Henrietta unnecessarily or get her facts wrong.

"Then at least that mystery is solved. Did Lord Northam say where he intended to go, or when he would be back, Joseph?"

"No, my lady. He wasn't one to chat with the grooms." Joseph looked down at his boots. "We were wondering whether to let Sir Robert know that the horse was still out there in all this snow. Mr. Coleman is worried about him."

"I'll tell Sir Robert," Lucy said. "One can only hope that Lord Northam has taken shelter in one of the houses nearby. Please inform me when the horse returns."

"Yes, my lady." Joseph bowed, then hurried back to the warmth of the stables.

"I can't see what else we can do, Henrietta." Lucy looked at Robert's cousin. "One must assume that Northam has the sense not to be out in this weather and that we will see him after the storm abates." She turned toward the path that had been cleared back to the main house, aware that the snow was now falling so heavily that it might soon be obliterated. "We should get back."

Henrietta didn't bother to answer, but she did start walking.

"Do you have any idea whom your husband might have

intended to visit?" Lucy asked as they marched briskly back toward the lights of the hall.

"As he didn't tell me he was leaving, then of course not," Henrietta sniffed.

"He has visited Kurland St. Mary on more than one occasion. It wouldn't be surprising if he had made some acquaintances in the surrounding countryside," Lucy suggested.

"Basil doesn't like country squires and would hardly go out of his way to encourage their pretensions."

"Then perhaps he went to the Queen's Head to arrange your passage on the mail coach back to London?"

"We're not leaving until I've had a word with my mother, who is behaving very unwisely."

Lucy kept her gaze fixed on the approaching house and swallowed all the things she would've liked to have said that were not her business. She'd learned to her cost that Robert's cousin was neither persuadable nor amenable. Her breath was far more useful in ensuring she reached home than in another pointless argument.

And if Northam was indeed dead, there was no point in antagonizing Henrietta when she was about to hear such devastating news. . . .

Robert sent the rector out to keep guard over the study while he stayed to watch Patrick examine Northam's body. When the doctor removed the dagger, he whistled.

"Mr. Harrington might use this as a letter opener, but it was definitely designed as a weapon. Look at the length and sharpness of that blade."

"Sharp enough to kill?" Robert repressed a shudder as Patrick wiped traces of blood off with his handkerchief.

"Obviously." Patrick studied Northam's chest. "From the angle of entry I'd say it was enough to stop his heart, but I'll know more when I examine him properly. Should I take the body down to my house, or do you think Mr.

Harrington would prefer to keep him at the rectory? Northam is a peer of the realm after all."

"It might be better for his wife to see him here before you get to work on him," Robert suggested. "She is somewhat emotional at the best of times."

Patrick grimaced. "So I have observed. She's not going to take this well, is she?"

"I can't think of many people who would rejoice in the murder of their spouse, Patrick," Robert said.

The doctor chuckled. "You'd be surprised." He measured the distance to the door. "Do you think we could manage to get him up those stairs together? I'd rather he didn't stiffen up in the rector's chair."

Patrick's wholehearted familiarity with death and all its horrors was probably a necessary part of his profession, but Robert would never get used to it. Repressing an instinctive desire never to touch another dead body again, he helped Patrick take Northam up to the best guest bedchamber, which was currently occupied by Captain Joshua Coles.

The captain, being up at Kurland Hall, was not around to object to his eviction. The rector instructed the maid to pack up Joshua's belongings and leave them on the landing for his wife to deal with on her return.

They laid the body gently on the bed and stripped him down to his nether garments. After Patrick studied the small entrance wound on Northam's chest, he brought the sheet up to Northam's flaccid chin and arranged his arms at his sides.

"The blade was so fine, there was very little bleeding."

"Is it possible that he fell on it himself?"

"If his heart suddenly stopped, or he had a seizure, I suppose he could have fallen forward and impaled himself on the blade, but it's unlikely. It looks like it was driven in with force and purpose." Patrick straightened and turned back to Robert. "But I'll need to examine him completely before I can fully answer your question. Do you want me to remain here so that I can speak to Lady Northam?"

"If you would." Robert checked that the maid and the rector had descended the stairs. "I'd appreciate it if you don't tell her exactly how he died."

"I'll have to tell her at some point." Patrick frowned. "She deserves to know."

"I agree, but she's not a military man. She'll need time to adjust."

"I have acquired some social skills, Sir Robert." Patrick went to wash his hands in the bowl of water the maid had provided. "I promise to be gentle."

By the time a note came from the rectory, Lucy was beginning to despair of dealing with Henrietta's antics for much longer. Her cousin had spent the last hour marching up and down Lucy's drawing room speculating as to where her husband might be and blaming Lucy for not knowing the answer. Beside Lucy and Rose, only Penelope, who was quite willing to make matters worse, and Sophia, who had tried to help and given up, remained in the room. Luckily, Aunt Jane had not yet put in an appearance, because she would not have tolerated Henrietta's behavior for a second.

James brought the folded note to Lucy and handed it over.

"The carriage will await you in front of the house, my lady."

"Thank you, James." Lucy read Robert's note and looked across at Henrietta. "It appears that Lord Northam might be at the rectory."

"Then we must go there immediately," Henrietta said. "Are you coming, Mama?"

"Yes, of course, my dear." Rose went to her daughter's side but was ignored as Henrietta rushed to reclaim her coat and bonnet from James.

"I'll accompany you, too," Penelope declared. "My husband is already there, and he has the gig without which I cannot get home."

Lucy smiled at her friend. "I'd much prefer it if you stayed here and acted as hostess in my absence, Penelope. You know everyone and can set them at ease."

"Don't you want Sophia to do that for you?" Penelope asked.

"I doubt I could manage as well as you, Penelope." Sophia spoke up. "You are far more . . . *assertive* than I could ever be."

Promising Lucy that she would preside over the teacups, Penelope remained in the drawing room with Sophia.

It took longer to dress in their thick winter clothes than it did to complete the drive down to the rectory. Despite the short distance, Lucy didn't think they would have made it on foot through the banks of snow and onto the country road without the horses.

At the rectory stables, Lucy paused to check that the missing Kurland horse was comfortably established in the Harrington stables—something that would cheer up the head groom and Robert. She had to assume that at some point during the christening ceremony, Basil Northam had turned up at the rectory and gone in to find everyone occupied at the church.

He was known as a man who liked to drink and had gained a considerable amount of weight over the past year or so. Had he been struck down by a seizure or had his heart failed? His anger over his mother-in-law's marriage and pregnancy had certainly been excessive enough to cause him harm.

Lucy made her way slowly into the house where she had grown up, and she spent a moment in the kitchen talking to the very young maid of all work. Even Lucy with her impeccable standards had to admit that Rose kept the house very well. She could find nothing to fault in the way

Rose treated her young stepsons, either. Both Michael and Luke adored her.

Henrietta's piercing scream sent her hurrying toward the back parlor, where Robert, Dr. Fletcher, Rose, and her father were already gathered.

"Lady Northam . . ." Dr. Fletcher said gently. "Please calm yourself. I understand that—"

Henrietta spun around and pointed a shaking finger at Lucy's father.

"You murdered him, didn't you? Of course you did! How could I even doubt it! Now you get everything!"

"With all due respect, Cousin, if Mr. Harrington wanted to murder anyone, the most obvious person would've been you, since you are your mother's direct heir." Robert spoke in his usual blunt way.

"You understand nothing!" Henrietta turned on him. "Where is the local magistrate? I wish to lay charges against Mr. Harrington immediately!"

Robert cast her a harassed glance. "I am the local magistrate."

"Then do your duty!" Henrietta snapped. "I expect you to charge that man with murder!"

"What makes you think Lord Northam was murdered, Henrietta?" Lucy confronted Robert's cousin. "Surely, you should listen to Dr. Fletcher before you start making accusations like that?"

"Well, of course he was! Why else would he have died? He wasn't *old*." Henrietta was quivering with rage. "He came here to have an amicable discussion with the rector and was killed in cold blood!"

"I thought you said you didn't know where your husband was?" Lucy asked.

"I know now," Henrietta retorted. "I should have guessed what had happened immediately!"

Robert glanced over at Dr. Fletcher. "Perhaps you might care to take my cousin upstairs to view the body. You can explain exactly how you think Lord Northam died and let her draw her own conclusions."

"I'll be more than happy to do that." Dr. Fletcher walked over to the door and held it open. "Would you care to accompany me, Lady Northam?"

After Henrietta's departure, Rose sank into a chair. Lucy went to Robert, who drew her over to the window so that they could talk privately.

"What on earth happened to Northam?" Lucy asked.

"He was stabbed in the chest with your father's letter opener."

Lucy stifled a gasp, her gaze instinctively drawn to her father's ashen face as he comforted his wife.

"Is it possible that Northam had some kind of seizure and fell upon the blade as he was about to use it?"

"I asked Dr. Fletcher the same question." Robert's grim expression gentled as he took her hand. "But he can't say for certain until he had examined the body in more detail."

She hated the note of sympathy in his voice as she battled her fear for her father. He might be older than Northam, but he was still a healthy man who enjoyed outdoor pursuits, and he was more than capable of defending himself. If he and Northam had gotten into a fight . . .

She clutched Robert's sleeve. "You can't arrest my father without any evidence, can you?"

He hesitated. "If Henrietta formally accuses him of murder, the law says I must investigate the matter thoroughly and, if necessary, send the guilty party to await trial at the quarterly assizes in Hertford."

She stared up at his inscrutable face. "You . . . *can't*."

"Lucy, I know that this is difficult for you, but—"

"There is no reason for my father to kill Northam! He doesn't need Rose's money, and Henrietta will inherit her share regardless of her mother's second marriage."

"Only if Rose doesn't change her will," Robert said carefully.

"Are you suggesting that she has?"

He took a long time to answer her, reluctance leeching from every word.

"I don't know if you remember this, but about a month ago I took Rose to Bishop Stortford to visit the Harrington solicitor."

"Why didn't he come to her at the rectory?"

"That's an excellent question." He hesitated. "Perhaps she didn't want anyone other than me knowing she had seen the man."

"But why?"

"I don't know, Lucy, but if she did change her will in her husband's favor and Henrietta and her husband somehow got wind of it, then your father might well be in a bit of trouble."

They both turned as Henrietta burst through the door and marched up to Robert. Seeing her husband's body hadn't dissipated her rage but only increased it.

"I told you he had been murdered, and we all know who was responsible, so do your duty, Cousin."

Robert glanced over at his father-in-law, who had risen to his feet and was standing beside his seated wife, one hand on her shoulder as if bracing for the worst.

"With all due respect, Cousin, we do *not* know who is responsible for your husband's death. As the local magistrate, it behooves me to investigate this matter further and decide whether to bring charges."

Henrietta started to interrupt, and he held up his hand.

"I understand that you are upset, but I will not be bullied into committing an innocent man to trial. We do not yet know what transpired at the hour of Northam's death. I will do my best to discover the facts, and only then will I make a determination as to the guilt or innocence of anyone here present."

"How can you be fair when you are married to the daughter of the murderer?" Henrietta asked.

"Because that is the oath I made to my king and country—to allow no man to be above the law and to treat everyone equally." Robert raised an eyebrow, his tone laced with ice. "Do you doubt my integrity?"

"Obviously." She glared at him. "Is there anyone else in this backward place who has the authority to override you?"

He bowed. "You can send to Hertford and speak to the chief justice of the courts. I'm sure he'd be delighted to come down here and deal with the matter for you personally—if he can get through the snow."

"What about the Earl of Harrington? He sits in the House of Lords," Henrietta persisted. "Isn't his word better than yours?"

Lucy laid a hand on Robert's sleeve as he stiffened. "In these parts, Henrietta, my husband's word is considered absolute. Perhaps you might allow him to investigate this matter as he sees fit?"

"I don't trust him." Henrietta took out her handkerchief and dabbed at her cheeks. "I will go to London and alert the authorities of this crime and maybe receive justice."

"I'm sorry to inform you that you are unlikely to get to London in this atrocious weather." Lucy glanced out of the window where the snow was falling steadily. "In truth, it will be difficult enough to get back to Kurland Hall."

"And, as the death occurred here in my jurisdiction, the London authorities would not be willing to investigate it for you," Robert added.

"Then I will return to Kurland Hall, speak to the Earl of Harrington, and ask him to deal with this matter for me," Henrietta announced, and headed for the door.

"Before you rush off . . ." Dr. Fletcher barred her way. "Do you have any wishes as to the disposal of your husband's body, my lady?"

Henrietta hesitated, her impatience at not leaving clear on her face. "What am I supposed to do with it?"

"Does he have a family plot that could receive his remains?" Dr. Fletcher persisted. "Or would you prefer that Mr. Harrington conduct a service here and bury him in Kurland St. Mary's graveyard?"

"As if I would permit my husband's murderer to pray over him," Henrietta snapped.

Aunt Rose stirred as if to speak and then sank back into her chair, her hand to her cheek.

"My lady, we cannot leave him upstairs," Dr. Fletcher said patiently. "Perhaps you might like to speak to our local undertaker, Mr. Snape, and hope he can find a solution to your dilemma?"

"If I must." Henrietta raised her chin. "Now get out of my way so that I can return to Kurland Hall."

Dr. Fletcher moved aside and allowed her to go past him before turning to Robert.

"I've got to return to the hall to pick up my wife. I'll be happy to take Lady Northam back with me."

"Thank you." Robert nodded. "I'd appreciate it."

Before he left, Dr. Fletcher crouched beside Rose's chair and took her hand in his.

"May I suggest that you take yourself off to bed, ma'am? You look worn out and you need your rest."

"I think I will, Dr. Fletcher." Rose stood with the assistance of her husband and doctor. Her usual smile was absent as she spoke to Robert. "I do so apologize for my daughter. She's obviously grieving and doesn't know quite what she is saying."

"It's all right, Aunt Rose." Robert bowed to her. "Don't worry, we'll sort everything out."

Lucy waited until everyone had left before turning to her husband. "Doesn't know what she is saying, indeed. Henrietta behaved appallingly!"

"I agree." Robert sighed. "This is a horrible tangle, though."

Lucy took his hand. "Then we will do what we do best—sort it through and solve the puzzle."

* * *

Lucy paused on the threshold and made herself study the figure on the bed. Northam's usually ruddy complexion had drained away along with his life, and he looked like a waxen image or a carving on a tomb. There were no obvious signs of violence, which made the sight easier to bear.

She walked over to the fireside, where Dr. Fletcher had folded Northam's belongings on the chair. Robert was downstairs attempting to find out when Northam had arrived from the stable hands. The kitchen maid claimed she had been busy upstairs making beds and had not heard a knock at the front door, or seen Lord Northam at all.

In Lucy's view, it made sense that Northam would time his arrival for when the majority of the family was in the church participating in Elizabeth's christening so that he could avoid them. Had he been looking for something specific in the rector's study? If Robert was correct and Rose had changed her will, had her son-in-law been seeking that?

But someone had come into the study and seen him there, and Northam had ended up dead.

Lucy picked up Northam's beautifully tailored coat and searched the pockets, revealing a handful of coins, a handkerchief, and a well-folded note. In his waistcoat she found his gold pocket watch and instinctively wound it up, the ticking sound breaking the unusual silence in the rectory. There was nothing concealed in his breeches, stockings, or boots.

Setting the watch and coins aside for Henrietta, Lucy opened the note.

Meet me at the Rectory, or leave the village, and let this matter rest!

Her breath caught in her throat and she rose to her feet, almost running down the stairs as she sought her husband. "Robert!" He was standing in her father's study frowning at the desk. He spun around as she approached, the letter held out to him.

"What is it?"

He bent his head to read the short script and then looked up at her. "Where did you find this?"

"In Northam's coat pocket."

"It suggests that someone asked him to appear at the rectory this morning." He studied her closely. "What's the matter?"

"That's my father's handwriting," Lucy blurted out. "I would recognize it anywhere."

Chapter 4

Robert went to close the study door and returned to his wife's side. She looked as if she was about to burst into tears, which was most unlike her.

"Steady on, my love. Are you absolutely certain that's his writing?"

"*Yes*, I spent too many years writing up his scientific notes and studies not to know his script." She reclaimed the note and read it through again. "It sounds like Father asked him to come here, which means you have the evidence you need to charge him."

"Not necessarily." Robert strove for an impartial tone. "The note is neither signed nor dated, which is rather important in matters of the law."

"But it *is* his handwriting," Lucy insisted.

"Who else would be able to swear to that in a court of law?" Robert asked.

"Rose, maybe?"

"A wife cannot incriminate her husband."

"But what about a daughter?" Lucy bit her lip. "Are you suggesting I keep my knowledge to myself?"

"I'm suggesting you don't say anything in public until we have had a chance to discuss the note with your father." He held her gaze. "But, if it becomes necessary,

I will expect you to offer your honest opinion on this matter."

"And send my father to gaol for a crime I am certain he didn't commit?"

"Lucy . . ." Robert reached for her hand, but she pulled away from him. "I am honor bound to investigate this matter. I cannot allow my feelings for you, or for your father, to prejudice my decisions."

"I almost wish I hadn't told you about the note, now." Lucy walked over to the window, presenting him with her back.

"We both know you have a strong sense of justice and would not willingly allow a murderer to go free," Robert said gently.

"But he's my father."

Robert walked over and placed his hands on her rigid shoulders. "Which is why we will both do our best in our own unique ways to prove that he didn't murder anyone."

She managed to nod, but he knew she wasn't truly convinced, and he attempted to occupy her thoughts in another direction.

"While you were viewing the body, I cleaned up the brandy and attempted to decipher the note Northam was writing at your father's desk."

As he had hoped, she turned toward him. "What did it say?"

"That he would call back later at a more convenient time, which seems odd as he must have known the rector was fully occupied with the christening and was not able to receive him at all today."

"I did wonder whether Northam deliberately came to the rectory when he knew no one would be here so that he could look for something," Lucy said. "Perhaps he wrote the note to make sure that if anyone saw him entering the house, he had a legitimate reason to be here."

"If your father did write that note to Northam," Robert reminded her. "Northam already had a reason to be at the rectory. That might be why he got up early—so that he could speak to the rector before the christening." Robert hesitated. "Your father was rather late arriving at the church."

"I know." Lucy's smile had gone. "But he is generally unpunctual unless it is an event he cares about, such as the hunt. Rose was late, too. Surely she would have noticed if her husband and her son-in-law were fighting in the study of her house."

"One would certainly think so. Now, do you want to come and talk to your father with me?" Robert asked. "Or would you rather I spoke to him alone and let you go upstairs and check on Rose?"

She turned toward him, her expression uncertain. "I don't want to see him. I couldn't bear . . ." She collected herself and resumed speaking. "I'll ascertain that Rose is resting, and maybe take the opportunity to ask her for her thoughts on this matter."

Robert cupped her chin and kissed her. "That's my girl. I'll meet you back here. At some point we should return home and seek out our other guests. They must be wondering what on earth is going on."

Robert found his father-in-law sitting in the back parlor, a glass of brandy in one hand and his nose in a book. He started when Robert closed the door and looked up.

"Ah! There you are. Have you made any progress in this appalling matter?"

Robert took the seat opposite. "I have some questions I would like to ask you, sir, if I may?"

"Naturally, go ahead." His father-in-law marked his place and set his book down on the seat beside him.

"Did you invite Northam to meet you at the rectory today?"

"Why would I do that?"

Robert offered him the folded note. "Because we found this in Northam's pocket."

The rector put on his spectacles and read the note. His brow furrowed before passing it back to Robert. "That certainly looks like my script, but I do not remember sending such a note to him. Why would I invite him here on such a busy and blessed day to discuss a subject that would only enrage him?"

"That's a very good question, sir," Robert agreed. "But if you didn't send him this note, how did it come to be in Northam's possession?"

"I don't know. But I suspect you are about to tell me that it makes it look as if I lured him here to his death."

As the rector was a very intelligent man, Robert wasn't surprised at his rapid assimilation of the facts.

"It does make you look guilty."

"I suppose the real question is why someone wanted Northam to die in my study so that I would be implicated in his murder."

"Or even easier, sir, did you end up in a fight with Northam and kill him over his wife's inheritance?"

The rector took off his spectacles. "You cannot truly believe that I committed such an atrocity, Kurland, can you?"

"I am merely telling you that to the majority, your decision to murder Northam would seem simple. He threatened your intent to keep money from the children of your second wife's first marriage, and you killed him to keep it."

"But I don't need her money," the rector exclaimed. "I don't even know the contents of her will!"

Robert made a mental note to inquire of his aunt as to whether that was true.

"Anyway, sir, while I investigate this matter I expect you to stay close to home."

"Like a guilty man?"

Robert fixed his father-in-law with a cool stare. "Like a gentleman who promises on his honor to respect my jurisdiction in this matter and would prefer not to be sent to Hertford gaol to await the assizes in the spring." He stood up. "If you can think of anything that would be helpful for me to know about this matter, please don't hesitate to call on me. And if you remember where the note Northam had in his possession might have come from, I'd be delighted to hear about that, too."

When Robert descended the stairs, Lucy was already in the hall putting on her bonnet. She glanced up as he approached, her expression half hopeful and half afraid, which tore at his heartstrings.

"Rose was fast asleep. I didn't want to awaken her."

"An excellent decision." He took his hat from her outstretched hand. "Your father doesn't recall sending a note to Northam asking him to meet him yesterday, but he did acknowledge that it was his handwriting."

She nodded and turned toward the door. "Did he have any notion as to how Northam might have obtained such a thing?"

"Not at this point, but he did promise to think about it." Robert followed her toward the kitchen. "I advised him to stay close to home until this matter is dealt with."

"Do you think he intends to run away?"

"Your father isn't a fool, Lucy," Robert said gently. "He is well aware of the legal peril he is in."

She didn't answer him as they entered the kitchen and she spoke a few words to the maid about her plans to feed the occupants of the rectory.

"I'll make sure the twins and Captain Coles remain at Kurland Hall, Maddy, which will give you much less to do until Cook and the parlor maid return this evening." Lucy smiled at the girl. "I'm sure you will cope admirably, but if anything goes amiss, please send a message up to me."

"Yes, Lady Kurland." Maddy curtsied. "I'll do that. Dr. Fletcher told me to check on Mrs. Harrington regularly and keep a look out for Mr. Snape."

Lucy gave a satisfied nod and went out the door toward the stable yard situated directly behind the house.

Robert caught up with her and directed her attention to the horse in the first stall.

"That must be the one Northam rode in on. The stable boy wasn't sure what time he arrived because he was too busy cleaning the yard for the arrival of the christening party. He noticed the horse was here only after everyone had gone back to Kurland Hall in the afternoon."

"Which means Northam could have arrived at any time after six in the morning, when the grooms are feeding and watering the horses," Lucy said as her father's head groom brought their gig out. "There is a morning service at eight, but Mr. Culpepper usually officiates at that one, whereas Father does High Mass at ten." She pursed her lips. "I would assume that Northam arrived after ten, because my father would not have left his study until the beginning of the service."

It occurred to Robert that his wife's intimate knowledge of the comings and goings of the rectory might prove very valuable when it came to establishing who had been where when Northam was murdered.

"Unless he killed Northam earlier, shut the door, and went about his business as if nothing had happened," Robert couldn't help but add.

"But any one of the rectory staff could have gone into his study to bank up the fire or fill the lamps and found the body," Lucy objected.

"Not if he'd locked the door."

He assisted his wife into the gig and went around the other side to climb up and take the reins. He could only hope that the road back to Kurland Hall was still open, because the snow had not stopped all day. He thanked the groom, clicked to the horse, and they were on their way out onto Church Lane and the country road beyond.

He wished he'd had an opportunity to ask Rose about her visit to the solicitor's office, because he had a sense that her answers might be important in unraveling what was going on. If she had changed her will and disinherited Henrietta, Northam would not have taken it well. Robert could just see him threatening the rector and them coming to blows.

But if Lucy's father had ended up in a fight not of his own making, and had accidentally struck a fatal blow, wouldn't he have admitted it by now? He was a man of the cloth, the son of an earl, and the brother of one, and would be treated with the consideration often offered to those of the landed gentry that was not afforded to the common man.

But he hadn't admitted anything even when Robert had offered him the opportunity to confess, which didn't help matters at all.

Lucy glanced up at her husband's thoughtful expression as he came around to help her out of the gig, which he'd brought to the more sheltered side of the house near the kitchens. She knew him well enough to tell that he was mulling over the events of the day and would not appreciate her offering him a thousand opinions until he'd settled on his own. It was hard holding her tongue when her father's very life was at stake.

"Shall we speak to the guests all together?" Robert broke his silence. "Or would it be better to keep as much as possible to ourselves?"

Lucy faced him. "Has it occurred to you that all our guests were present at the rectory today?"

"What of it?"

"As Northam was murdered there, any one of them could have done it."

"I suppose you are right." He raised an eyebrow. "Which means that when we tell them that Northam is dead, we should watch them all very carefully indeed."

"And not assume that any of them are less capable of murder than my father," Lucy reminded him.

His slight smile vanished. "He is still the prime suspect, Lucy. I don't think there is a jury in the country that wouldn't convict him on what we already know."

She stamped her foot. "You said you would strive to remain balanced in your inquiries!"

"And I will." He held her gaze. "If my methods upset you, perhaps you might consider stepping back and letting me deal with this matter alone?"

"Are you telling me not to interfere?"

"I know you too well to imagine that such a command would be listened to, my dear. I am merely asking you to allow me to investigate this murder as I think fit."

"And keep my nose and opinions out of it," Lucy said flatly.

"As if you would." He kissed her nose. "Now, come into the house. It is far too cold to be arguing on the step."

She went inside because she was starting to shiver, aware that he hadn't promised her anything and hadn't rescinded his demand for her not to involve herself. James got up from the table and came forward to take her bonnet and damp cloak. She thanked him, took off her wet boots, and left them in the scullery.

When they reached the entrance hall, Lucy immediately heard Henrietta's strident tones and looked over at Robert.

"I suspect we might find all our guests gathered together in the drawing room listening to Henrietta. She's probably already told them my father is a murderer."

Robert grimaced. "I had hoped Patrick would persuade her to take a calming sedative and go to bed." He took Lucy's hand. "Perhaps we should hurry along and see if we can repair the damage she has undoubtedly caused."

When they entered, Henrietta was pacing the hearth rug as she spoke, gesticulating wildly as she responded to questions from her enthralled audience. Lucy had been to several plays in London, and Robert's cousin would have made a fine tragic actress. Sitting right in the front was

Lucy's uncle David, the current earl, who was listening attentively.

He turned as they approached and fixed his cold stare on Robert.

"What is this I hear of my brother murdering Lord Northam in cold blood?"

"That is not proven, my lord, but Northam is indeed dead." Robert settled his irate gaze on his cousin. "Perhaps you have said enough, Henrietta. You are obviously overwrought and should retire."

"You will not get rid of me that easily, Robert Kurland!" Henrietta stamped her foot. "I have a right to receive justice, and I do not believe you are willing to provide it for me."

"And you believe the Earl of Harrington will serve you better? When you accuse his only brother of murder?" Robert snapped. "Come now, Cousin. Surely as a member of your family I have both your interests and those of my wife's close to my heart."

"I don't trust you," Henrietta hissed.

"But I do." The earl spoke up. "I have no intention of usurping Sir Robert's authority in this case, Lady Northam, so you should cease your supplications."

Henrietta threw up her hands, glared at them all, and stormed out of the room, discreetly followed by one of the footmen Robert had already asked to keep an eye on her.

"I do apologize." Robert looked at the earl, the Stanfords, Captain Coles, and the Harrington twins. "I was hoping to discuss this matter with you all in a more private manner. I didn't anticipate that my cousin's grief and anger at her misfortune would manifest itself in such a way."

Luke Harrington raised his hand. "She said Father murdered Lord Northam. Is that true?"

Robert turned to the boy. "As I said, Northam is dead, but as no one has confessed to actually killing him, I would not like to speculate."

"Good riddance," the earl said shortly. "I never liked the man."

"Hear, hear," Andrew Stanford murmured.

Luke glanced at his twin, who poked him in the side. "We saw him."

"Saw whom?" Lucy asked. "Lord Northam?"

"Yes. We were out riding, and he crossed our path."

"Where was he going?" Lucy exchanged a startled glance with Robert.

"To the Queen's Head, I think." Luke frowned. "There's not much else on the road he was taking."

"Perhaps he was going for a gallop in the fields?"

"Not if he was going that way," Michael added his voice to his twin's. "Too much snow."

"He was definitely not heading for the rectory?"

"No, or we would've passed him directly on Church Lane. He was turning away from the village, not toward it."

"At what time did you see him?" Robert intervened.

Luke and Michael consulted in low tones. "Around nine? The church bell chimed the hour just as we spotted him."

"Then he wasn't going to the eight o'clock service," Lucy murmured to Robert. "Not that I believe him to be a religious man."

Robert turned to the other guests. "Did any of you see Lord Northam leave the house this morning?"

Sophia raised her hand. "I think I might have seen him. I came down early to let Hunter out, and I heard the outer door bang as I went toward it. There were footsteps in the snow ahead of me and a cloaked figure hurrying toward the stables." She wrinkled her nose. "I'm not exactly sure of the time, but it was not long after eight."

"Which would make sense if the twins saw him around nine," Sophia's husband interjected, his keen lawyerly gaze fixed on Robert. "I assume that as the local magistrate you have to investigate this matter. If I can offer you any assistance, please let me know."

"I appreciate that." Robert bowed to his friend.

"I am more than willing to offer my aid as well," the earl spoke up. "Ambrose is my brother, after all, and I cannot quite see him as a murderer, can you?"

"No, my lord, I cannot," Robert agreed. "But a murder did occur in the rector's study, and it must be dealt with fairly."

Lucy saw all the men in the room nod in agreement and wondered whether she was the only person present who simply wished the whole matter would go away. Her gaze fell on the stricken faces of the twins, and she went over to them as Robert continued speaking to the earl.

"Can we go home, Lucy?" Luke, as always, spoke first. "Father will need us."

"He asked me to keep you here for a while," Lucy said carefully. "He doesn't want you to worry."

"But he's been accused of murder! Lady Northam said he stabbed her husband in the chest."

Lucy held Luke's frightened gaze. "Do you truly believe our father could do such a thing?"

"Not really, but Lady Northam made it sound like he did," Michael said miserably. "If we were at the rectory, we could look for clues and help prove his innocence."

"But you can accomplish that here, too," Lucy suggested. "I can't leave Elizabeth for long, which means that Robert will need your help. In fact, you can help him right now by writing down exactly what happened when you saw Northam this morning."

"I'll do that," Michael volunteered, and rose to his feet. "We really do want to prove Father's innocence."

"I'll tell Robert you are willing to aid him." Lucy smiled at them both. "He will be delighted."

After settling Michael and Luke at her writing desk in her small sitting room at the back of the house, she returned to the drawing room. Her uncle beckoned to her, and she went over to sit with him.

"This is a bad business, Niece, a very bad business indeed." He took her hand and patted it. "Northam was a most unpleasant individual, but murdering him? What on earth could've brought my brother Ambrose to such a point? Lady Northam insinuated that he was determined to steal her mother's fortune and settle in on the twins, but why would he need to do that? My father left him very well provided for."

"I know, Uncle," Lucy agreed. "I don't know a single reason why my father would have killed Basil Northam. He is far too peaceful and spiritual a soul."

"Spiritual? Hardly that." The earl gave an unexpected bark of laughter. "Too indolent, you mean? He never wanted to go in the church, he had his heart set on the military, but my father insisted, and he was right to do so."

He glanced toward the window. "I wish I could go up to London, find my brother an excellent lawyer, and employ a retired Bow Street Runner to investigate this matter for our family, but Kurland will have to do."

"My husband is very conscientious and will solve this murder in his own indomitable way," Lucy reassured the earl. "He has already had considerable practice in doing so." She nodded at Andrew Stanford. "And we do have one of the best barristers in London right here among us."

"Indeed, we do." The earl sat back. "Now you will have to excuse me. I need to go upstairs and tell Jane what has occurred."

"She has not come down since we ate after the christening?" Lucy asked. "Is she feeling well?"

"She was rather tired." The earl grimaced. "This business with Julia has worn her out."

"You don't think the matter can be resolved between them?" Lucy asked tactfully. "Is the engagement truly at an end?"

"It is, and Julia is adamant that she will not change her mind. Penzey was distraught, and she refuses to even see him." He sighed and stood up. "I just pray his family doesn't take us to court over any of it."

Lucy rose with him. "Is Max sleeping as well?"

The earl paused and looked around the room. "I have no idea. We quarreled quite badly earlier at the luncheon, and he stormed off in something of a rage."

Lucy patted his sleeve. "Don't worry, Uncle. I will find out where he is and make sure he comes down for his dinner."

After checking that Robert was aware dinner would be served in an hour, Lucy went to speak to her cook and housekeeper and then went upstairs to knock on Max's door. The snow was still falling, enveloping the house in an unusual silence as if the whole place were holding its breath. The christening day seemed to be lasting forever.

Lucy knocked again and went in to find no sign of her cousin. His bed was made, and his eveningwear sat ready, warming by the fire. She checked the wardrobe and found the clothes he'd worn to the christening. His everyday clothes, heavy coat, and boots were missing. She rang the bell, and Frederick, who was looking after him during his stay at Kurland Hall, came up from the kitchens carrying a kettle of hot water and a fresh towel.

He started when he saw Lucy. "My lady. Is there something amiss?"

She pointed at the bed. "Do you know when Mr. Harrington went out?"

"I thought he was here, my lady." He held up the water. "I haven't seen him since this morning when I helped him get dressed for the christening."

"Did he not come up here to change after lunch?"

"If he did, he didn't call for me." He fidgeted with the towel draped over his arm. "Is everything all right, my lady?"

Lucy smiled at him. "When Mr. Harrington does come in, please tell him dinner will be served at seven."

"I'll do that, my lady." Frederick bowed and went out, leaving her in possession of the room.

Lucy walked over to the window and pushed aside the heavy curtains. If Max was out in the snow, she hoped he'd found shelter. He wasn't familiar with Kurland St. Mary and its outlying villages and could easily have gotten lost. But why had he gone out in the first place? Surely even a man who lived mainly in London would know not to wander off in a snowstorm.

But he'd been miserably unhappy since he'd arrived, and the crackling tension between him and his father all too obvious. She could only hope he'd escaped to the Queen's Head and was currently drowning his sorrows in ale with the village locals. She paused, her gaze drawn to the fire, which needed building up.

Reluctant to call Frederick back up the stairs, she knelt on the hearth rug and attended to the matter herself. A curl of half-burned parchment caught her eye, and she picked it out of the grate and smoothed it with her fingers. It appeared to be some kind of IOU or gambling debt. The section that hadn't caught fire revealed half of Max's scrawled hereditary title, Viscount Cruise, and the letters *Nor*.

Lucy sat back on her heels. Was it possible Max had owed *Northam* money? Both her uncle and aunt had indicated that Max was seriously in debt and resented being held accountable for it. What might Max have felt being forced to come to Kurland St. Mary only to discover one of his creditors staying in the same house?

Had he been angry?

And why had he burned the IOU? Had he found a way to finally settle his debt?

Chapter 5

Dinner was a somewhat subdued affair. Lucy's aunt Jane stayed in her room, there was still no sign of Max, and even the twins behaved themselves. Lucy longed to spend some time in the nursery with her children, but she also had matters to discuss with her husband that would have to wait until her guests had been attended to.

Luckily, Andrew and Sophia Stanford and Captain Coles were willing to carry the brunt of the conversation between them, which meant Lucy had merely to reply and smile at various intervals while her mind seethed with possibilities. Robert, too, seemed distracted, which wasn't surprising considering the impossible situation he had been placed in.

"Where is Max?" Robert suddenly asked.

"I'm not quite sure." The earl looked over at Lucy, a question in his gaze. "Did you find him, Niece?"

"Unfortunately not." Lucy met Robert's gaze. "It appears that Max might have gone out at some point."

"In this weather?" Robert frowned. "That is hardly advisable."

"I quite agree," the earl said, nodding. "I do hope the young fool has found shelter."

"I'm sure he has, Uncle." Lucy tried to sound reassuring. "If he rode out over Kurland land, there are plenty of cottages and farms nearby, and three local villages to find shelter in."

The earl threw his napkin down on the table. "That boy is determined to cause his mother unnecessary anxiety. I'm not going to mention this to my wife, who is already tired enough, and I would ask you all to do the same."

Robert inclined his head. "With all due respect, sir, wouldn't your countess rather know that her son is currently out in a snowstorm?"

"If the need arises for her to know, I can assure you that I will tell her myself." The earl rose to his feet, his expression icy. "Good evening, Kurland." He turned to Lucy. "Please inform me when my son returns, however late that might be."

Lucy nodded as her uncle exited the room, shutting the door behind him with a definite bang.

"I believe the earl and his son were at odds today, which perhaps explains his current disposition and concerns," Lucy said to no one in particular. "I wonder if I should send a message down to the stables to check whether Max took one of the horses."

"I'll do that." Robert set his glass back on the table. "I can tell you one thing, my dear, I do wish our guests would be a little bit more considerate of my livestock."

"I can't help but agree with you," Lucy said. "No horse or rider should be out in this storm."

Captain Coles cleared his throat. "If you like, Kurland, I'll pop down to the stables and deliver your message myself." He tapped his thigh. "I'm not used to being cooped up all day and could do with some exercise."

"There should still be a clear path to the stables," Robert said. "If you wish to brave the elements, then go ahead. Personally, after years of traipsing through inhospitable mountain ranges in all kinds of inclement weather with the regiment, I have grown rather fond of my own fireside."

Captain Coles grinned through the candlelight. "I can't blame you for that when the company in your house is so delightful."

"Delightful?" Robert's bark of laughter almost made Lucy smile. "You are stuck here in the middle of an investigation into a murder, my friend. I can assure you that things are generally much more sedate than this!"

After the guests had finally dispersed to their various bedchambers and Coles had set off for the stables, Robert found a quiet moment to retreat to his study, take a glass of brandy, and attempt to write up his notes about the murder of Lord Northam. The day appeared to be endless. He wasn't entirely surprised when his wife peeped in through the door, and he beckoned her inside.

She still wore the new bronze silk dress she'd acquired for the christening, and her hair was in elaborate ringlets very different to the braided coronet she usually favored. Despite Elizabeth's rushed arrival, she looked remarkably well, which pleased him greatly.

"Am I interrupting you?" She approached his desk, the silk of her skirts rustling gently as she moved.

"I've just about finished." He set his pen to one side. "Is there something you want to tell me?"

In reply, she handed over a badly scorched piece of parchment. "I found this in Max's room when I was making up the fire."

He put on his spectacles to better read the damaged script, and frowned. "I assume this is an IOU. Is Cruise Max's courtesy title?"

"Yes, and the man he apparently owed money to has a name that starts with Nor."

"You think that's Northam?"

"Why not?" She raised her eyebrows. "We know that he is a gambler, and we also know that Max is in debt."

"We can't make that assumption until we talk to Max."

Robert sat back. "Where on earth do you think he's gone?"

"Perhaps his flight has something to do with Northam's death."

"That is a remarkably long leap to make, even for you, Lucy."

"But don't you think it's peculiar?" she challenged him. "That Max is nowhere to be found and Northam is dead?"

Robert shrugged. "As you said, Max has been fighting with his father all day. His disappearance is far more likely to be tied to that than Northam's death. If he's been missing since after the christening, he might not even know that Northam *is* dead."

"But we do know that he came back here, changed his clothes, and took the time to attempt to burn this IOU."

"Perhaps Northam decided to forgive him the debt, or Max found a way to pay it off?" Robert suggested.

"I can't see Northam forgiving Max anything, can you? My uncle is extremely wealthy. In the end, as a gentleman, he would probably feel obliged to pay Max's debts of honor. Northam would know this."

"Then maybe Max begged his father to give him the money to pay off Northam while they were here, and thus cleared the debt? That would certainly explain why the two of them were barely on speaking terms."

Lucy sighed. "You are determined to be difficult about this, aren't you?"

"Not at all. I am merely exploring one of several hundred reasons for what might have happened, none of which involve your cousin Max murdering Lord Northam."

"I never suggested Max murdered him!" Lucy protested. "Although he was at the church for the christening, and thus could have seen Northam. He did have a very good reason for wanting Northam gone, because he was in debt to him and in trouble with his father."

Well used to his wife's ability to construct theories from the flimsiest of facts, and aware that quite often she was right, Robert held his tongue.

"I suppose you are going to tell me I am being fanciful again," Lucy said.

"No, but I would urge you to remember that the simplest explanation is usually the correct one. Do you really wish your cousin Max to be guilty of murder?"

"No! I'd rather a complete stranger had found his way into my father's study and killed Northam for no reason at all."

Robert had to smile at her acid tone. "Unfortunately, there are many people who could have murdered Northam. The rectory was a very busy place this morning, what with the church services and the christening. Half the village was in the churchyard, and all the local gentry and our houseguests at least attended the christening. As we don't know exactly what time Northam died, it could be anyone." He glanced down at his notes, which were more a series of frustrating questions than anything useful. "And we haven't even discussed why Northam apparently visited the Queen's Head."

"We should go there tomorrow," Lucy said with a decisive nod.

"*We* will do no such thing. I will go and you will stay here in the warmth and care for our guests."

To his surprise, for once she didn't argue her case.

"I told the twins you would welcome their assistance in this matter."

"What an excellent idea! They know all the locals and will probably learn far more than I ever will because of my position."

"They are very worried about Father."

"Understandably so." Robert paused. "I promise I will do my best to reassure them and provide plenty of opportunities for them to rush about the estate helping gather information."

She smiled at him, and despite his worries he had to smile back.

"We will get through this, my love."

"I know." She came to stand beside him. "I have a great deal of faith in you, Robert. I just cannot see my father as a murderer."

He reached for her hand and brought it to his lips to kiss. "Just remember, we're a long way from me hauling your father off to Hertford to stand trial. In truth, we have barely begun the investigation."

The next morning, the snow had finally stopped, leaving the house and estate cocooned within ten-foot-high drifts, treacherous-covered ditches, and almost impassable roads. The daily mail coach from London was not expected to reach the Queen's Head any time soon if at all, and the Kurland staff were busy attempting to clear pathways between the house, the stables, and down the drive to the county road.

After visiting his children in the nursery and firmly refusing Ned's urgent pleas to be allowed to accompany him, Robert went down into the hall to put on his thickest coat and warmest hat. Joshua emerged from the breakfast room and stopped to speak to him.

"Where are you off to this fine morning, Kurland?"

"I'm visiting the Queen's Head in the village." Robert wound his scarf around his throat several times.

"Would you like some company?" Joshua offered. "After my time in India I'm rather enjoying all this snow."

"I think I'd prefer the heat, but you are more than welcome to join me."

If Max was at the Queen's Head as Lucy suspected, having Joshua with him might make it easier to persuade the young man to return to the hall.

Within a quarter of an hour they were in the gig with the oldest and surest of the Kurland horses carefully pick-

ing its way down the closely packed snow on the drive.
Joshua had taken the reins at Robert's request and seemed
in no hurry to press the horse or demand more than was
safe in such a hostile environment. The journey to the
Queen's Head was normally accomplished in less than ten
minutes but took them three times as long in the snow.

The stable yard was unusually quiet with neither the
mail coach nor the local farmers coming into the village
for the market or to deliver supplies to the shops. Mr.
Jarvis came out to greet Robert.

"Good morning, Sir Robert."

"Good morning, Mr. Jarvis." Robert gestured at the entrance to the inn. "May we come inside?"

"You're right welcome, sir. There is some mail for you
from the Friday coach, which was the last one to get
through. Is that what you're after?"

Robert stepped over the threshold and embraced the
rush of heat and the scent of wood burning in the vast fireplace of the taproom.

"I'll definitely take the mail off your hands, but I did
have another matter I wished to discuss with you."

"Then come on through to the kitchen, sir, where Mrs.
Jarvis can make you some mulled wine and a bite to eat."

Robert took off his hat and, ducking his head to avoid
the beams, went through to the back of the building, the
oldest part, and into the large kitchen, where he was
greeted with a shriek from the landlady.

"Sir Robert! How lovely to see you! We walked up to
the church yesterday to take a peek at the christening, but
the weather being what it was, we didn't get to see much
of your precious darling daughter, although Lady Kurland
looked very well, didn't she, Mr. Jarvis?"

"Yes, my dear, she certainly did."

Robert smiled. "Good morning, Mrs. Jarvis. May I introduce my friend Captain Coles?"

"Ma'am." Joshua doffed his hat. "A pleasure."

Mrs. Jarvis patted her hair and fluttered her eyelashes. "You're a lovely one, aren't you? Are you an army man like the major here?"

"Yes, indeed. We served in the same regiment."

"I believe I saw you arrive on the coach the other day," Mrs. Jarvis said.

"Yes, I came down for the christening. I'm Miss Elizabeth's godfather."

Before Mrs. Jarvis could ask any more questions, Robert cleared his throat.

"Might I ask if you had a Mr. Max Harrington staying with you last night?"

Mr. Jarvis frowned. "What did he look like, sir?"

"Dark hair, brown eyes, about my height, and in his early twenties." Robert supplied the details.

"I think he did come in for a tankard of ale or two, but he left at some point. I did warn him not to go out in the storm, but he wasn't willing to listen to me, sir."

"Right top lofty he was," Mrs. Jarvis added. "And downright rude to my staff."

"Sounds just like Max," Joshua murmured into Robert's ear.

It was Robert's turn to frown. "How late did he leave?"

"He was gone before I closed up early, so maybe between eight and nine o'clock?" Mr. Jarvis looked at his wife for confirmation and received a nod.

"Aye."

"Did he speak to anyone?"

"I saw him with that Lord Northam," Mrs. Jarvis said. "But maybe that was the night before?" She grimaced. "I kept out of his lordship's way as he tended to be a bit over familiar."

"It definitely could not have been Northam last night," Robert said firmly. "He was not available." He returned his attention to Mrs. Jarvis. "Did you see a lot of Lord Northam here?"

"Unfortunately, yes. Now, I know he is connected to

your family, Sir Robert, but I can't let any of my maids near him. He is also rude and inconsiderate to the ostlers and stable hands."

Mrs. Jarvis's refreshing frankness was sometimes a trial for Robert, but on this occasion he was more than happy to encourage her to keep talking.

"I can only apologize for his behavior. Did he meet anyone else here besides Mr. Harrington?"

"Indeed, there is a gentleman staying with us who came down on the mail coach seeking Lord Northam. I sent one of the post boys up to Kurland Hall with a message, and Lord Northam came down to see Mr. Penarth." Mr. Jarvis pursed his lips. "They were shouting so loudly the whole inn could hear them. Mr. Penarth had booked to leave on the mail coach today and was most annoyed when it didn't turn up."

"Then he is still in residence?" Robert thanked Mrs. Jarvis for the cup of spiced mulled wine she handed him.

"I assume so, seeing as he hasn't paid his bill yet or found anyone willing to take him back to London."

"Would you inquire as to whether he might speak with me on a matter of some urgency?" Robert asked.

"I'll go and knock on his door right now, sir."

Mr. Jarvis departed on his errand, and Robert sipped the excellent wine as Joshua flirted amiably with the innkeeper's wife.

Mr. Jarvis returned and nodded at Robert. "He'll be down in a moment, sir. Would you care to go through to the private parlor at the rear of the house to receive him? It's nice and warm in there."

Leaving Joshua in the kitchen, Robert took his wine with him through to the private parlor and stood in front of the roaring fire considering what he had learned. His concern for Max had only increased. Where was the dratted boy, and how was he mixed up with Northam? How was he going to return to the hall and admit to the earl and countess that he had no idea where their son and heir had gone? If he'd sent someone down to the Queen's Head yesterday evening to check whether Max was there, this crisis would have been averted.

The fact that Northam and Max had been seen together the night before the christening was rather unexpected. Perhaps Lucy had been right that the name on the IOU she'd found was Northam's. Max had returned to the hall, accompanied his family to the church for the christening the next morning, and had ample opportunity to sneak off to confront Northam and kill him.

The door creaked open and a diminutive well-dressed man with a rotund build and a balding head came into the room. He wore the sober clothing of a London business-man and carried a silver-topped cane.

"Sir Robert Kurland? I believe you wished to speak to me on a private matter concerning Lord Northam?"

"Indeed, yes. Thank you for agreeing to see me." Robert bowed. "I understand you met with Lord Northam yesterday morning. Would you be prepared to divulge the reason for your meeting?"

Mr. Penarth raised an eyebrow. "It was a private matter, sir. I cannot see quite what it has to do with you."

"Lord Northam is married to my cousin, thus the matter does involve my family rather intimately," Robert said. "I am merely attempting to clarify some facts."

Mr. Penarth's amiable expression disappeared. "Lady Northam is well aware of the reason for my visits to her husband. If you wish to inquire as to what those reasons are, I suggest you apply to her if she is your kin. I don't take kindly to threats, sir."

Not being a man good at prevarication and unnecessary flummery, Robert set his jaw.

"May I be frank with you, Mr. Penarth? I am the local magistrate and I am investigating a matter pertaining to Lord Northam. This matter requires me to demand an-swers to somewhat impertinent questions, which might later be important in a court of law."

"Has Lord Northam dirtied his financial reputation in this small village as well as the whole of London?" Mr. Penarth shook his head. "I can't say I'm surprised." He gestured at the two chairs beside the fire. "Shall we sit down and see if we can aid each other and resolve this matter amicably?"

"Thank you." Robert took the seat. "Did you come down from London, Mr. Penarth?"

"Indeed I did, sir." Mr. Penarth nodded. "I reside in Bethnal Green and I work in the city of London as a financier."

"How did you come to know Lord Northam?"

"He approached my consortium about a financial matter—a loan, so to speak, that he was having problems sourcing elsewhere."

"From what I know of him I can quite understand why his bank was reluctant to lend him a penny," Robert murmured. "But, please continue."

"We tend to deal with high-risk clients, Sir Robert, and after discussing the matter with my partners, we agreed to offer Lord Northam a loan."

"Presumably with very high interest rates. I assume he accepted your offer?"

"He did, with a promise that we would be paid back handsomely well within the specified time limits." Mr. Penarth sat back, his fingers laced together on his protruding stomach. "The first two repayments came in on time, and then there was nothing more. As per the terms of our agreement, our company accountant wrote to Lord Northam requesting immediate settlement of the entire debt. The letter was returned unopened. We added additional interest for each late day, but nothing worked."

"Did you take him to court?"

"We tend not to bother with such institutions, sir, seeing as they tend to favor the rich and aristocratic at the expense of the poor man in the street." Mr. Penarth paused. "We have other methods of extracting payment."

"Violent ones?"

Mr. Penarth met Robert's gaze, his bland expression belied by the coldness in his eyes. "We do not condone violence, sir, but occasionally things do boil over when the bailiffs arrive to confiscate a defaulter's belongings."

"Did Lord Northam eventually cooperate with you?"

"No, sir, which is why I came down to see him in person. We had a man watching his house. I was alerted to his sudden desire to leave town and followed him here." He paused. "It seems that the scheme Lord Northam borrowed money to finance was rather more complicated than he'd originally let on."

"In what way?" Robert asked.

"It involved the arrival of a cargo from overseas that Lord Northam had persuaded several of his peers to invest in—except neither the ship nor the cargo actually existed."

"Good Lord." Robert tapped his fingers against the arm of his chair. "What in heaven's name was Northam thinking?"

"From what I can gather, sir, he simply intended to make a profit. He spent the money we gave him on registering fake shareholders and ship owners to create the impression that the cargo was very valuable and that any sensible investor would want to be involved in the deal."

"But where did all the money go?" Robert wondered. "And how did Northam think he would make a profit from such an egregious scheme?"

"As far as we can tell, having just acquired the books, he did very well out of it—well enough to pay us back in full and take a tidy profit. Except he didn't pay us back all that we were owed." Mr. Penarth grimaced. "Now that the ship is supposed to have docked and the cargo sold, his investors are probably aware that they have been fleeced, too."

"Which is why I assume Northam decided to leave London."

"Exactly, Sir Robert. May I ask if you purchased shares in this endeavor?"

"No. I wouldn't trust Northam to give me advice on the cut of my coat let alone my finances." Robert shuddered. "However, I would be very interested in learning the names of the shareholders."

"I am more than willing to send you a copy of the list when I return to London." Mr. Penarth hesitated. "Did Lord Northam attempt a similar extortion scheme here? Is that why you are asking all these questions? Because if so, despite my reservations about the law, I am more than happy to be called as a witness for the prosecution."

After considering Mr. Penarth and weighing his options, Robert answered frankly.

"Lord Northam is dead."

Mr. Penarth's hand closed around his cane, but other than that he exhibited no sign of shock at Robert's blunt disclosure.

"Are you at liberty to disclose how he died?"

Robert eyed him keenly. "Why do you ask?"

"Because when a gentleman such as Lord Northam is struck down at a relatively young age in the middle of a financial scandal, one cannot help but wonder why." Mr. Penarth paused. "Did he kill himself?"

"My doctor believes he was murdered."

"By whom?"

"That is unclear."

Mr. Penarth smiled. "With a man as disliked as Northam, I suppose the possibilities are endless." He reached into his coat pocket. "I should give you my card. It has both my business and home addresses on it. I will send you the information on the shareholders when I return to London."

Robert took the engraved card and turned it over in his fingers. "One last question, Mr. Penarth. When you spoke to Lord Northam yesterday, how did you leave things with him?"

"I told him to repay the money he owed me. He implied that he would soon be richer than Croesus and that if I left him alone, he would certainly consider paying me back at some point." Mr. Penarth's mouth twisted. "I gave him a date on which I would require full payment with interest, and he told me to go to the devil."

"Did he elaborate on how he intended to acquire this mythical fortune to pay you back?" Robert asked.

"Family money, I believe. His wife is from a wealthy industrial family, and she had expectations to inherit very soon." Mr. Penarth paused. "Forgive me, you said you were connected to Lady Northam by marriage. Do you by chance know of this fortune he mentioned?"

"I know of 'a' fortune, but not one Lord Northam has any claim to."

"Then he was lying. I thought as much, which is why I insisted on full payment by the end of the year." Mr. Penarth slowly stood up. "Ah, well. I'll have to take my chances with all his other creditors after his estate goes through probate. Not that I should imagine there will be any money there for the taking."

"I tend to agree with you. Lord Northam has been living on borrowed money and borrowed time for decades." Robert rose, too, tucking the business card in his waistcoat pocket. "I doubt you will be returning to London today, Mr. Penarth. The county road is currently impassable."

"So I understand. I sent one of the ostlers out this morning looking for available transport, but no one is prepared to risk such a journey in this weather." Mr. Penarth shivered. "I don't enjoy the countryside, Sir Robert. Town born and town bred, and that's all there is to it."

"If there is no further snow tonight, you will probably be able to travel tomorrow," Robert advised him. "I'm sure Mr. and Mrs. Jarvis will take good care of you until then."

"They have been most kind." Mr. Penarth turned to the door. "Was Lady Northam present when her husband was killed?"

"No, from what we can ascertain, Lord Northam died shortly after he visited you here yesterday. He was at the rectory."

"Is the rector under suspicion?" Mr. Penarth asked.

"Mr. Harrington is certainly one of the people who have been asked to account for their whereabouts," Robert said diplomatically.

"Harrington?" Mr. Penarth looked back over his shoulder after opening the door. "I believe one of the names on Lord Northam's list was a Harrington." His shrewd eyes narrowed. "What a remarkable coincidence."

Chapter 6

Deciding that as he'd already reached the village he might as well call in on the rectory, Robert directed Joshua to drive down the high street. Although there were cart ruts in the packed snow, there was very little sign of life, and most of the shops were closed up.

Joshua alighted from the gig, handed the reins over to the stable boy, and followed Robert into the rear of the rectory, stamping the snow off his boots on the kitchen mat.

"Is everything all right?" he asked Robert as they left their hats and cloaks to dry out beside the warmth of the kitchen fire.

"I'm getting rather worried about the whereabouts of Max Harrington," Robert confided. "I fully expected to find him at the inn sleeping off a night of excess drinking. I can't think where else he might be. It's not as if he knows the area well or has any acquaintances among the gentry."

"Young men are remarkably resilient," Joshua reminded him. "You know that as well as I do, having commanded a few in your time." He grimaced. "Not that I'm going to miss that part of the job. I always had a healthy appreciation that I was outnumbered by my men and that one false step might lead to mutiny."

Robert paused. "You aren't going back?"

"On my return, my father informed me that he couldn't afford to pay for any further advancement in my career. And, as the war has ended and promotions on merit will be as rare as hen's teeth, I suspect I'll be stuck as Captain Coles for the remainder of my military career."

"That is a shame. You are an excellent officer."

Joshua smiled briefly. "Thank you. The rest of the regiment is currently serving in India. It seems pointless to incur all that extra cost to go all the way out there again simply to assess my chances of promotion when I know it won't happen."

"Forgive me for asking," Robert said cautiously. "Is your father still in good health? You sound concerned for him."

"I am rather worried." Joshua hesitated. "He seems very withdrawn. With my sister Marion having recently married, I suspect he is quite lonely. He says her wedding bankrupted him, but I doubt that."

"Maybe he simply wishes you to come home."

"Perhaps. I must confess that I have no intention of forcing him to hand over money he insists he doesn't have, but I would like a look at the family accounts." He let out a frustrated breath. "I've never been terribly impressed by his financial acumen. He was left a considerable fortune by my grandfather, and somehow it has dwindled away to nothing."

"Lord Northam gained a considerable dowry when he married my cousin, but he managed to fritter that away in ten years." Robert patted Joshua awkwardly on the shoulder. "I'm sure you'll come about."

"Let's hope so." Joshua followed him along the hall to the back parlor that Robert's aunt Rose usually occupied. "Otherwise I will soon be looking for an occupation that pays a reasonable wage."

Robert went in and found the room empty. He turned around, excused himself to Joshua, and headed back to the rector's study. After he knocked on the door, he was given permission to enter and found the rector sitting at his desk writing.

"Thank goodness you are here, Kurland!" His father-in-law waved his quill pen in the air. "I was just writing a note to Dr. Fletcher."

"What's wrong?" Robert said sharply.

"Rose is not well at all." The rector frowned. "I am very worried about her."

"Then I will go to Dr. Fletcher's immediately and bring him back here." Robert offered. "We only just arrived in the gig."

"I'll go," Joshua said from the doorway. "Dr. Fletcher lives opposite the school, yes?"

"He does." Robert nodded and walked toward Joshua. "Are you sure—"

Joshua lowered his voice. "The rector looks rather upset, Major. Perhaps he would appreciate your company."

Reluctantly, Robert conceded that it was his place to remain at his father-in-law's side rather than rushing off to fetch the doctor. He was far better at action than in dealing with the emotions of others, which was why he had wanted to be a soldier in the first place.

"I'll stay," he said abruptly. "Tell Dr. Fletcher not to bother getting out his own rig and bring him straight back in mine," Robert conceded.

"I will." Joshua offered him a smart salute. "I'll be as quick as I can."

For the first time, Robert wished he'd accepted Lucy's offer to join him on his excursion. She was remarkably good at dealing with people who needed careful handling. He turned back to the rector, who had remained behind his desk, his hands folded together and staring at nothing.

"When did my aunt become unwell, sir?" Robert asked.

"She hasn't been well since the christening. This morning, when she attempted to get up, she fell into a deep swoon. I had to call her maid to help me get her back into bed."

"She is probably grieving for her son-in-law and worrying about her daughter," Robert suggested.

"Grieving Northam? She disliked him intensely—thought Henrietta had wasted herself on the man." The rector shook his head. "She is upset that Henrietta has not bothered to call on her. She wishes to be a comfort to her daughter but is also reluctant to stir up Henrietta's somewhat exhausting emotions."

"With all due respect, sir, I think Aunt Rose is better off not seeing Henrietta, who is still convinced you are a murderer after her mother's fortune," Robert replied.

He went over to the sideboard and poured his father-in-law a brandy. "Have you eaten today?"

"Not yet—what with Rose being ill. I haven't had the time."

"Then I will go and fetch you some food. I find things always look better on a full stomach."

He brought back a platter of bread, cheese, and pickles and set it at the rector's elbow.

"Here you are, sir."

"Thank you. Did you come to speak to me about Northam's death, or were you just passing by?"

"Actually, I came to ask if you'd seen Max today." Robert helped himself to a small brandy to ward off the cold. "He's still missing."

"Max is? Good Lord. How is my brother taking it?"

"He doesn't yet know Max hasn't been found." Robert grimaced. "I was hoping he'd called in here or maybe borrowed a mount from you."

"Not to my knowledge." The rector ate some of the bread and a sliver of cheese. "The last time I saw Max was at the church after the christening arguing with his father."

"Did your brother mention why Max and he were at odds?"

"Gambling debts, I believe. Not that such things should trouble David, as he has very deep pockets indeed."

"Perhaps he didn't appreciate his son wasting his money on such matters. I don't think I would be very pleased if Ned grew up to be an inconsiderate wastrel."

"Max is hardly that."

"Did you ever see Max speaking to Northam?" Robert asked as the rector stacked some of the pickle on the bread and topped it with cheese.

"I don't believe so." His companion paused to chew. "Why do you ask?"

"We suspect Max owed Northam money."

The rector sat back and looked at Robert. "Are you trying in your roundabout fashion to suggest that *Max* might have murdered Northam?"

"I can't discount the possibility, sir." Robert shrugged. "His nonappearance is hardly helping his case."

"But David would be devastated!"

Robert fixed his companion with a stern look. "You'd rather be convicted of a crime you insist you didn't commit than entertain the notion that a member of your family is the culprit instead?"

"I just don't believe any Harrington is capable of such a thing."

Hearing the sound of approaching voices and somewhat irritated by the rector's stubbornness. Robert cleared his throat.

"There is one other matter I wished to ask you. Did you at any time invest in a venture proposed by Northam?"

"I-I—" The rector spluttered, his hand coming to his throat as he began to cough.

Dr. Fletcher came through the door; eased past Robert, who had risen to his feet; and pounded the rector hard between the shoulder blades.

"There you are, sir. Get it out." He repeated the maneuver until the rector gave one final violent cough and straightened again, his eyes streaming.

"Thank . . . you, Dr. Fletcher."

"Probably a piece of food went down the wrong way." Dr. Fletcher eyed his patient carefully. "Take a drink, and you should be fine now."

Robert, who had stepped out of the way, watched the rector. If he attempted to repeat his question and his father-in-law started choking again, Dr. Fletcher would intervene and tell him to go to the devil. Robert decided that the horrified look on his father-in-law's face was enough for him to deduce that if the rector wasn't involved in the fake scheme, he certainly knew all about it.

Lucy set her sleeping daughter back in her cradle, smiled at the nurse stationed by the fire, and tiptoed out of the room. She hesitated on the landing before descending the stairs. Should she go and inquire after her aunt Jane? She hadn't seen her since the christening celebrations. But what if she asked about Max's whereabouts? Lucy still had no idea where her cousin was or whether Robert had located him at the Queen's Head.

Just as she contemplated descending the stairs, a slight noise from below made her pause and ease farther back into the shadows. Henrietta, now dressed in the black gown Lucy had lent her, was leaving her room. Lucy frowned. There was supposed to be a footman stationed at the door to offer Robert's cousin his assistance and a maid in the room itself to prevent such excursions.

Glad of her soft kidskin slippers, Lucy glided silently downward, keeping her distance from Henrietta, who was moving cautiously toward the servants' stairs. She wasn't dressed to go out, but perhaps she intended to claim her cloak and boots from the kitchen scullery, where such things were left to dry.

To Lucy's surprise, Henrietta stopped abruptly before the end of the corridor, opened one of the doors, and went inside. It took Lucy a moment to realize she'd gone into the apartment set aside for the Earl and Countess of Harrington. Was she intent on renewing her pleas to the earl to investigate his own brother, or did she have another reason for being there? Lucy went to the door, paused for less than a second, and then continued onward through the servants' door. The bare stairwell had two doors leading off it, one of which went into the dressing room between the bedchambers.

Lucy cautiously eased the door open and peered through the crack. There was no sign of the earl or countess, although one of the cupboards stood open. She picked up her skirts and ran toward the cupboard, positioning herself behind the door where she could clearly hear Henrietta speaking from within the bedchamber.

"You will help me, or I will tell my cousin Robert the truth."

Lucy held her breath but failed to hear any reply from her aunt.

"I am not funning with you, my lady. If you don't want the high and mighty Harrington family embroiled in a scandal, then you will make certain that my husband's murder is avenged by incriminating the rector. Do you understand me?"

"Get out."

Lucy barely had time to hide before the dressing room door opened and was quietly shut behind her aunt Jane, whose face was rigid with anger. Her aunt stared into space, her fingers clenched into fists as if she was attempting to master her formidable temper. When the exterior door slammed, presumably behind Henrietta, the countess let out a breath and returned to the bedroom, leaving Lucy alone.

Lucy remained where she was until her knees stopped shaking, then she quickly let herself out of the servants' door before resuming her search for Henrietta. To her surprise, Henrietta had returned to her room, where the startled footman jumped to his feet when she wished him a good day. Lucy intended to have a word with her staff about guarding Henrietta far more carefully. She wished Robert would return home. She had a lot to discuss with him.

To her relief, he arrived back in less than an hour. His expression was not forthcoming as she followed him up to their bedchamber, eager to tell him what had transpired during his absence. She then found he had news of his own.

"Aunt Rose was taken ill this morning. Dr. Fletcher is attending her. I asked him to let us know how she was feeling as soon as he could."

"Poor Rose," Lucy said with a sigh. "I suspect the anxiety about her current situation plus her pregnancy are making her ill. I wonder if I should go down to see her."

"Perhaps you could wait until we hear from Dr. Fletcher?" Robert suggested. "If he thinks Rose needs female companionship, I'm sure he will mention it. Mrs. Culpepper has already promised to pop in regularly."

"Then I will await his report." Lucy studied her rather stern-looking husband. "Are you very worried about her?"

"Yes, but I'm also concerned about Max. He wasn't at the inn or at the rectory."

Lucy bit her lip. "Then where on earth is he?"

"I wish I knew." Robert unwrapped his scarf and warmed his hands in front of the fire. "If you approve, I would like to send Luke and Michael out to search for him in the surrounding villages."

"I think that is an excellent idea," Lucy agreed. "They have nothing to do but worry themselves silly at the moment, and they are driving me to distraction."

Without replying directly, Robert started speaking again.

"At the Queen's Head this morning, I met a very interesting man named Mr. Penarth who not only knew Northam but had loaned him a considerable amount of money, which had not been repaid. He followed Northam down from London to collect on his debt and was soundly rebuffed." Robert eased off his boots. "I got the distinct impression that Mr. Penarth would not hesitate in the slightest to deal harshly with any client who was foolish enough not to pay back his debts."

"Did he physically threaten Northam?"

"If he did, he certainly wasn't going to admit it to me. In truth, he was extremely pleasant, but I know a hard man when I see one." Robert turned to look at her. "If he wanted Northam dead, I doubt he would dirty his own hands, but it would still happen on his orders." He set his boots to dry in front of the fire.

"Did you ask him what he was doing at the time of the christening?"

"Not yet." Robert discarded his coat and went through to the dressing room. "He can't leave the village until at least tomorrow morning. I didn't want to scare him off while he was being so accommodating."

"But what about the money owed to him?"

He *said* he would attempt to retrieve it from the estate, but I didn't believe him. I suspect he will pursue Henrietta for the debt regardless." He selected a new coat and put it on without bothering to call for Silas, his valet. "He seemed to believe she was well aware of her husband's schemes."

His quick smile was constrained. "I'm torn between warning her to be careful of him and leaving her to fight her own battles."

"She seems quite confident enough to fight for herself," Lucy said as she smoothed the shoulders of his coat. "I just overheard her threatening my aunt Jane."

Robert frowned. "Why the devil was she out of her room? Didn't we set a guard on her?"

"I'm not sure what happened with that, but I certainly intend to find out," Lucy said severely. "Henrietta told Aunt Jane that if she didn't help her prosecute my father, then she would embroil the Harrington family in a scandal."

Robert paused as he buttoned his coat. There was a look on his face Lucy couldn't quite decipher. "Were those her exact words?"

"I believe so." She regarded him closely. "Why?"

He shrugged. "No matter. It just complicates things a little further, doesn't it?"

"I would say so." It was her turn to pause. "You don't sound very surprised. Is there something you aren't telling me?"

He walked back through to their bedchamber and started taking items out of his discarded coat and placing them in his pockets.

Lucy followed, but he continued with his task as if she hadn't spoken.

"Robert . . ."

He finally looked at her. "There is nothing that needs to concern you at this moment. If that changes, I promise I will tell you."

"So there is something." Lucy couldn't help asking. "Does it have to do with more evidence against my father?"

"As I said, as soon as I have proof of what was said to me I will discuss it further." He consulted his pocket watch and looked over at her. "You promised to allow me the discretion to manage this investigation as I chose."

"I promised you no such thing." Lucy glared at him. "But I can see that you have made your decision, and that there is no point in arguing with you further."

She headed for the door, her head held high, and he gently caught her elbow.

"Lucy, please believe me when I say I don't want your father to be tried for murder."

She shook off his hand and continued on her way. She'd intended to ask his advice as to whether she should approach her aunt about what she had overheard, but if her husband intended to be difficult, she was quite prepared to make that decision by herself.

Robert stared at the closed door in frustration. Half of him wanted to go after his wife and tell her what Mr. Penarth had said about the list of investors in Northam's fraudulent scheme, while the other half insisted he wait in case he simply made matters worse. He wished Max Harrington were available for a little chat. He had a sense the boy would be far more forthcoming than his rather formidable father who, as a peer of the realm, was remarkably secure in his lack of accountability to anyone except his monarch or the House of Lords.

It seemed unlikely that Max himself would invest in anything when he was already in debt, but had he gone into debt because he'd given all his money to Northam? Or worse, had Max somehow used his father's money with the earl none the wiser?

Despite the Earl of Harrington's status, Robert realized he was going to have to face him with some rather hard truths, both about the nonappearance of his son and his potential involvement in a sham investment scheme. With that in mind, Robert checked his appearance in the mirror, straightened his cravat, and went to find his most eminent guest. He'd faced down Napoleon's finest troops at Waterloo; one soon-to-be irate earl should not be that difficult.

Facing his wife if he had to tell her that the rector was a murderer was a far more terrifying prospect.

Chapter 7

"Are you suggesting Max's disappearance has something to do with Northam's murder?"

Robert regarded the earl, who was visibly angry. He'd asked Lucy's uncle to meet him in his study before they ate the midday meal and was wondering if he should have left it until the earl had eaten his fill and was in a better temper.

"I am not saying that, sir. I am merely telling you that Max has been missing since the christening and that he was seen at the Queen's Head talking to Northam the night before he died."

The earl took a quick turn of the room before coming to a stop in front of Robert again.

"Why would Max want to murder Northam? Such a suggestion is absurd!"

"Which is why I was hoping you could clear up this matter for me, sir," Robert said evenly. "If Max owed Northam money, I'm sure you would've been aware of it."

"Max owed a lot of people money," the earl snapped. "He has poor judgment in both his choice of friends and his current entertainments."

"But did Max ever tell you he was in debt to Northam specifically?"

"He—" The earl stopped speaking and glared at Robert. "Do you seriously imagine I am going to incriminate my own son?"

Robert didn't look away. "You would prefer your brother to be prosecuted instead? I understand family loyalty, sir, but in this instance I would be sincerely grateful if you could just tell me the truth."

"And let you haul Max off to gaol?"

"As a peer's son, that is most unlikely to happen, and you know it," Robert countered. "I have no intention of accusing anyone of anything yet. I am simply attempting to gather evidence, and that involves inquiring into matters that some of us might prefer to remain private."

The earl let out an irritated breath. "Then so be it. Max wasn't pleased to see Northam here in Kurland St. Mary. When I inquired as to why he had been spending time with a known blaggard, Max predictably told me to go to the devil."

"Which indicates that they were at least acquaintances."

"Of course they were. They both love to gamble. If Max did owe Northam money, I wouldn't be surprised to hear it."

Robert bowed. "Thank you for that, sir. I appreciate your honesty."

He received a ferocious glare in return. "Then I trust you to treat my words with the respect they deserve and not draw any unwanted or hurried conclusions!"

"I certainly won't do that." Robert paused. "My first concern is to ascertain where Max has gone. This isn't the best weather for him to be out in unfamiliar territory."

"I agree."

"I've asked the twins to ride out and search for him in the surrounding countryside. They know the land intimately, and all the dwellings, so if he has stayed overnight with someone, they will soon find him."

"Good, and then perhaps he can answer for himself and

put an end to all this pointless speculation. Good day to you, sir." The earl inclined his head a barely civil inch and turned to the door, his intention to leave quite obvious.

Robert didn't have the heart to stop him and ask about the fraudulent shipping scheme. If his son were not only missing but also possibly involved in a murder, he too would have problems maintaining his temper. The earl and Max might be at odds now, but they had previously enjoyed a good relationship, which had reminded Robert of his strong connection with his own father.

He'd sent a note down to the stables to ask the head groom to help out with the search for Max, and was confident that if Lucy's cousin were still in the vicinity, he would be found.

"Dr. Fletcher is here, Sir Robert." James came into the room. "Do you wish to speak to him?"

"Yes, send him in, and lay another place at the table. He'll probably be staying for lunch."

He sat behind his desk, his fingers drumming an irritable tattoo on the mahogany surface until Patrick came in and shut the door.

"How is my aunt?"

"Not well." Patrick brushed at the snow on his coat. "I've recommended that she stay in bed for the foreseeable future."

"Is it possible that she might lose the child?"

"Yes, and her life if she isn't careful." Patrick let out an irritated breath. "Can you see to it that her daughter is not allowed to upset her?"

"I'll do my best to keep them apart, but unless I lock Lady Northam in her room, I cannot guarantee she won't get out," Robert said.

"It would be far better for her mother if she was left alone until this matter about Northam's murder has been solved."

"I'll ask Lady Kurland to keep an eye on Lady Northam, then. She is far more persuasive than I am." Robert paused. "Do you think Rose would appreciate a visit from me?"

"No." Patrick gave him a stern look. "I'll wager you would be badgering her about Northam's death."

"The trouble is, she does have some very important information that might help clear this matter up more quickly," Robert admitted

"Then write her a letter and I'll deliver it myself." Patrick sniffed the air. "Is that roast pork I smell?"

Robert sighed and stood up. "I have no idea, but I'd trust your nose anywhere. Come and eat with us. Then you can tell my guests to leave Aunt Rose alone in person."

Lucy approached her aunt Jane's bedchamber with some trepidation. She knew the earl had been asked to speak to Robert in his study, and that it was the perfect time to question her aunt, but she was still somewhat nervous. She tapped on the door and was given permission to enter.

Aunt Jane sat by the fireside, her embroidery on her lap and her spectacles perched on the end of her nose. She looked up at Lucy and smiled.

"I have been the most reclusive of guests, have I not? David said you were worried about my nonappearance. I had already planned to come down for luncheon and contrive to be more sociable."

"I'm glad to hear it." Lucy took the seat opposite her aunt and studied her carefully. There was no trace of the anger she'd witnessed earlier or any indication that her aunt would ever stoop that low. "I was wondering if anyone had told you about Max."

"Has he turned up?"

"Unfortunately not. But the twins are going to look for him this afternoon, and I'm sure they'll find him tucked up safe and warm in someone's house."

"I do hope you are right." Aunt Jane set her embroidery

hoop down. "I must confess to some anxiety as to his safety. My husband brushes it off as just another example of Max's immaturity, but I am not so certain. As a child he often ran away when he was in trouble."

Lucy hesitated. "Do you think he is in some kind of trouble now?"

"I know that he was disturbed to find Lord Northam here, as was I," Aunt Jane said carefully.

"We were certainly not pleased to see him either," Lucy confided. "He was not invited to the christening but turned up with his wife to upbraid Rose for daring to marry my father. We've been trying to get rid of him ever since." Lucy grimaced. "Not in *quite* such a manner as murdering him, but all the same. Robert suggested there were some very good reasons why Northam decided to leave London."

"Indeed." Aunt Jane nodded. "I am well aware of why he needed to leave, and the last place I expected to see him was here in Kurland St. Mary. Max was absolutely furious."

"Do you think it is possible that Max might have argued with him?" Lucy asked carefully.

"Are you suggesting my son might have murdered Northam?"

"I suppose I am." Lucy didn't flinch from her aunt's questioning stare. "It is strange that Max has not been seen since the murder was discovered."

Aunt Jane's composure finally cracked. "If Max did such a thing for what he considered justifiable reasons . . . what would happen to him?"

"You'd have to ask Robert about that," Lucy said diplomatically. "But I doubt an earl's heir presumptive would be confined to gaol."

Aunt Jane nodded and picked up her embroidery again. "Then let's hope he can be found, and he can explain himself."

Lucy stood and stared down at her aunt's bowed head.

"Knowing Max, he has probably found himself a warm place to wait out the storm and will be horribly unimpressed by all the furor surrounding his disappearance."

Her answer elicited a small smile from her aunt. "I'm sure you are right. What with Max's disappearance and Julia being so unwell, I scarcely know how to go on right now." Aunt Jane stiffened her spine. "But I cannot wallow in despair. That doesn't help anyone."

"Indeed." Lucy nodded. "I must go and make sure that Cook is ready to serve lunch."

"I will be down in a moment myself, my dear."

Lucy descended the stairs in a somewhat pensive state. She was about to head for the kitchen when she noticed Robert coming out of his study with Dr. Fletcher, whom he'd obviously asked to stay and eat with them because the good doctor was always hungry. He looked up at her with a grave expression, sent Dr. Fletcher on his way, and came over to her.

"What's wrong?"

"I just had the oddest conversation with my aunt Jane."

He took her hand, drew her back into his study, and shut the door.

"What happened?"

Lucy looked up into his concerned blue gaze. "She seemed to suggest that Max had good reason to kill Lord Northam. She even admitted knowing that Northam had been forced to leave London. Mayhap we have been looking at this murder in the wrong light." She drew a quick breath. "What if Uncle David paid off Max's gambling debts on the understanding that Northam left town only to arrive here and find the very man Max intensely disliked attending an event in Kurland St. Mary?"

"You think that might have been enough for Max to lose his temper and kill Northam?"

"It's possible." Lucy shrugged. "I don't want anyone in my family implicated for murder, but it certainly sounds likely, doesn't it?"

"Yes," Robert said simply.

"And earlier I heard Henrietta threatening Aunt Jane about exposing the Harrington family, which surely strengthens my theory?"

"Indeed."

"Is that all you have to say?" Lucy glared at him.

"At this point you usually accuse me of disagreeing with your premise, but when I agree with you I am still wrong?" He kissed her forehead and offered her his arm. "I need to think about all this. Shall we go into the dining room and speak again after we've eaten?"

"I hardly think I will eat a thing," Lucy confessed. "But appearances must be maintained, and we still have a house full of guests."

"I really would like to speak to Rose," Robert confided as he walked with her across the hallway. "Knowing what was in her new will would help matters enormously."

"Mayhap you could write to her?" Lucy suggested.

"That's what Dr. Fletcher suggested. Perhaps I'll do that this afternoon." Robert opened the door into the dining room for her and stood back. "After you, my dear."

"Thank you."

Captain Coles was helping himself to a plateful of food from the dishes lined up on the sideboards. Dr. Fletcher was already eating. There was no sign of the Harringtons or Henrietta Northam.

"Good afternoon, Lady Kurland, Sir Robert. I hope you don't mind me helping myself," Joshua said cheerfully.

"Not at all." Lucy smiled at him.

He took his seat at the table and set down his plate. "I was wondering if I might ask you a favor, my lady. My belongings are still at the rectory, and I suspect it might be preferable for me to remain here at the hall until Mrs. Harrington is feeling more the thing. Would it be possible for me to go down to the village and collect my possessions?"

"Of course, Captain Coles," Lucy responded, guilt settling over her. "I do apologize. I meant to extend an invitation to you to stay here this morning, and I quite forgot."

"You have quite a lot on your mind right now, my lady," Captain Coles said diplomatically. "I am more than willing to fetch my own bags." He glanced over at Robert. "I understand that there is a Kurland horse in the rectory stable, so I will walk down to the village and ride back with the noble steed and my possessions."

"Good. You can take a letter to my aunt for me." Robert took the seat opposite Captain Coles. "Make sure you come into my study before you leave, and I will have it ready for you."

Lucy had barely started eating when the door flew open and her brother Michael came in unwrapping his scarf, bringing the cold bite of winter with him.

"Lucy! We found Max! He was at the Bellweathers. He took shelter when the storm came down and has been there ever since!"

"Well, that at least is excellent news." Lucy smiled approvingly at him. "Where is he now?"

"He wouldn't leave with us. Luke told me to come and tell you what was going on and that he would remain there and keep an eye on Max."

"Good thinking, and well done." Robert stood up. "I think I'll go and persuade him to come back myself." He glanced over at Lucy. "Perhaps you might ask your uncle if he wishes to accompany me?"

"I'll go and speak to him immediately." Lucy glanced regretfully at her uneaten food. "I'll send a message down to the stables to get your gig ready while you write your note to Aunt Rose."

Despite the earl having chosen to accompany Robert, he maintained a very chilly silence as Robert drove the gig down through Kurland St. Mary and out toward Lower Kurland, a hamlet with a small population clustered around a manor house and a chapel. The depth of the snow and the need to keep the wheels of the gig within the two frozen ruts of the road kept Robert too busy to worry about the lack of communication.

The sight of smoke from the chimneys of Bellweather House was a welcome one as Robert carefully turned the gig and set off along the short elm-lined drive. He tried to remember the last time he had visited the owners, but as he let his father-in-law run the local hunt he rarely had occasion to socialize with the Bellweather family, who were all horse and hound mad.

"Where exactly are we?" the earl asked as Robert took the gig around the side of the house to the expansive stables.

"Bellweather House in Lower Kurland," Robert answered as a groom came to stand at his horse's head. "Since I no longer host the Kurland hunt, Mr. Bellweather has taken on the responsibility of hosting many of the events. I understand from the rector who is master of the hunt that he does it very well."

"It looks like Max fell on his feet," the earl murmured as they were ushered into the warmth of the house and left to await their host in the magnificent paneled entrance hall.

"Sir Robert!"

Robert looked up as Mr. Bellweather descended the stairs surrounded by a sea of well-behaved dogs.

"Good afternoon, sir. May I introduce you to the Earl of Harrington?" Robert turned to his companion. "This is Mr. Arthur Bellweather, my lord."

"A pleasure." The earl inclined his head. "I understand that my son is currently residing with you."

"Indeed he is," Mr. Bellweather said heartily. "He was rather cold and wet when he arrived, but he has thawed out nicely, and has been an extremely pleasant and polite guest."

"I'm glad to hear it," the earl said gruffly and bowed. "Thank you for your assistance, sir."

"You are most welcome, my lord. It is easy to get lost in these country lanes when you are not familiar with them—especially during a winter storm." Mr. Bellweather gestured to the right. "Would you like to come through to the drawing room where my family and your son are currently gathered?"

Robert followed the earl and his host down the corridor that led into a sunny room overlooking the snow-covered garden at the rear of the house. The sound of laugher made him pause on the threshold and look over to the fireplace, where Max and Luke Harrington were holding court with the Bellweather ladies.

Max jumped to his feet, his smile fading as he spied his father. "Sir."

"Good afternoon, Max." The earl still sounded exquisitely polite. "I am glad to see that you are unharmed. I do hope you have thanked your hosts for taking such good care of you?"

"Of course, sir." Max bowed at Mrs. Bellweather and her daughters. "I never expected such delightful company in my hour of need."

Miss Hermione Bellweather tittered and glanced fleetingly at her mother, who answered Max. "It was our pleasure, Mr. Harrington."

Robert stepped forward. "Mrs. Bellweather, may I introduce you to the Earl of Harrington? He has been most concerned as to his son's whereabouts."

"Indeed I have, ma'am." The earl took his hostess's hand. "Thank you for your kindness to my son."

"As I said, my lord, he has been a credit to your family." Mrs. Bellweather curtsied and then beamed at Max, who went rather red. "Would you care for some tea?"

"That would be most appreciated." The earl sat down

opposite his son, who was regarding him warily. "It is remarkably cold out there today."

"Indeed."

While the social niceties were being exchanged, Robert took the opportunity to speak quietly to Luke.

"Congratulations on finding your cousin."

Luke grimaced. "We'd almost decided to turn back, but Michael wanted to speak to Miss Hermione on some ridiculous matter, so I agreed we would call here. We tried to get Max to leave with us, but he refused outright, and we could hardly drag him out in front of the Bellweather family."

"You did exactly the right thing," Robert said. "If you wish to take yourself back to Kurland Hall, then please go ahead. The earl and I will ensure that Max returns with us."

"Thank you." Luke nodded. "Shall I take Max's horse with me?"

"If it is from the Kurland stables, then yes, please," Robert said. "I am rather tired of my guests borrowing my horses and failing to return them."

Luke was still grinning as he made his excuses to his hosts and headed out to the stables. Robert noticed that Max was watching his cousin carefully and made certain that Luke was not pulled into any clandestine conversation before he left. He wished he could speak to Max alone before the earl got to him, but he knew that was unlikely. He decided to do everything he could to prevent them from exchanging confidences and aligning their stories.

After a courteous half hour, the earl and Max finally stood up to take their leave of the Bellweathers. Robert followed them closely out to the stables. Max made no attempt to escape his father's watchful presence and chatted amiably about the shocking weather. Robert reminded himself that if Max was truly innocent, and had simply lost his way in the snow, he wouldn't need to be worried.

To Robert's relief, the earl hardly spoke to his son on the drive home, leaving Robert to concentrate on the treacherous road and the sudden onslaught of snow flurries sliding off the banks in the bitter wind. He was grateful to see the gates of Kurland Hall come into view through the encroaching dusk, and thoroughly appreciative of the work his staff had done to clear the paths up to the house and to the stables.

He pulled up at the side of the hall to allow the earl to descend but caught hold of Max's arm before he could follow suit.

"Would you mind accompanying me to the stables, Max? I might need help with the horse."

"Of course, sir." Max sat back down.

Robert drove the last few hundred yards to the stable block, where he brought the gig undercover and got down to help Max before one of the grooms appeared to complete his task.

"Well, I'll be off to the hall, then," Max said jauntily. "My mother will be waiting to ring a peal over my head for worrying her."

"Max?" Robert raised his voice as his companion headed for the exit. "May I speak to you for a moment?"

Max turned reluctantly, his hands deep in his pockets, and his chin sunk into the scarf around his neck. Robert gestured toward the head coachman's office, and his companion followed him inside.

"What is it?" Max asked.

"How well do you know Lord Northam?"

Max's skin slowly reddened. "What on earth does that have to do with anything?"

"I understand from your father that you might have owed Northam money," Robert added.

"Even if that's true, what's it got to do with you?"

Robert regarded him carefully. "Perhaps we could start with you explaining your movements after the christening on Sunday? Mr. Jarvis at the Queen's Head said you were drinking in the taproom and left somewhat worse for wear at a late hour."

"So what if I did?" Max's expression turned sullen. "I didn't want to come to Kurland St. Mary in the first place. I did my duty by attending the christening as my father ordered. After that, surely my time was my own?"

"It depends on what you did with it," Robert answered. "You came back to the hall long enough to change your clothing and then left, presumably to drown your sorrows at the inn. What happened after that?"

"I was deep in my cups and I lost my way back to Kurland Hall." Max met Robert's stare with one of his own. "I ended up in Lower Kurland and the Bellweathers let me stay the night. What else is there to say?"

Well used to dealing with junior officers, Robert raised his eyebrows and remained silent until Max started to fidget.

"I don't know what you want me to tell you, sir. Did Lord Northam accuse me of something?" Max snorted. "He's a fine one to talk."

"What do you think Northam might be accusing you of?"

Max half turned away. "All the things he's guilty of, like cheating at cards and refusing to pay his gambling debts."

"I thought you were the one unable to pay your debts," Robert said softly. "Didn't your father cut off your allowance?"

"I—" Max stopped speaking and drew an agitated breath. "If you want to accuse me of something, Sir Robert, could you just say it in plain language? I'm tired, I want to go to bed, and I still have to deal with my parents."

"Are you aware that I am the local magistrate in this area, charged with investigating crimes and empowered by the king and parliament to ensure justice?" Robert asked.

"Why are you telling me this?" For the first time, Max looked completely bewildered. "It's no secret that I don't like Northam. I warned him not to enrage my parents when I discovered he was here in Kurland St. Mary, but that is hardly a crime, is it?"

"It depends what you did to ensure that he understood your warning. Do you owe him money?"

"Yes, but that's neither here nor there. All gentlemen gamble—even you I'll wager." Max shrugged in an unconvincing way. "I admit that seeing him here, gloating and threatening to directly ask my father for money, was infuriating. But there was very little Northam could actually do to follow through on his threats, and my father would've sent him away with a flea in his ear."

"When did you last see Lord Northam?"

"At the Queen's Head the night before the christening. I arranged to meet him there."

"Why?"

Max looked longingly toward the door, and Robert tensed.

"Why are you asking me all these ridiculous questions?" Max burst out. "Did the innkeeper inform you that I lost my temper with Lord Northam? Is that now the sort of crime the local magistrate has to investigate?"

"You didn't see Northam on the day of the christening?" Robert persisted.

"No! And if you don't believe me, go and bloody ask him! He's the criminal here, not me!"

"I can't ask him."

"Why not? Has he run away again? He left London in disgrace, you know." Max laughed. "You'd better check your pockets, Sir Robert, and the strong box, because I have no doubt that Northam would happily steal from his own family."

Robert held Max's furious gaze. "I can't ask Lord Northam any questions because he is dead."

Max gulped hard, his mouth hanging open before he pivoted and ran for the door. Luckily, Robert had been anticipating that very thing and stuck out his booted foot, tripping Max and bringing him down to the floor with a resounding crash.

Mr. Coleman came in and looked down at the thrashing figure.

"Do you need a hand, sir?"

"Yes, can you get him back on his feet and ask two of the grooms to walk him over to the hall for me?"

"Yes, Sir Robert." Mr. Coleman whistled loudly for his grooms and kept a firm foot on Max's neck until he was able to stand. "Take him to the hall, lads, and await Sir Robert there."

"Thank you." Robert was just about to follow Max when Mr. Coleman stepped in front of him.

"Begging your pardon, sir, but I was wondering if you could explain how the horse Captain Coles brought with him was the one that was taken out of my stable first?"

Robert paused. "What?"

"Captain Coles took out a horse the morning of the christening, and that other gentleman, whom we think was Lord Northam, also took a horse." Mr. Coleman gestured at the stalls. "But the one Captain Coles brought back was the one Lord Northam took out."

"Are you sure?" Robert frowned.

Mr. Coleman chewed thoughtfully for a moment. "I wasn't the one who noticed it, sir. That was young Joseph, so I can't really say whether it is true or not."

"Are both horses unharmed?"

"As far as I can tell, they are both in good health."

"Does it really matter, then?"

"Well, no, sir, it's just something of a puzzle."

Robert looked past Mr. Coleman toward Max and his companions. "A puzzle I'll happily leave to you while I try to ascertain who is responsible for Lord Northam's death."

"As you wish, sir."

Robert hurried after Max, knowing that he'd have to allow the earl to be present for any further questioning of his son, and already knowing that his guest might make that very difficult.

Chapter 8

Lucy took one look at her husband's face before she dashed ahead of him and Max to open the door to his study.

"Will you fetch your uncle, please, Lucy?" Robert asked. "He will probably wish to be present for this conversation."

"He just went upstairs. I'll go and speak to him immediately," Lucy said.

She ran up the stairs so quickly that she was breathing hard when she knocked on the door of the best guest chamber. Aunt Jane opened the door, her eyes widening as she took in Lucy's expression.

"David said that Max has been found. Is everything all right?"

"I'm not sure." Lucy took a deep breath. "Robert would like my uncle to join him in the library."

Aunt Jane raised her chin. "*We* will be down directly." She shut the door gently in Lucy's face.

Lucy wasn't quite sure how Robert would feel about the countess joining them, but she was confident that he would skillfully extract her from the conversation if it became necessary. Not that he stood a chance of preventing

Lucy from hearing what was going on. Had Max confessed to something? Was that why Robert had thought it necessary to have him accompanied by two of the grooms?

She went back down the stairs and let herself into the study. Robert sat behind his desk and Max sat in front of him. His lip was bleeding, and he looked as if he had the beginnings of a black eye.

"My uncle will be down directly, Robert," Lucy said, and received a nod in return. "Should I perhaps take care of Max's injuries before his parents see him?"

"Be my guest." Robert studied her cousin. "Max has given me his word that he has no intention of attempting to run away again."

Lucy left the study and repaired to the kitchen for some hot water and a cloth to bathe Max's torn lip. She took a moment to confer with James as to the whereabouts of Henrietta, who had apparently remained in her room all day and barely eaten. Lucy knew she would have to speak to the widow soon, but she found herself surprisingly reluctant to do so.

"Mr. Snape did call, and Lady Northam asked for the body to be prepared to send back to the family estate up north where the dowager Lady Northam resides," James informed her as he handed over the basin of water and a bottle of witch hazel from the still for the bruises. "Mr. Snape said he would confer with Dr. Fletcher."

"I'm glad Lady Northam has come to a decision about that," Lucy said as James held the kitchen door open for her. "Perhaps you might bring some tea and coffee into Sir Robert's study in about half an hour?"

"Certainly, my lady."

Lucy had just finished tending to Max's wounds when his parents appeared in the study. Despite her best efforts, Aunt Jane immediately rushed to her son's side.

"What on earth happened? Were you set upon by thieves?"

Robert cleared his throat. "Unfortunately, that was my doing. Max attempted to leave before I finished questioning him."

"Indeed." Lady Jane drew herself up, her blue gaze narrowed. "And who pray gave you the authority to attack my son?"

Robert had the grace to blush. "Ah . . ."

"Sir Robert has the power of his office behind him, my dear," the earl said, his expression equally uncompromising. "Perhaps he felt he had just cause." He turned to his son, who had sunk deeper into his chair. "I am waiting for an explanation, Maximillian."

"He said Lord Northam was dead," Max muttered. "I wasn't . . . expecting that."

"So you decided to run away? Did you *want* Sir Robert to believe you were guilty?"

"Guilty of what?" Max looked at everyone's faces. "Being glad that Northam is dead? I *am* glad, and I don't care who knows it!"

"You said you owed money to Lord Northam?" Robert reasserted control over the conversation.

"Well, he *said* I did, but as I'd already discovered, he cheated, I refused to pay up."

"Gentlemen usually pay their gambling debts as a matter of honor," Robert reminded him.

"But Northam wasn't honorable, so why should I pay him a single penny?" Max sat forward, his gaze on Robert. "You sound just like my father."

"I *said* that if you could prove beyond dispute that Northam had cheated, you should make your evidence public, but if you had nothing more than a suspicion, no one would believe you," the earl intervened.

Max flung up his hands. "Everyone knows Northam cheats."

"Then why did you play cards with him?" the earl demanded. "Perhaps your gullibility deserved to be fleeced."

"That's so *unfair*—"

Robert cleared his throat before the earl and Max could start arguing in earnest.

"If you had already refused to pay Lord Northam, why did you agree to meet him the night before the christening?"

Max reluctantly returned his attention to Robert. "Because I wanted to warn him not to engage with my parents."

"And did Northam agree to do that?"

"Of course not. He laughed in my face." Max scowled. "I told him—" He paused and sat back. "To leave them alone."

"Or you would do what?" Robert asked.

Max glanced over at his mother, who was sitting beside Lucy, her hands clasped tightly in her lap.

"I told him I would challenge him to a duel."

Lucy was close enough to hear her aunt's sharply indrawn breath.

"As if he would have taken a challenge from a youth such as yourself," the earl scoffed. "No wonder he was laughing at you."

Max shot to his feet. "I'm not a child! I'm perfectly capable of killing a man!"

Robert stood, too, and shot the earl a quelling look. "Please sit down, Max. Are you telling me that you were completely unaware of Northam's death until I mentioned it to you in the stables?"

"How would I have known?" Max asked. "I went to the christening, as ordered, and then back to Kurland Hall. I couldn't stomach the thought of seeing the Northams after the luncheon, so I changed my clothes, left the house, and went into the village."

"And spoke to no one except the landlord of the Queen's Head?"

Max shrugged. "I spoke to the other patrons in the taproom, but I can't say I asked for their names or a formal introduction." He glanced over at his parents. "Do I really have to sit here and be accused of murder, Father? Isn't there anything you can do to persuade Sir Robert I'm not a suspect?"

"Sir Robert is perfectly entitled to ask all the questions he wants, my boy," the earl said. "And I would suggest you curb your impertinence."

Max let out an aggrieved sigh and slumped back in his seat.

"There is one more thing I wish to ask you about," Robert said.

"What now?" the earl murmured with a distracted look at his wife. "Isn't this bad enough as it is?"

Robert produced the IOU that Lucy had recovered from the fire. "Do you recognize this, Max?"

He brought it over to where Max was sitting and waited as he read the scorched parchment.

"It looks like a gambling note," Max said after a long pause.

"With your name and perhaps Northam's on it?" Robert suggested.

"Where did you find this?" Max handed it over to his father and looked up at Robert.

"I think you know."

"Did Northam have it?"

"I found it." Lucy spoke up. "It was in the fireplace in your room. Did you destroy it after you'd spoken to Lord Northam?"

"No!" Max turned to his father. "If it is my promissory note, I gave it to Northam! Why on earth would it be in my possession?"

The earl's expression became even grimmer. "That is exactly the point, Max, and why Sir Robert is beginning to believe you might be a murderer." He turned to Robert. "I trust that anything that has been said here this afternoon will remain in confidence until this matter has been fully investigated?"

"Of course, my lord." Robert bowed.

"I assume that you will want Max to stay close to Kurland Hall?"

"In the circumstances, that would be advisable."

"Are you saying you believe I killed Northam, Father?" Max was ashen. "Is that what you think me capable of?"

"You did just say you were willing to kill him in a duel, Max, so which is it?" Robert asked.

"They aren't the same thing!" Max shouted. "One is an honorable action and the other the act of a coward!"

The earl ignored his son's outburst, his attention fixed on Robert. "I will make sure he is in my sight at all times."

"Thank you." Robert looked at Max. "Is there anything further you would like to tell me about this matter?"

"Before you send me off to gaol?" Max stared at Robert. "I didn't bloody kill him!"

"I have no intention of sending you anywhere," Robert said calmly. "I am relying on your good sense to understand why I consider you a suspect. If you have any evidence to suggest otherwise, trust me, I would be delighted to hear it."

"Come on, Max." The earl gestured toward the door. "I'll accompany you up to your room."

After they left, Aunt Jane rose to her feet and approached Robert's desk. "We will talk to him privately, and hope he is more forthcoming to his parents than he has been to you." She inclined her head toward Robert. "Thank you for your patience in this matter, sir."

"Thank you for your understanding." Robert bowed. "You must know that the last thing that I want is for a member of my wife's family to be implicated in this matter."

"Which is why I trust you to find out the truth," Aunt Jane said. "I no more believe my son is a murderer than I believe my brother-in-law is."

She left the room, leaving Lucy staring at her husband.

"Do you really think Max murdered Northam?" Lucy asked when she was certain her aunt was out of earshot.

"I don't know." Robert shoved a hand through his hair. "It seems unlikely, but he does have a reason to hate Northam."

"And he had the opportunity to sneak into the rectory during the christening and meet Northam in my father's study. He might even have sent that note to Northam inviting him to the rectory," Lucy said. "Max has something of a temper, which Northam would probably have enjoyed provoking."

"Until he found himself dead." Robert grimaced.

"If Max did kill Northam, it might explain why the burned promissory note was in his fireplace."

"Yes, as Max said, if he had given it to Northam the only way he could've gotten it back is *from* Northam, voluntarily or involuntarily. Maybe he didn't pay back his debts in cash, but in kind." Robert sighed. "Max incriminated himself there, didn't he?"

"If he did murder Lord Northam, will you be able to prove it?" Lucy asked carefully.

"The evidence is circumstantial at best." Robert glanced up at her. "And, as he is the son of an earl, unless he actually confesses, I suspect not. Your uncle is a very influential man in political circles and has the ear of the monarch. I doubt we would find a court in the land willing to convict him."

"Even though it would exonerate my father, I still can't quite see Max as a murderer." Lucy spoke in a rush.

"The thing is, Lucy, neither can I." Robert reached for her hand. "And therein lies our problem."

Chapter 9

After listening to Max passionately defending himself, Lucy finally felt capable of dealing with Henrietta. After a quick visit to the nursery floor to ascertain that both her children were happy and well, she went down to Henrietta's bedchamber and knocked on the door.

When there was no reply, she went in and found Henrietta sitting in a chair beside the fire in her night robe, her hair still falling around her shoulders. She looked pale and irritable but not unwell.

"Have you eaten today, Henrietta?" Lucy asked as she straightened the bedsheets and pillows. "Shall I ask Cook to send up a tray?"

"Why would I need to eat when I am caged up here like a bird?" Henrietta demanded. "My husband has been murdered, and the entire village seems determined to exonerate the rector."

"You are not caged. You are more than welcome to come down to the drawing room and mingle with the other guests if you wish."

"And have to look into the faces of the Harringtons?" Henrietta sniffed. "The very family who have murdered my dear departed Basil? I assume the rector is still pretending he knows nothing about my husband's death and is happily going about his business as a man of God."

Lucy took the seat opposite Henrietta. "How do you imagine my father managed to kill Lord Northam while he was engaged at the church baptizing his granddaughter?"

"He had plenty of opportunity to murder him before the service. Basil left this house hours before the christening."

"Do you really think no one would have noticed your husband arriving in the busy rectory or heard him and my father arguing?" Lucy asked. "I find that quite unlikely."

"Well, of course you do." Henrietta shot her a glare. "If my mother is stupid enough to comply with her new husband's wishes and leave him all her money, it is your family who stand to benefit to the detriment of mine."

"Did your mother suggest she was thinking of doing such a thing?"

"Her solicitor wrote to me about some legal matter, which, on further correspondence, alerted me to the fact that she had been tampering with her will." Henrietta dragged a handkerchief from her sleeve and dabbed at her eyes. "Dear Basil warned me that she would likely do something stupid if she ever married again, and he was correct."

"Your mother's money is her own," Lucy pointed out. "From what I understand, you have already been handsomely compensated by her estate."

"That is none of your business," Henrietta snapped. "And Robert should not be discussing our family finances with you."

"You believe my father is so desperate for money that he would murder your husband for it?"

"Yes." Henrietta held Lucy's gaze. "Have you spoken to him about his finances lately? From what I understood from my late husband, your father is barely able to pay his bills."

"I don't believe you." Lucy was tired of being polite to the recent widow when she was being offered nothing but insults in return. "You are just afraid that your mother won't leave you everything."

"And why shouldn't I be afraid? Do you have any idea what happens to women like me if their husbands can't pay their debts? I'll be banished to Yorkshire, forced to economize, and have to rely on a board of trustees for my son to make financial decisions for me for the rest of my life!"

"That is unfortunate, but perhaps you should have thought of that before you ran through all the money you had already been given?"

Henrietta took a sharp breath. "You Harringtons are all the same! Out for yourselves and be damned to anyone who gets in your way!"

"I understand that you dislike my father, but to malign the entire Harrington family is completely unnecessary," Lucy countered.

"You think the Earl of Harrington and his wife are perfect, do you?" Henrietta laughed. "They are just as bad as your father. Even if the rector is guilty of murder, they will cover it up, mark my words."

"I don't think Robert will allow that to happen," Lucy reminded her. "He is, after all, your cousin."

"And he's married to you, and rumor has it that the earl has picked him to stand for parliament in his safe seat. One has to wonder how far my dear cousin is willing to turn a blind eye in order to secure his new political career."

"I can assure you that Robert would do no such thing." Lucy glared at her companion. "He is an honorable man who always upholds the law."

Henrietta stood up. "Then ask him whether the Harringtons are acquainted with the gentleman currently installed in the Queen's Head."

"Who would that be?" Lucy asked innocently.

"A Mr. Penarth."

"I believe Robert has already spoken to him."

"And received a bunch of half-truths and lies, no doubt." Henrietta climbed back into bed and drew the covers up. "Ask him who Mr. Penarth really came to Kurland St. Mary to see. Then perhaps you might begin to see things more clearly."

"I was just about to go and visit Mr. Penarth." Robert looked over at his wife, who had come to find him in his study. He noted that her color was high and her bearing almost military, which usually meant she'd been arguing with some unfortunate being. "I am quite willing for you to accompany me if you wish."

"Thank you. Henrietta is insisting that Mr. Penarth knows my father, although how that can be, I am not sure."

Inwardly Robert sighed as he rose to his feet. Attempting to keep things from his wife rarely worked out for the best. "He might have been involved in a scheme Mr. Penarth financed."

"The one involving Northam?" His wife frowned. "You didn't mention that earlier."

"I was hoping to have more information on it before I . . . bothered you with the details." Robert braced himself as she advanced toward him.

"In truth, you didn't want to upset me, did you?"

"You are correct."

She placed her hand on his waistcoat. "Please don't keep me in ignorance about such matters."

"I didn't want to worry you."

"Which is no excuse, because I will worry anyway." She straightened his cravat. "If my father is caught up in these matters, I would rather know."

"What else is Henrietta suggesting?" Robert asked.

"Just that you, I, and the entire community of Kurland St. Mary are determined not to convict anyone for murdering her husband."

"When in fact the issue is that we have too many suitable candidates and the problem is narrowing down who had the opportunity and the motive." Robert kissed the top of her head and stepped back. "Now, do you want to accompany me? There has been very little snow this afternoon, but I don't want to be out for too long after it gets dark, and we need to be back in time for dinner."

When they drew up at the Queen's Head it was still remarkably quiet, as the coaches were unable to get through and most of the local farms were snowed in. One of the ostlers came out to take the horse's head, allowing Robert to help Lucy down from the gig.

They were greeted warmly by Mr. and Mrs. Jarvis, who insisted on offering them mulled cider while one of the maids went to inquire if Mr. Penarth was willing to see them. She came back quickly and asked if they would mind accompanying her upstairs, as Mr. Penarth was indisposed.

Robert held the door open for his wife and followed her into the best bedchamber, which smelled of mustard and camphor. Mr. Penarth was sitting in front of the fire, his feet in a basin of steaming water. In his right hand he clutched a large handkerchief.

"I do apologize for not getting up to greet you, Lady Kurland," he said, his voice hoarse between coughs. "I find myself rather unwell." He indicated the table beside him that held a bottle of whisky and a tin full of some kind of lozenge. "Mrs. Jarvis and her staff are taking very good care of me, but I don't think I'll be able to leave for at least another day or so."

"I am sorry to hear that, sir." Robert instinctively backed up a step as Mr. Penarth sneezed loudly. "We are more than happy to wait until you are recovered before bothering you with our questions."

"I wanted to see you, Sir Robert." Mr. Penarth paused to blow his nose. "I managed to get a message through to my secretary in London. I expect his reply to my letter in the next day or so."

"Thank you for doing that." Robert bowed. "Have you had any more thoughts as to Lord Northam and his financial matters?"

"Nothing in particular, Sir Robert, but after further consideration, I am fairly certain there was a Harrington on that investors list."

Beside him Lucy stiffened, and Robert laid a calming hand on her arm.

"Then I look forward to seeing it." He paused. "Did you meet with anyone apart from Lord Northam while you were here?"

Mr. Penarth looked up. "Such as?"

"Any members of the Harrington family?"

"You're a clever man, aren't you, Sir Robert." Mr. Penarth nodded. "I thought as much. I did happen to meet a Mr. Max Harrington, but we spoke only for a moment. I saw him arguing with Northam, and I made a point to make Mr. Harrington's acquaintance before I ventured back upstairs."

"What did you talk about?" Robert asked

"Lord Northam. Mr. Harrington was more than willing to share his grievances with me." Mr. Penarth paused to sneeze into his handkerchief. "He was also well on the way to being in his cups, and perhaps rather more loquacious than he should have been."

"Did Max mention that he was in debt to Northam?" Lucy asked.

"Not directly, but as I'd overheard a goodly part of his conversation with Northam, I was aware that he was."

"Did he ask for your help?"

Mr. Penarth shrugged. "He was more intent on reliving his grievances than asking me for anything. I'm not even sure he knew who I was."

"You didn't tell him?"

"I attempted to explain my interest, but as I mentioned, Mr. Harrington was already rather drunk."

Robert grimaced. It sounded just like Max.

"When Mr. Harrington was speaking to Lord Northam, did he threaten him?" Lucy asked.

"Ma'am, they were threatening each other, but I did hear the boy mention a duel." He grimaced. "Northam laughed."

Mr. Penarth started coughing again, and Robert gave Lucy a harassed glance. "Perhaps we should come back tomorrow, sir."

"As you wish." Mr. Penarth waved a hand in their general direction and kept on hacking. "A pleasure, Lady Kurland, Sir Robert."

Robert paused on the landing at the top of the main staircase and faced Lucy.

"At least Mr. Penarth confirmed what Max said about his conversation with Northam."

"But is that good or bad?" Lucy asked.

"That depends whether you believe Max is capable of murder. He definitely spoke to Northam, he attempted to fight with him, and he was angry."

"If that is the case, why didn't he kill Northam right then and there?" Lucy asked. "I can almost see Max losing his temper and lashing out in a rage, but waiting until the next day and luring his prey into a trap? That doesn't seem like him at all."

"I can't argue with your logic." Robert frowned. "I'm still not sure Mr. Penarth is telling us everything."

Lucy glanced at the closed door. "We can hardly go back in there and bully a sick man, can we?"

"Unfortunately not." Robert hesitated. "Did you notice that when I asked if he'd met any members of the Harrington family, he didn't answer me immediately?"

"Do you think he also met my father?"

"If he is on the list of contributors to Northam's fake trading deal, then why not? Mr. Penarth might have had more than one reason to come to Kurland St. Mary and collect on his debts."

Lucy started down the stairs. "Perhaps it is time for us to speak to my father again. He is supposed to be coming up to the hall to tell us how Rose is faring this evening, so we had better get back."

Robert followed her down the stairs. In all the upheaval, he'd forgotten the rector was coming to dinner. If he had his way, he'd make sure any conversation between them took place when his wife was occupied elsewhere.

Robert came down to dinner early while Lucy went up to supervise the nursery and put Ned to bed. He met Joshua in the drawing room along with the Fletchers and the Stanfords. There was no sign of his father-in-law or the earl and countess. After making sure they all had a drink, he turned to Joshua.

"Did you manage to retrieve your possessions?"

"Indeed, I did." Joshua pointed at his shirt. "I now have clean linen and can return the things I borrowed from you. I left your letter with the kitchen maid, who promised to take it up to Mrs. Harrington when she woke up."

"Thank you."

"Has Max turned up yet?" Joshua asked.

"Yes, you missed that little drama while you were out. He was discovered warm and dry and being very well taken care of at Bellweather House. The earl and I went over there and brought him safely home."

Joshua lowered his voice. "Did he say anything about Northam?"

"What about him?"

"With all due respect, Kurland, I'm not stupid. Max disappeared conveniently around the time Northam was killed, and we both know he was in debt to the obnoxious man."

"How did you know that?" Robert asked, intrigued.

Joshua shrugged. "Because I heard Max and his father arguing about it on the way to the christening. We were in the same carriage." He paused to look Robert in the eye. "Is it possible that Max was involved in Northam's death?"

"I don't care to speculate about such a serious matter," Robert said. "The earl and his son are very aware of my position, and that's all you need to know right now."

"Understood, Major." Joshua offered him a smart salute. "I'll keep my nose out of it."

"I'd prefer it if you continued to keep your eyes open." Robert offered his fellow soldier a faint smile. "I could do with all the assistance I can muster."

Robert turned as the rector came into the drawing room, followed closely by his brother and the countess. Had they been discussing the current situation together? If that was true, Robert wasn't sure he appreciated it. He went over to the rector.

"Good evening, sir. I hope you bring good news of my aunt?"

His father-in-law sighed. "She is resting comfortably in her bed. Mrs. Culpepper has come to watch over her while I am absent, for which I am very grateful."

Dorothea, the curate's wife, was an amiable soul quite unlike her sister, Mrs. Fletcher, who was rather more exacting. Robert knew that his aunt was in excellent hands. He glanced over at the clock on the mantelpiece, noting that he had at least a quarter of an hour before dinner was served. He touched the rector's shoulder.

"Would you mind coming to my study? There is something I wish to discuss with you."

"As you wish."

There was a note of resignation in his father-in-law's usually jovial voice and a decided slump to his shoulders as he followed Robert out into the hall and to his study.

Robert shut the door. "I hate to ask you this, but do you know a Mr. Penarth?"

To his astonishment, the rector nodded. "Unfortunately, I do. I was involved in a trading venture that turned out to be a complete fraud. Mr. Penarth wrote to me about a month ago to request my assistance in bringing the perpetrator of the scheme to justice."

"Ah, thank you for your honesty." Robert cleared his throat. "Did the venture affect your finances?"

"Yes, rather badly, in fact." The rector grimaced. "I've had to reduce my spending quite considerably."

"With all due respect, sir, I do have to wonder what induced you to back a scheme headed by Lord Northam."

"I wasn't aware that he was part of it. I was approached by another partner." His father-in-law took a hasty turn around the room. "My brother said that you believe Max might have killed Northam. Is that true?"

"He admitted to owing money to Northam and threatening him," Robert said. "And he did arrange to meet Northam at the Queen's Head the night before the christening, where, according to witnesses, they argued loudly."

The rector shook his head. "Max isn't the kind of boy who would kill anyone."

"You'd be surprised what 'boys' can do, sir," Robert countered. "I had many such as Max under my command in the cavalry. They can be ferocious fighters."

"I'd much rather I was convicted of murdering Northam than Max. At least I've had a long and enjoyable life."

Robert paused. "Is that a confession, sir?"

"Of course not!" The rector looked affronted. "I'm merely hypothesizing."

"Then perhaps you could refrain from doing so and accept that a man such as yourself, who has been left in financial straits, would have just cause to be angry at the person who swindled him, and might just be considered a murderer?"

"I appreciate your attempt at logic, Kurland, but I didn't kill him."

"Even though your financial losses were significant?" Robert persisted.

His father-in-law shrugged. "As you well know, my wife is in possession of a substantial fortune. Even if I were penniless, I suspect she would be more than willing to pay the bills."

"Does she know about your current financial position?"

For the first time, the rector looked uncomfortable. "Considering her present affliction I have chosen not to inform her of that, or of your continuing suspicions. I do not wish to adversely affect her health."

"Is it possible she might have discovered the information by herself?"

"How so?" The rector frowned.

"From her daughter? The woman who was married to Northam?"

"I hadn't thought of that. If Henrietta has communicated with my wife, I can guarantee that I will have been portrayed as a villain." The rector paused. "And, now that I think about it, Rose *has* written to her solicitor recently."

Robert marveled both at his father-in-law's blithe belief that there was no evidence to convict him of anything and his willingness to incriminate himself.

"Lord Northam was discovered dead in your study, sir. He is responsible for your loss of income. A jury might easily believe that you had a motive for murder."

"Yes, yes, I know all that, but—"

Robert interrupted him. "Then please be aware that both you and Max are under suspicion, and behave accordingly. This is not some amusing academic exercise in logic. This could result in your conviction for murder!"

He strode toward the door and opened it wide. "Dinner will be served very shortly. Perhaps we should make our way to the drawing room before Lucy wonders where we are."

Chapter 10

"I am determined to see Rose." Lucy faced Robert across the breakfast table, glad for once that they were both early risers and that none of their guests had yet emerged from their rooms. "Dr. Fletcher said she is more settled now and that, as long as I don't agitate her, I can pay her a visit."

Robert raised an eyebrow. He'd been in a bad mood ever since he'd emerged from his study with her father the evening before.

"You're not exactly known as a calming influence, my dear. Are you sure that you should go?"

"I beg your pardon? You appear to be the one causing all the trouble in this household." Lucy set down her knife with a clatter. "I don't know what you said to my father last night, but he was very upset during dinner. Even a mention of Ned failed to cheer him up."

"Your father is a suspect in a murder. He seems unwilling or unable to take the accusations against him seriously. I had to remind him that whatever I think of Max's story, a jury is still more likely to convict *him*."

"Well, no wonder the poor man looked so miserable, and you are suggesting I am the one who lacks tact!" Lucy shot back. "Weren't we supposed to speak to him together?"

Her husband avoided her gaze as he refilled his coffee cup. "I don't believe I said that."

"Perhaps I just assumed that we would, seeing as this matter concerns both of us?"

"I took the opportunity to speak to him before dinner." Robert sipped his coffee. "You were otherwise engaged."

"With your children, both of whom were very disappointed that their own father could not find a few minutes to come up and say good night to them."

Robert grimaced. "That's quite unfair, Lucy. I went up to see them after dinner."

"When they were both fast asleep."

There was a small taut silence before Robert continued speaking.

"Your father says he hasn't told Rose about any of this, which strikes me as ridiculous."

"Why? Most men don't share information with their wives," Lucy countered. "They think we need protecting from the harsh realities of life. My father is no different, and you are a fine one to talk."

"But Rose is eminently capable, and probably a better financial manager than your father will ever be. Damnation! If he sold off half the bloodstock in his stables, he could pull himself out of debt in an instant, but that would never occur to him."

Lucy rose and shoved in her chair. "You are in a most disagreeable mood this morning."

"Because I'm sick and tired of your family thinking they are above the law," Robert snapped. "I am trying to make allowances, but—"

"It is not my family's fault that your cousin married a cheat and a swindler. Perhaps you should think on that!" Lucy retorted, turned on her heel and left the room.

A walk down to the rectory through the snow would help calm her spirits and allow her to think through the events of the last few days. She had a sense that she was missing something obvious, and that Robert's frustration, however badly expressed, mirrored her own. The specter of death had come close to her and Kurland St. Mary before but had never involved so many members of her and Robert's families. Whichever way she shook the puzzle, someone she cared for was implicated in a murder.

Lucy put on her stoutest boots, warmest coat, and bonnet and set off down the drive toward St. Mary's Church. It sat on the corner of the Kurland estate opposite the rectory her father had rebuilt in the modern style less than twenty years ago.

If her father and Max hadn't murdered Northam, and she was quite convinced on that, who had? She stopped suddenly and stared out over the bare tree-lined horizon. What about Mr. Penarth? Northam had been afraid enough to flee London rather than face the provider of his loan. It would've been easy for Mr. Penarth to walk down to the rectory, let himself in while everyone else was busy with the christening, meet Northam as arranged, and kill him.

Mr. Penarth had already told Robert that he doubted the courts would get his money back for him, so why not take justice into his own hands? He could have killed Northam and been away back to London the next day on the mail coach without anyone being the wiser. The only reason he was still trapped in Kurland St. Mary was because of the appalling weather.

Had Robert bothered to ask anyone at the Queen's Head whether Mr. Penarth had ventured out the morning of the christening? Lucy set off walking again. After she visited Rose at the rectory, she would continue on to the inn and ask those important questions herself.

"Kurland, might I have a word?"

The Earl of Harrington appeared at the door of Robert's study, where Robert had retreated after his bruising encounter with his wife over breakfast. He was already regretting his argument with her. The last thing they needed was to be on opposite sides in this matter when there was so much at stake.

"Please, come in." Robert stood and waited until his guest was seated before sitting down again.

"I have something to tell you that is dashed awkward, but it needs to be said." The earl met Robert's gaze. "I was the one who paid off Max's debt to Northam."

For a moment, Robert simply stared at him before he managed to speak.

"Would you care to explain how that came about, my lord?"

"It's quite simple, really. I became aware that Max was in trouble. Although I had threatened not to pay any more of his gambling debts, I was merely attempting to frighten him."

"Frighten him into doing what exactly?"

"Keeping within the bounds of his exceedingly generous allowance." The earl's easy smile dimmed. "I thought that if I tightened the screws a little, Max would come to his senses. That's why I refused to listen when he asked for an advance on his allowance and ordered him to accompany us to the christening."

"I see." Robert was in no hurry to end the conversation.

"But when I discovered that Northam of all people was here in Kurland St. Mary, I was anxious to avoid any confrontation between him and Max that might disrupt your celebrations."

"How considerate of you." Robert inclined his head a deliberate inch.

"I sought Northam out the evening before the christening and paid off the debt in full." The earl's expression twisted. "He was quite insufferable about it, of course."

"I can imagine."

"I didn't tell Max until this morning." The earl dropped his gaze to his hands. "As you might imagine, he was quite angry with me."

"One might hope he would've been grateful."

"At some level I suspect he is, but he insists his gentlemanly pride is hurt. You know how young men can be." The earl twisted his signet ring around his finger. "I wanted you to know about this because if there was no debt owing, then Max had no reason to wish Northam dead, and you can take him off your list of suspects."

Robert let the silence grow between them until the earl was forced to look up at him.

"You are suggesting that although Max admitted arguing with Northam, he did nothing more than that and was unaware that Northam had been killed until I told him so at the stables."

"Yes, that's it, exactly." The earl nodded vigorously, rose to his feet, and started for the door. "I'm glad you understand your familial obligations. I'll still keep an eye on Max, just to make sure he doesn't do anything stupid, but apart from that we can consider this matter closed, yes?"

Robert didn't attempt to detain the earl as he left the room, because what was the point? The man was doing everything he could to safeguard the future of his only son. The question was, how much of what he had said was true?

"Devil take it!" Robert smacked his palm down on the surface of his desk.

He wished Lucy were home, but she'd gone to the rectory to speak to Rose, and he wasn't expecting her back for quite a while. He read through the letters Dermot had left for him to sign on his desk and then sealed them. The house was quiet, and he wondered if any of his guests had come down for breakfast. With Lucy being absent, it was his duty to attend to them.

After picking up the letters, he took them through to the hall, where James would arrange for them to be taken down to the mail coach, if it ever turned up. He paused, his attention on the slow murmur of voices from the breakfast room. Did he really want to face the Stanfords and the Harringtons when his ability to believe that the earl was telling the truth was superficial at best?

He turned abruptly and went up the stairs. He would make up for missing his children's bedtime the night before by visiting them in the nursery. There at least he wouldn't have to pretend to be anything but himself.

"Thank you, Maddy." Lucy smiled at the kitchen maid, who had accompanied her to Rose's bedchamber. "Perhaps you might make some tea and bring it up?"

"Yes, my lady. Mrs. Culpepper said to tell you that she would be back later to sit with Mrs. Harrington while she has her dinner, and to take your time."

"Thank you."

Lucy tapped on the door and went in to find Rose sitting upright in her bed against a pile of pillows. She had her sewing basket beside her and a book facedown on the counterpane. Her smile brightened when she saw her guest.

"Lucy! How very kind of you to visit me when I know you must be busy with your guests. Ambrose said that no one has been able to leave the village since the christening and that they are all still staying with you."

"As it is mostly family, I can't say that it has been difficult." Lucy bent to kiss Rose's cheek and sat on the chair beside the bed. "They are very well behaved."

Rose chuckled. "Well, I am grateful that you had room for Captain Coles. The poor man had to retrieve his clothing from us yesterday."

"As he is a military man, I doubt it caused him too much distress." Lucy looked more closely at Rose, noting the dark shadows under her eyes and the tight lines around her mouth. "How are you feeling?"

Her companion grimaced. "I fatigue very easily, and getting out of bed makes my head swim, which is most inconvenient." She rested a hand on her rounded stomach.

"My other pregnancies were easy compared with this one, but I am a great deal older."

"Dr. Fletcher believes that if you obey his every instruction you will do very well," Lucy said encouragingly.

"Dr. Fletcher is remarkably bossy. He wants me to spend the next four months in bed." Rose said. "It is not natural for me to lie around doing nothing, and it simply makes me worry even more."

Lucy took Rose's hand and squeezed it. "Having experienced my own anxieties during my pregnancies, I can only sympathize."

"Ambrose is very troubled," Rose confided. "He feels somewhat responsible for my predicament."

"As he should," Lucy said. "You are carrying his child."

"A child neither of us expected." Rose let out a long breath. "He says he is delighted, but knowing what happened to your mother, Lucy, I do wonder if he fears the same thing might happen again."

"It won't happen," Lucy said with far more confidence than she felt. "Dr. Fletcher and Grace Turner will not allow it."

There was a tap on the door, and the maid brought in the tea Lucy had requested. After pouring them both a cup, Lucy settled back in her seat.

"How is Henrietta?" Rose asked.

"She is . . ." Lucy considered her words carefully. "Rather distraught."

"Is she still blaming Ambrose for her husband's death?"

"Yes. She seems to think that the whole village is conspiring to prevent her from prosecuting him. I have tried to reassure her that Robert is her cousin, and that he will do his best to obtain justice for Northam, but she refuses to believe it because he is married to me."

"Henrietta was always stubborn," Rose remarked. "She seems unable to understand that quite a lot of people disliked her husband intently."

"Although I hesitate to speak ill of the dead, he certainly wasn't beloved," Lucy agreed. "But he was Henrietta's husband, so perhaps she saw a better side of him than we did."

"I doubt he had a better side." Rose set her cup down on the tray beside her bed. "He was always disrespectful, discouraged me from forming a relationship with my grandchildren, and resented my spending any money that wasn't on him or Henrietta. Sometimes I begged her to speak up and defend me, but she never would. She became as bad as he was."

"I'm sorry," Lucy said softly, aware that Rose's color had risen. "I didn't mean to distress you. Perhaps we should talk about something else."

"*I* am sorry that my daughter and her late husband brought their ill will and troubles to Kurland St. Mary. You cannot imagine my embarrassment when they chose to berate me in front of my own husband about my condition." Rose's fingers tightened on the counterpane. "And to insinuate that poor Ambrose had married me for my money and intended to use it to benefit his own family was *inexcusable*."

Lucy nodded, unwilling to add to Rose's grievances or agitate her further. After a moment, Rose resumed speaking.

"Dr. Fletcher said that I was not to allow Henrietta to visit me, and I am beginning to believe he was right. I must confess that I don't want to speak to her, Lucy. I cannot find it in myself to offer her the sincere condolences and support that any mother should offer her child on such a sad occasion."

"Considering how she and Northam have behaved toward you, Rose, I cannot fault your decision," Lucy said. "Dr. Fletcher is right. Your health and the health of your child must come first."

She poured Rose some more tea and spent several minutes describing how Ned had climbed up the ladder into the hayloft without telling anyone, creating a panic in the stable yard when they discovered he was missing. She was relieved to see Rose laugh more easily, and even more reluctant to ask any of the pointed questions hovering on the tip of her tongue.

Despite her best efforts to be sociable, Lucy could see Rose was already beginning to tire. She decided it would be better to leave her to rest. She assembled all the tea things on the tray and set it next to the door to carry down.

"It has been delightful, but I have to go home, Rose. Robert is expecting me, and I don't want to be walking through another snowstorm."

"You are more than welcome to borrow our gig," Rose offered. "I know your father wouldn't like you being out on foot in this weather."

"It would take longer to get the horse and gig out than it will for me to walk home," Lucy said. "But thank you for the offer." She went to kiss Rose's cheek. "I will tell Robert that you are looking very well indeed. He will be most relieved."

"He is a good boy," Rose said. She pointed at her bedside table. "Captain Coles delivered a letter from him."

"Robert wanted to visit you, but Dr. Fletcher told him to write rather than bother you in person," Lucy said.

"Please tell him that I will write back. There is a lot to say. I have been too tired to get out my writing desk and apply myself in earnest to the task of replying."

"I'm sure he will understand." Lucy hesitated. "Is there anything you wish me to tell him?"

Rose raised her chin. "You can tell him that I did change my will, and that I don't regret it for an instant."

Lucy was pondering Rose's final remark as she made her way down the stairs. She left the tray in the deserted kitchen and was just about to leave when her father came in through the back door with his dogs. He'd obviously been out riding and still carried his whip.

"Ah! Lucy." He smiled but didn't quite meet her eyes.

"Have you been visiting Rose? She looks much better today, doesn't she?"

"Yes, indeed." Lucy didn't move as he attempted to get past her. "Is it true that you owed Lord Northam money?"

His brows came together. "I don't think that is any of your business, my dear, is it?"

"If it led you to fight with Lord Northam in your study and kill him, then yes."

Her father drew in a harsh breath. "It's come to this, has it? My own daughter believes I am a murderer? Shame on you, Lucy Harrington, shame indeed. Your sister Anna would never have believed such a thing of me."

He whistled to his dogs and marched away from her. Undeterred, she followed him right into his study.

"Why should I not ask you these questions? If you didn't murder Northam, someone else did. You seem unwilling to make any effort to discover who that was!"

His face settled into familiar stubborn lines. "Maybe it's because I believe in the power of the law and that no jury would convict me of such flimsy evidence!"

"It's more than that. Do you think your brother will save you?" Lucy finally had his attention. "Not at the expense of his son, Father. If he has to choose between you and Max to satisfy Robert's desire for justice, then I can assure you that he will not choose you."

"Go home, Daughter." Her father's tone was icy. "Go and attend to your family and leave matters of the law to those far more capable of logic than you will ever be."

Lucy met his furious gaze. "I'll go, but I suggest you put that supposedly superior intellect of yours to work and try to remember exactly what happened the morning of the christening and who you allowed into your house, because if you don't, you will be standing trial for murder."

She stomped out of the house toward the street that went to the Queen's Head. The snow had been cleared from the road, but a sharp frost overnight had made the ground as smooth as a mirror, and she had to watch her step. Despite her father's harsh words, Lucy was pleased that she wasn't either crying or cowed. Living with a man who appreciated her had taught her not to care for her father's unfavorable opinion of her.

"Lady Kurland!"

She looked up to see Captain Coles waving at her. He was dressed warmly in his military greatcoat and appeared oblivious to the biting wind that had reddened Lucy's cheeks and made her nose and ears tingle.

"Good morning, Captain. You are out bright and early."

"I'm not used to being cooped up, my lady. I felt the need to stretch my legs and offered to walk down to the inn to see if any letters or parcels had got through."

"That was kind of you." She gestured back at the rectory. "I was just visiting Mrs. Harrington, who was very apologetic that you had been turned out of your room."

"It was of no matter. I could hardly stay there demanding to be waited on while the lady of the house was incapacitated, now, could I?" He offered her his arm. "Are you returning to the hall, or do you have other errands to run? I am more than willing to accompany you before I visit the inn."

Lucy took his proffered arm and placed her gloved hand on his sleeve. "In truth, I was headed that way myself."

"Then we can proceed together." Captain Coles started walking. "I must say that I am enjoying my first winter in England for many years."

"If you intend to stay here, Captain, you will soon get used to it and wish yourself in warmer climes." Lucy's breath puffed out in a little cloud as they walked up the incline. "My brother, Anthony, is stationed in India with your old regiment and he seems to be enjoying himself immensely."

"He's young." Captain Coles chuckled.

"And he hasn't yet had to fight in an actual war." Lucy gripped his arm more firmly as her foot slid from under her. "I pray he never does."

"Amen to that." He headed toward the stable yard of the inn. "I suspect it will be easier to navigate the cobbles and straw than the slope on the street entrance."

Lucy stepped over the threshold and sighed as the smell of the wood fire, brewed hops, and ash engulfed her. The hatch to the cellar was open, which suggested that Mr. Jarvis was occupied down there, so Lucy navigated her way to the kitchen at the back of the house.

Mrs. Jarvis welcomed her and Captain Coles with her usual enthusiasm.

"Have you come to see if the mail has gotten through yet? Because I'm afraid it hasn't—although we did get news that the mail coach is going to attempt to get here tomorrow if there is no snow overnight." She pointed at the table. "Now, sit yourselves down and I'll get you both a warm drink to set you back on your way to the hall. How are your children, my lady?"

"They are both very well, thank you." Lucy received her cup of warmed whisky and ginger and sipped it carefully. "How is Mr. Penarth?"

"He's still coughing fit to burst." Mrs. Jarvis shook her head. "But he is determined to get on the first coach back to London, I can tell you that."

"Which day did he arrive?" Lucy asked after another fortifying drink.

Mrs. Jarvis frowned. "The day before the christening, I think?" She turned to Captain Coles. "You arrived on the same coach, sir, didn't you?"

"Yes, I did. Mr. Penarth was a very pleasant traveling companion."

"Did he mention to either of you why he was coming to Kurland St. Mary?" Lucy asked.

"He indicated that he had business here, but not with whom. That's all I remember," Captain Coles said.

Mrs. Jarvis nodded. "He said the same to me."

"Did he venture out into the village at all?"

"He did, my lady, but only on foot. Mr. Jarvis offered him a horse, but he said he couldn't ride."

The horrified expression on Captain Coles's face was identical to the one Robert would've had at the idea that someone had never learned to ride. If Mr. Penarth had stepped out, he could easily have located the rectory.

"Mr. Penarth grew up in London. He's probably never needed to mount a horse in his life," Lucy said. "I do hope he enjoyed his walks. Kurland St. Mary is a very pretty village."

"He did tell me he went into the church, my lady." Mrs. Jarvis was back to stirring something on the stove. "He even asked me what time the services were held—although he doesn't look like a very godly man to me."

"Perhaps he has hidden depths," Captain Coles said with a smile. "One never quite knows when a man will develop a taste for religion."

"Do you wish to speak to Mr. Penarth, my lady?" Mrs. Jarvis asked.

"No, I don't wish to disturb him, but please tell him I called and that I was inquiring as to his health." Lucy finished her drink and rose from the table, pulling on her gloves. "Thank you for the most welcome beverage. I expect someone will be down tomorrow to see what the mail coach will bring."

"That will probably be me." Captain Coles grinned and bowed to his hostess, who blew him a kiss.

When they exited the inn, the sun was attempting to break through the clouds, making the hard frost glint like crystal. Lucy retied the ribbons of her bonnet and turned toward home, her hand tucked securely in the crook of Captain Coles's arm.

"Robert said that you don't intend to rejoin your regiment," Lucy remarked as they inched their way down the slope toward the shortcut through the church graveyard.

"My father can no longer afford to help me pay for a new commission. Without war prizes or indeed a war to advance promotion, I'm destined to be stuck as Captain Coles for the rest of my life."

"Will you miss your regiment?"

"I'll miss my friends and the camaraderie," Captain Coles confessed. "But my father needs my help with his estate, which has suffered some severe financial losses in the last few years. I suspect there is very little money left, but with good management and time I hope to provide us both with a sufficient income to live modestly, if not excessively."

"I'm sure you will achieve your goal," Lucy said. "I know my husband thinks very highly of you indeed."

"Sir Robert is a good man and he was an even better officer. Hard, but fair."

"When your future is more settled, we would enjoy welcoming you and your father at Kurland Hall."

"Thank you, my lady." Captain Coles smiled down at her. "I am looking forward to watching my delightful new goddaughter grow up to become as wise and beautiful as her mother."

Lucy blushed and concentrated on the route ahead as they made their way between the church and the graveyard and emerged on the drive up to Kurland Hall. Smoke billowed from the many redbrick Tudor chimneys and the emerging sun reflected off the diamond-paned windows that faced the park.

"It is a fine house," Captain Coles remarked as they drew nearer.

"I have grown very fond of it myself," Lucy confessed. "Although it can be confusing for guests, what with its many staircases and doors."

"I enjoy a puzzle." Captain Coles opened the side door with a flourish and stepped back. "If you'll excuse me, I promised to go and tell Mr. Coleman if his package from London had arrived."

"Thank you for escorting me home." Lucy smiled up at him.

She entered the house, shedding her gloves and untying her bonnet as she walked through to the kitchen, where her staff was busy preparing the midday meal. After a quick conversation with her housekeeper and cook, she proceeded through into the main hall. She was just about to go upstairs when her husband appeared and beckoned imperiously at her from his study door.

After their disagreement earlier that morning, she contemplated pretending that she hadn't seen his rather autocratic gesture, but curiosity won out, and she went toward him.

"Lucy, thank goodness you are home." He ushered her into his study and shut the door firmly behind her. "Just after you left, the earl asked to speak to me in private and confessed that he had paid off Max's debt to Northam."

"What?" Lucy spun around from warming her hands at the fire. "When?"

"He said he met with Northam and paid off the debt but neglected to mention it to Max until this morning."

Lucy frowned. "Even if that is true, which I sincerely doubt, it hardly exonerates Max. If Max didn't know the debt had been paid off until today, then his previous actions are still questionable."

"That was my first thought." Robert leaned back against the door, his arms folded over his chest. "The earl suggested that by paying off Northam, Max was now free of suspicion and that I should take him off my list of suspects."

Lucy stared at him in silence. "But that makes no sense."

"It does to the earl." Robert shrugged. "All he cares about is making sure Max is protected. I can understand his view, but I can't say I agree with him."

"Did my uncle say exactly *when* he paid Northam off?"

"He said he went to the inn the evening before the christening and met Northam there."

"It appears that half our guests claim they were at the Queen's Head that night, and yet none of them remember or mention seeing one another." Lucy wrinkled her nose. "Perhaps we should ask Mr. Penarth about that as well."

"I assume he's still at the inn?" Robert asked.

"Yes, indeed. I went to inquire as to our mail after visiting Rose. Mrs. Jarvis said he was planning on leaving tomorrow if the mail coach showed up as promised."

"Then I must endeavor to speak to him before he departs." Robert walked over to his desk. "I must tell you, Lucy, that your uncle's behavior does not sit well with me."

"How so?"

"He implied that I should conveniently overlook his son's possible guilt because I am connected to the Harrington family, yet he seems to forget that I am also connected to the family of the man who was murdered."

"My uncle has a very high opinion of his worth and standing in the world. He probably meant no offense but assumed you would inevitably bow to his superior rank." Lucy walked over to his desk. "And the thing is, Robert, we already know that if Max was brought to trial it would never go ahead. My uncle would call in some favors, and the case would be dismissed."

"I am fully aware of that, but I still don't like it." Robert's mouth set in a firm line. "I didn't say anything to the earl, but at this point I have no intention of letting Max Harrington get away with anything."

Chapter 11

Robert waited to see if Lucy would rush to defend her family, but to his immense relief she did nothing more than nod, sit down, and arrange her skirts before looking up at him again expectantly.

"Please excuse my manners. I should have asked you how Rose was before ranting about the Harringtons," Robert said.

"It's quite all right. If I had been here when my uncle tried to sell you such a ridiculous tale, I doubt I would've been capable of keeping my opinions to myself."

Robert smiled. "I must confess that I was astounded at my own restraint, but I decided it was far better for him to believe that the matter was settled than for me to point out the error of his ways."

"I also saw my father at the rectory." Lucy grimaced. "We argued quite dreadfully. I attempted to direct his attention to the fact that he might be convicted of murder and that perhaps he should stop taking the matter so lightly. I suggested that if he thought his brother was going to save him rather than Max, then he was mistaken."

"I suspect he didn't appreciate your sentiments?"

"He told me to go home and mind my own business."

"But you were right to say that to him." Robert gestured at the door. "The earl proved this morning that his only real concern is for his son. He didn't mention your father once."

"But what if my father truly believes his brother will save him?" Lucy asked slowly. "It isn't out of the realm of possibility. If my father agrees to take the blame for Northam's death, thus freeing Max from any threat of a trial, then my uncle might well be inclined to help acquit him."

"That's a remarkably cynical assessment, my dear."

"But it might also be true." Lucy held his gaze. "I know my father's family better than you do, and they will do anything to keep the Harrington name unblemished. It would also explain why my father is happily ignoring the implications of being accused of murder. He doesn't think justice really applies to *him*."

For the first time, Robert heard the hurt behind her words and studied her more closely. Whatever had happened at the rectory that morning had affected his wife more deeply than she was prepared to admit. Her father was a selfish man who rarely acknowledged the burden he had thrust on his oldest daughter when her mother had died birthing the twins.

But what to say to her? He wasn't known as a sympathetic man, but he hated seeing his wife hurt.

"Your father is a fool," he said gruffly. "You should pay no heed to him."

She offered him a quick smile. "Thank you. I must admit that for the first time in my life I was more than willing to wash my hands and walk away as directed. He has Rose to fight for him now, and my allegiance is to you, and our family."

"Which is exactly as it should be," Robert said firmly. "You are valued here, my dear, never forget it." He cleared his throat and sought desperately for a new subject. "Did Rose mention if she'd had a letter from me?"

"She received it, and she intends to write back to you at some length." Lucy hesitated. "She told me to tell you that she did alter her will, and she doesn't regret it."

"Ah." Robert nodded. "Was that all she said?"

"Yes. She was becoming agitated about how badly Henrietta and Basil had treated her. I didn't want to make her ill, so I didn't press too hard."

"I understand." Even though he appreciated Lucy's concern for Rose's health, he wished he'd been there. He suspected Rose would've been more forthcoming with some direct questions from him. "I hope she writes back to me soon and clarifies her remarks. For all I know she could've left everything to Henrietta and cut out the rest of her family and your father completely."

"From what she said about the Northams, I suspect that isn't the case," Lucy said. "In truth I was quite surprised about how angry she was with Henrietta. She has no desire to see her at all."

"I can't say that alarms me. Henrietta is hardly likely to make her mother feel better."

"But Rose was quite unlike herself," Lucy continued. "Perhaps her concern for her own health and her new husband has finally made her see the Northams with new eyes. In the past, she has always been the first to defend Henrietta."

As the clock on the mantelpiece chimed the hour, Robert rose to his feet and went over to his wife. "Rose is tougher than she looks."

"As are all women." Lucy took his proffered hand and stood up. "Do you want me to speak to my uncle about Max, or should I leave things as they are?"

"Leave them." Robert glanced out the window. "If the weather keeps improving, our guests might be able to depart in a day or so, and good riddance to the lot of them."

"But then Max will be gone, and I doubt he would be willing to return to Hertford for a trial." Lucy paused. "Is it worth appealing to Max's better instincts? Would he care if his own uncle was prosecuted for a crime he committed?"

"Having spoken extensively to Max, I'm not sure he has developed a better side, and even if he did, you can be sure the earl would never let him express his opinions if it meant he implicated himself."

Lucy sighed. "I fear you are correct." She headed for the door. "Are you going to speak to Mr. Penarth today?"

"I think I must." Robert held the door open for her. "If he intends to leave tomorrow, this might be my last chance."

"Has it occurred to you that Mr. Penarth could've murdered Northam?"

"I suppose he could have." Robert paused. "Do you have any evidence to suggest that he did?"

"Mrs. Jarvis said he went out walking in the village after he arrived and that he was very interested in the church."

"Which means he probably had a fair idea where the rectory was." Robert nodded. "He didn't strike me as the kind of man to do his own dirty work, but I might be wrong. He certainly disliked Northam, and had a good reason to wish him dead."

"That's what I thought."

Robert touched her shoulder. "Lucy, you do realize that your father and cousin are still the most likely to have killed Northam, don't you?"

She raised her gaze to meet his. "There's no need to treat me like a child, Robert. I am fully aware of that, but you cannot allow your fixation on my family to rule out other options."

"I take your point." He dropped a kiss on the top of her head. "I will go and speak to Mr. Penarth immediately."

She watched him walk toward the rear of the house, his dogs at his heels, and turned to the stairs. She was about to go into the nursery to see her children when Betty, her maid, came running toward her.

"My lady, can you come with me right now? Lady Northam is having some kind of fit!"

"Of course." Lucy picked up her skirts and hurried after her maid. There was a footman stationed outside Henrietta's door, which was wide open.

"I went in to see if she needed any linen washing, my lady, and she was screaming fit to burst," Betty gasped.

"Get someone to fetch Dr. Fletcher as quickly as possible."

"Yes, my lady." Betty ran off.

Lucy stopped in the doorway and surveyed the wrecked room before focusing her attention on Henrietta.

"What in God's name are you doing? Are you ill?"

Henrietta spun around, her eyes glittering. She had a broken chair leg clenched in her hand like a weapon.

"Go away!"

"You are destroying my house. I am going nowhere," Lucy said staunchly. "If there is something troubling you, then tell me what it is and I will try to help you."

"You can't help." Henrietta threw the chair leg to the ground. "The only person who can help me is dead." She stared straight at Lucy. "The bastard hid it from me."

"Hid what?" Lucy asked.

"What I was owed! The night before the christening, he told me he had secured the funding necessary for us to leave for the continent and that I should ready myself to leave." She pointed at the chest of drawers she'd obviously ransacked. "He said the money was in his strong box, but I found it this morning, and it is unlocked and empty."

Henrietta stared blankly at the disruption she had created. "He's double-crossed me again, hasn't he?"

Lucy stayed where she was, blocking the exit, her gaze fixed on her guest who had now sunk to the floor, her hands in her lap.

"Is it possible Northam took the money with him when he left that last morning?" Lucy asked tentatively.

"If he did, it wasn't returned to me when I received his possessions. I suppose it is possible that someone at the rectory stole it." Henrietta looked up at Lucy. "We already know your father is a murderer, so why not a thief?"

"I was the one who checked Lord Northam's belongings after he died, and there was no money on him except the coins I returned to you." Lucy hesitated. "Did your husband use the money to pay off Mr. Penarth?"

Lucy braced herself as Henrietta slowly rose to her feet and began tidying the room. Lucy started to help her, one eye on the clock as she wondered how quickly Dr. Fletcher could get to the hall. Henrietta's behavior went far beyond the usual grief exhibited by a widow. In truth, she appeared quite unhinged.

"Basil would never willingly give Mr. Penarth a penny. The man is corrupt." Henrietta finally spoke as she shut the last drawer of the tallboy.

"Perhaps he thought it was the only way to stop Mr. Penarth from pursuing you both." Lucy folded Henrietta's skirt and put it back in the wardrobe. "If the debt was paid off, you could've returned to your home in the north rather than having to flee the country."

"There isn't enough money in the whole estate to pay off that bastard Penarth. And Basil would never have settled for a tame life in the country. It would have bored him immensely." Henrietta turned to face Lucy. "It's far more likely that the rector stole the money before he murdered my husband."

"Why on earth would your husband take the money to the rectory when it was meant to finance your trip to the continent?" Lucy countered.

Henrietta shrugged. "Perhaps Basil wanted to flaunt his newly found wealth in front of your father."

"But why?"

"Because, according to Basil, the money was from the

Earl of Harrington." Henrietta's smile was not pleasant. "He probably wanted to gloat."

Lucy opened and closed her mouth as Henrietta's smile widened.

"I told you that the earl and your father were both up to their necks in this, didn't I? It's a pity you chose to ignore me." She walked over to the window and opened the curtains. "It still looks remarkably cold out there but not impassable. I'm sure that if my mother made the effort she might condescend to visit me, and express her insincere condolences in person."

"Rose is not allowed to leave her bed," Lucy said firmly. "Dr. Fletcher will not permit it."

"How convenient." Henrietta shoved the other curtain back so hard the brass rods squeaked. "Then I will have to go and visit her."

"Dr. Fletcher is not allowing any visitors."

"Betty said that you were at the rectory this very morning!" Henrietta spun around. "Does my own mother not wish to see me?"

"She does not wish to see anyone, Henrietta. Even Robert had to write her a letter. I suggest you do the same."

"And have it thrown in the rubbish before she reads it by her devoted husband?"

Lucy met Henrietta's gaze. "If you wish to write, I promise I will deliver the letter into her hands."

"As if I would trust you." Henrietta tossed her head.

There was a knock on the door and Dr. Fletcher came in, his keen gaze sweeping the disordered room, the broken chair, and the ripped bed hangings.

"Good morning, Lady Kurland, Lady Northam. How may I be of service?"

"Good morning, Dr. Fletcher." Lucy returned her attention to Henrietta. "If you don't trust me, perhaps you would trust Dr. Fletcher to deliver the letter?" Lucy gestured at the doctor, who had set his bag on the bed. "He can also confirm that your mother is not to receive visitors. I spent ten minutes with her this morning, and she was quite exhausted."

"Lady Kurland is correct, my lady." Dr. Kurland opened his bag. "Your mother needs to rest quietly."

"So that she can birth that revolting child who will take away my inheritance?" Henrietta sniffed. "I can't say I care whether it lives or dies."

Dr. Fletcher's startled gaze met Lucy's, and he stepped between her and Henrietta.

"With all due respect, my lady, I am trying to preserve your mother's life."

"If she stays alive long enough to have a proper conversation with me about what she has done to her will, then I'll take the risk of her and that brat dying because of it."

"And I will not," Dr. Fletcher snapped. "If you attempt to visit my patient I will stop you."

"How?" Henrietta raised her chin and glared at the furious doctor. "Will you lock me up? Will yet another miscarriage of justice occur because I *dared* to disagree with the mighty Harrington family?"

"Why don't you write to your mother first?" Lucy hastily intervened. "I'm certain she will answer all your concerns. If you still feel that you must see her in person, then we can consult with Dr. Fletcher, Robert, and my father to see if there is a way to manage it."

Henrietta stomped over to the writing desk in the corner of the room. "I will not be put off for much longer, Lucy. If my mother doesn't answer my questions, I will demand to see her, and to hell with her delicate health!"

When Henrietta's back was turned, Lucy motioned for Dr. Fletcher to join her outside the room. He picked up his bag and followed her, his expression stormy.

"I cannot believe a daughter would have such little care

for her mother's health." He started speaking the moment the door closed. "She is an incredibly selfish woman."

"Lady Northam seems most unlike herself," Lucy confessed. "When I arrived, she was searching for something and had almost destroyed the room."

"Grief sometimes makes people behave quite irrationally," Dr. Fletcher mused, "but in this case it seems more than that."

"She is so . . . angry," Lucy blurted out. "It's as if she is fueled with rage rather than sorrow and consumed with the desire to hurt others."

"I cannot disagree with you. The last thing we need is for her to seek out her poor mother," Dr. Fletcher said. "Is Sir Robert here? I need to speak to him about making sure Lady Northam is kept safely at Kurland Hall."

"My husband just set out for the Queen's Head," Lucy replied.

"Then I will leave him a note in his study and return this evening after I've seen all my patients."

"Thank you." Lucy offered him a warm smile. "If Lady Northam becomes . . . violent, or insists on seeing her mother before you come up with a plan, what should I do?"

He delved in his bag and offered her a bottle. "Give her laudanum if you can. If she attempts to hurt anyone, have James or one of the footmen secure her in the cellars."

"Do you really think that is necessary?" Lucy asked.

"You tell me."

Lucy grimaced. "When I entered her bedchamber she had the leg of a chair in her hand and was attempting to break through the paneling on the wall. She swung around to confront me, and for a moment, I was fearful that she meant to attack me."

"Then you have your answer." Dr. Fletcher bowed. "Good morning, my lady. I'll see myself out after I've left Sir Robert my note."

After the doctor had gone, Lucy made sure that Henrietta's door was locked from the outside and that Fred, the footman stationed there was fully aware of his responsibilities. The thought of Henrietta running through the house in a rage filled Lucy with horror.

She set off down the stairs to her parlor, aware that a period of calm reflection was necessary to enable her to continue her day. Henrietta had inadvertently confirmed that Northam had received money from the Earl of Harrington, but did that exonerate Max? And had Basil really taken the money down to the rectory merely to brandish it in her father's face? That seemed odd. In Lucy's mind it still appeared far more likely that Northam had attempted to buy Mr. Penarth off. Whether he had succeeded remained to be seen.

She paused in the hall and gazed over at the door of Robert's study. She wished he hadn't left so quickly. There were several things she'd like to ask Mr. Penarth as well.

Robert drew up the gig in the stable yard of the Queen's Head and waited as Mr. Jarvis came to stand at the horse's head.

"Morning, Sir Robert! Here again?" He winked. "You and her ladyship thinking of moving into my premises, are you?"

"It sometimes feels like that," Robert acknowledged as he got down. "I might as well rent your best bedchamber while I'm here and save myself all this effort."

"Mr. Penarth's still in that one, sir, but never you mind, we'll find you a nice warm place to sleep in the stables." Mr. Jarvis chuckled as he handed the horse over to one of his ostlers. "Are you here to inquire about the mail coach?"

"Yes, and I'd like to see Mr. Penarth if he can spare me a moment." Robert removed his hat as he stepped through the door into the beam-lined taproom.

"As the mail coach is planning on being here in the

morning, Mr. Penarth is determined to be on it. He blames the countryside for giving him a cold, although in my opinion the air is far better out here." Mr. Jarvis took Robert's hat. "I'll go and see if he's up, sir."

Robert warmed his hands by the fire in the taproom and responded to several greetings from the elderly villagers who tended to congregate in the inn whenever it was cold and wanted good food and company.

Mr. Jarvis returned. "He'll see you, Sir Robert. Says for you to go on up, as he's in the middle of packing."

"Thank you." Robert retraced the now-familiar route up the stairs to Mr. Penarth's bedchamber and knocked politely on the door.

"Come in, sir," Mr. Penarth called out to him. "And please excuse my mess."

"You appear to be feeling much better, Mr. Penarth," Robert said as he surveyed the occupant of the room. "I am glad to see it."

"My fever has abated sufficiently for me to travel back to London." Mr. Penarth folded a coat and placed it in his trunk. "I must confess that I'm glad to be leaving. If the coach gets through tomorrow, as promised, the mail will probably bring that information you wanted about the fraudulent shipping scheme."

"I'm looking forward to seeing it." Robert paused. "As to that, did you come to Kurland St. Mary just to see Northam, or did you have other business here with the rector?"

"You're a sharp one, aren't you, sir?"

"I do my best." Robert bowed.

"There is always pleasure in killing two birds with one stone." Mr. Penarth set a pair of boots on the hearth. "I had communicated with Mr. Harrington about his losses previously. When he mentioned his connection to Northam and his willingness to inform against him, I decided to follow Northam here and see them both."

"Did you set up a meeting with Mr. Harrington before you arrived?"

"I sent a message to inform him that I was on my way to Kurland St. Mary, but I didn't specify a time to meet. My primary goal was to find Northam."

"Understandably." Robert nodded. "Did you visit Mr. Harrington in the rectory?"

"I spent a most convivial hour with him the day before the christening. He is a very learned man, and we discovered a shared love of horse racing. He wrote a letter detailing his concerns about Northam and offered to stand as a witness against him if the matter ever came to trial."

"Did you also find time to speak to the Earl of Harrington?"

Mr. Penarth paused as he buttoned a shirt. "I don't believe I did. Why? Is he suggesting otherwise?"

"He says he came to the Queen's Head on the evening before the christening and met with Northam."

"I don't recall seeing him here, and I spent the majority of the evening in the taproom keeping one eye on Northam and the other on the door." Mr. Penarth set the shirt to one side. "I suppose the earl might have spoken to Northam while I was engaged with his son, but, no." He shook his head. "That couldn't have happened. Northam left first."

"Did Northam attempt to pay off any of the money he owed you when you spoke to him?"

"He had none to offer me." Mr. Penarth's faint smile faded. "In truth, as I said, he seemed even more defiant than he had done in London. Which made me wonder why he was so confident he could evade me. Did his wife's mother offer to pay off his debts if he left the country?"

"Not as far as I know."

"Then one has to assume that he had at least gathered together enough money to leave. I wonder where he got it?

Because, as you mentioned, any such largesse should rightfully belong to me."

"I am beginning to have suspicions that he did find money somewhere." Robert admitted the bare minimum of the truth. "But I am still unsure how he came by it."

"Maybe that's why Northam came to Kurland St. Mary in the first place," Mr. Penarth commented. "To call in a debt."

"Which ended up with him being murdered."

"I can't feel sorry for the man," Mr. Penarth said. "He had no thought to those whose wealth he stole with his lies. In truth, he laughed and called us all fools for lending him the money in the first place."

"Did you see him on the day of the christening?" Robert asked.

"Not to speak to—we had said everything that needed to be said. But I was taking my morning constitutional along the high street when I saw the activity at the church and stopped to take it in. I noticed Northam walking toward the rectory and disappearing into the garden."

"Can you remember what time it was?"

"Just before twelve, I believe."

"Thank you." Robert bowed. "I appreciate your willingness to help in this matter."

"I don't like being swindled out of my money, Sir Robert, but in this instance I believe that Northam got the comeuppance he richly deserved." Mr. Penarth shut the lid of his trunk with a flourish. "I only wish I'd been there to see it happen."

"Are you quite certain you weren't?" Robert asked. "You were in the vicinity, and you admit to seeing him enter the rectory. What was to stop you following him in, killing him while everyone else was at the church, and leaving on the mail coach, no one the wiser the next day?"

"Nothing, I suppose." Mr. Penarth met Robert's searching stare and had the temerity to chuckle. "Except I didn't do it. I suggest you deal with the facts, Sir Robert, unpalatable as they are. Lord Northam was murdered by your father-in-law, the rector, who had a very good reason to wish him dead and the perfect opportunity to execute his plan."

"What makes you think that?"

"Now, come on, sir. You are a sensible man, and a magistrate in your own right. Mr. Harrington lost a lot of money because of Northam and is married to Lady Northam's mother. The best way to keep the money safe in his hands was to kill that leech Northam. I'm heartily glad that he did it."

"The money will be inherited by Henrietta Northam, not by her husband," Robert pointed out.

"But by law, Northam controlled her fortune, didn't he?" Mr. Penarth said. "He could take it, leave her and his children to starve in a gutter, and no one could lift a finger to stop him."

"Neither her mother nor I would have allowed such a thing to happen."

"That's all very well, Sir Robert, but legally you wouldn't stand a chance. Northam could get away with anything— he's already spent one fortune. What's to stop him running through another one? Now Lady Northam's future is in the hands of Mr. Harrington, you, and any trustees the courts appoint for her son. Her husband's death ties her hands completely, which I cannot help but be amused by."

Mr. Penarth bowed. "I wish you well with the case, sir. If there is anything further I can help you with, please write to me at my London address, and I will be happy to assist you if I can."

After a long moment, Robert returned the bow. "Good morning, Mr. Penarth."

Robert walked out of the room with the irritating suspicion that he had been soundly trounced and sent about his business by a master deceiver. It was an unsettling feeling, and he didn't like it at all.

By the time he reached Kurland Hall, he was still

seething, and not inclined to feel merciful when he discovered his doctor's message on his desk. He strode back into the hall and found James.

"Where is Lady Kurland?"

"She's in the nursery, sir. Do you want me to fetch her?"

"Her ladyship is not a dog," Robert snapped. "When she comes down, please ask her to come to my study."

"Yes, sir. Sorry, sir."

James disappeared at some speed, and someone cleared his throat behind Robert.

"That was slightly unfair, my friend." Andrew Stanford came toward him. "The poor man was merely trying to help."

"I know." Robert stared at his friend. "Do you have a moment? I'd like to ask your opinion about something."

Andrew followed Robert into his study. "As long as you promise not to bite my head off, I'm happy to help."

"What are the chances of a murder case against a peer's oldest son and heir coming to trial?" Robert said bluntly.

"Good Lord." Andrew blinked. "You think Max Harrington murdered Northam?"

"It's possible." Robert took a short turn around the room. "What if he did?"

"With all due respect, my friend, for such a case, he would have to be caught in the act by at least a hundred nonbribable witnesses, and even then he might still get off." Andrew shook his head. "And with the Earl of Harrington's political influence and friendship with the monarch? You are correct, such a case would never come to trial."

"Damnation." Robert shot his friend a ferocious scowl. "I feared you would say that."

"Then I am sorry to disappoint you." Andrew bowed. "Is there anything else?"

"No, but thank you for giving me the unvarnished truth."

"That's what friends are for." Andrew paused. "Are you quite certain it is Max Harrington? I can't quite see him murdering anyone in cold blood."

"Neither can I, to be honest, but he's the most likely suspect I have at the moment."

"Apart from the rector, I assume?"

Robert frowned. "Why do you say that?"

"Because as a prosecutor I usually assume that if someone is murdered in a specific place, then the owner of that space is usually responsible."

"If Mr. Harrington goes to trial, I expect the jury will agree with you," Robert said gloomily. "How am I supposed to tell my wife that I am sending her father to the assizes?"

Andrew patted his shoulder. "If it comes to that, I suspect Mr. Harrington would also benefit from his brother's influence and either be exonerated or given a very light sentence indeed."

"Do you truly believe that?"

"Indeed, I do, and, if he does come to trial, please call upon my professional services to defend him."

"Thank you, Andrew," Robert said gruffly.

"You are most welcome, my friend." Andrew glanced out the window. "If the weather holds up, Sophia and I are hoping to leave in the next day or so. We are anxious to see our boys, and painfully aware that we have greatly outstayed our welcome."

"Not at all." Robert opened the door of his study and spotted his wife coming down the stairs. "It has been a pleasure."

After Andrew spoke briefly to Lucy, Robert ushered her into his study and shut the door.

"What now?" she asked.

"I was about to ask you the same question. Dr. Fletcher left a note telling me to lock my cousin in the cellar if she attempts to see her mother. What the devil happened while I was out?"

"Henrietta ransacked her room looking for money she insisted Northam had received, which was supposed to pay for their passage to the continent."

"Money from the earl?"

"I assume so. She couldn't find it and grew extremely agitated and angry. I asked Betty to send for Dr. Fletcher, because I was afraid she had gone mad."

"Dear God." Robert shoved a hand through his hair. "Did she threaten you?"

"When I arrived, she had a broken chair leg in her hand and she was attempting to cave in the wall." Lucy's lips tightened. "She also told Dr. Fletcher that her desire to speak to her mother was more important than Rose and the baby's health and that she didn't care if they died." She wrapped her arms around her waist. "It was horrible."

Robert instinctively pulled her close. "I can see why Patrick recommended the cellars."

"I tried to suggest that Basil might have used the money to pay off Mr. Penarth, but Henrietta insisted he would never do that."

"Mr. Penarth received nothing from him. I asked that very question this morning. He also insisted he never saw the earl with Northam that evening."

Lucy's brow creased. "Then, is my uncle lying?"

"Why would he lie?" Robert groaned. "I tell you, Lucy, I am damned near sick of the lot of them."

"I can't help but agree with you." Lucy met his gaze. "But what are we going to do to resolve this?"

"First, I think we need to speak to the earl again."

"Agreed." Lucy gave a decisive nod. "He is obviously trying to hide something. Did you ask Mr. Penarth about his own movements that morning?"

"He said he saw Northam entering the rectory while the guests were arriving at the church but that he didn't pursue him because he had nothing else to say to the man."

"He saw Northam arrive on foot just before the christening?" Lucy frowned. "But Michael and Luke saw him near the rectory on horseback much earlier."

"So they said." Robert looked at her. "Did Northam make two separate appearances at the rectory? And if so, where did he go in the middle?"

Lucy headed for the door. "Perhaps you should speak to the earl while I go and talk to the twins."

Chapter 12

"I thought we had decided that the entire matter was closed, Kurland." The earl shot Robert an irritated glance as he paced the study.

"I never agreed to that, my lord, and with matters such as murder, new evidence means that I am obliged to continue to ask questions."

"What about this time?"

"You claim that you went to the Queen's Head the night before the christening and paid off Lord Northam, correct?"

"Yes, what of it?"

"No one saw you at the inn that evening. I have several witnesses who are willing to testify that you were not there." Robert held the earl's furious gaze. "Did you really pay off that debt, my lord?"

"Of course I did! Are you calling me a liar, sir?"

"Perhaps you have simply misremembered the day and the time when you met with Northam?" Reluctantly, Robert attempted to be diplomatic.

"What if I did?" The earl sat down heavily on the chair in front of Robert's desk.

"Then I need to know the truth," Robert continued. "I already have an idea of when the meeting took place."

"Do you now." The earl loudly exhaled. "Northam refused to speak to me that evening either here at Kurland Hall or at the inn. As a last resort I wrote to him and asked to meet at my brother's house."

"While pretending to be your brother?" Robert asked.

"Yes, we have very similar handwriting. It was easy enough to copy my brother's style."

"And that meeting was set before the christening?"

"I didn't specify a time. I assumed that Northam would be attending the christening and that when I saw him walk out I would follow him into the rectory."

"But Northam wasn't invited to the christening."

"I am aware of that now."

Robert frowned. "Forgive me if I sound confused, but how did you deliver the money if Northam didn't turn up?"

"When I discovered he wasn't at the church, I went over to the rectory and saw him entering the house through the back garden. We had a very short conversation, which culminated in me giving him the money and walking back to the church."

"With all due respect, my lord, why didn't you tell me this sooner?"

"Because it looks bad, doesn't it?" The earl sat back, a challenge in his gaze. "That I was there in the rectory with Northam just before he died."

"May I ask how much money you gave him?"

"Five hundred pounds."

"That . . . seems excessive, my lord."

"Max lost very heavily, and Northam added interest." The earl rose to his feet. "With hindsight, I admit that I should have mentioned this sooner, but your obsession with the truth puts my family in a very difficult position— a position I was attempting to avoid."

Robert rose, too. "Lord Northam was murdered, sir. Perhaps you might consider *that* before you worry about anything else."

"Northam was a fool and a liar whose schemes finally

caught up with him. His death doesn't bother me in the slightest. It would be far better for all concerned if this matter could be laid to rest along with the body as a regrettable but unsolvable crime." The earl shrugged. "Even if I did pay Northam off, you can't prove that my son had anything to do with his death."

"I am quite aware of that," Robert said icily. "Is there anything else you would care to reveal that you have previously forgotten?"

"There is nothing," the earl snapped. "And damn your impertinence, sir."

He marched out of the study, slamming the door behind him. Robert let out a curse and went to find Lucy.

"Are you quite sure you saw Lord Northam at nine on the morning of the christening?"

Lucy had found her brothers in the library playing cards and betting with hastily scribbled bank notes.

"Yes." Luke set his cards facedown on the table. "He was going toward the Queen's Head."

"On horseback?"

"He wouldn't have gotten very far otherwise. The snow was still falling, and the drifts were high," Michael added.

"But it definitely was Lord Northam?"

"Yes, we saw his face, clear as day. He obviously recognized us, because he immediately picked up his pace."

Lucy looked up as Robert entered the room. One glance at his furious face told her that his interview with the earl had not gone well. The twins stared cautiously at him and then back at Lucy.

"Is there anything else you'd like to know, Lucy?" Michael asked. "Otherwise, we can go—"

"No, stay a moment." Robert held up his hand. "You saw Northam going toward the Queen's Head, correct?"

"Yes, sir." Both blond heads nodded.

"When you arrived back from your ride, was his horse in the rectory stables?"

The twins exchanged a glance. "There was definitely a Kurland horse in our stables later. We saw it after the christening," Luke said.

"Were you aware that Northam was in the rectory that morning?"

Michael raised a hand. "I thought I heard voices in Father's study when I was coming down the stairs to leave for the church, but I assumed it was Father and Mr. Culpepper." He swallowed hard. "I suppose it could've been anyone."

"Did either of you see the Earl of Harrington or your cousin Max at the house?"

"No," the twins spoke at the same time.

"Thank you." Robert nodded. "The sun has finally come out. You should take the opportunity to go for a ride."

Michael and Luke shot to their feet. "Yes, sir."

Lucy waited until they shut the door behind them before turning to Robert.

"I assume my uncle retracted his claim?"

"He said he wrote a note asking Northam to meet him in the rectory on the morning of the christening."

"The note I thought my father had written?" Lucy pressed a hand to her chest. "I suppose their handwriting must be very similar."

"Or he asked your father to write it for him."

Lucy continued to stare at him, so he carried on speaking.

"Northam had refused to meet with the earl, so he claims he pretended to be your father to lure him in. But Northam didn't attend the christening, so your uncle sought him out at the rectory, saw him approaching the house through the garden, and paid him off then."

"Why did he lie about meeting Northam at the inn?"

"Why do you think? Because of his obsession with not dirtying his family's name and being caught at the scene of a murder. I tell you, Lucy, I was not convinced of Max's guilt, but the more the earl obstructs me, the more I tend to wonder why."

Lucy reached out to cover his clenched fist with her hand and struggled to think what to say. Before she could frame a sentence, Robert drew in a ragged breath and sat back.

"So Northam leaves Kurland Hall around eight in the morning, is seen by the twins heading toward the Queen's Head at nine, and is back in the rectory before the christening ends, where he is murdered in your father's study."

"As far as we know," Lucy interjected.

"Indeed. Two questions still need answering. Why did it take Northam so long to reach the village from here even in the snow, and why did he go to the Queen's Head?"

"Presumably because he had business there."

Robert shook his head. "Mr. Penarth denies seeing him at the inn on the day of the christening."

"Well, he would, wouldn't he?" Lucy argued. "Maybe Basil was attempting to placate Mr. Penarth with the promise of money from the earl."

"But at that point, Northam presumably thought he was due to meet your *father*, not his brother."

"Then perhaps he believed my father was going to give him money as well?" Lucy made herself voice the difficult question.

"It's possible—although your father is not flush in the pocket right now because of Northam."

"Maybe Basil thought my father would pay him off with Rose's money?"

"Pay him off for *what*?" Robert asked, aware that his voice was rising.

"I don't know—maybe just to go away and leave Rose alone." Lucy threw up her hands.

"That's far more likely. But I doubt my aunt keeps the kind of money in the house that Northam needed." Robert paused. "That's another thing. The earl said he didn't know Northam was going to be in Kurland St. Mary for the christening yet somehow managed to have five hundred pounds on his person in order to pay him off."

Lucy gawked at him. "Five hundred pounds?"

"Which leads me to doubt the earl's story again." Robert groaned. "And where *is* this mythical five hundred pounds? It certainly wasn't on Northam's body when we found him."

"Which means someone in the rectory stole it from the body before we arrived, or Northam found some way to hide it," Lucy mused.

"Or he gave it to someone else." Robert stood up. "I think we need to speak to Mr. Penarth again one last time, don't you?"

When Lucy and Robert arrived in the gig, the Queen's Head appeared busier than it had for days. Two of the ostlers were stacking parcels and boxes against the wall, presumably awaiting the arrival of the mail coach in the morning. There was no sign of either the owner or his wife when Robert headed straight up the stairs toward Mr. Penarth's room.

Even though the door was slightly ajar, Robert knocked anyway, but he didn't hesitate to go on through. He stopped immediately and looked around.

"Where is he?"

"His trunk is here and the fire is still made up," Lucy said. "Perhaps he went for a walk in the village."

Robert strode over to the wardrobe and opened the door. "His hat and greatcoat are missing."

"Then let's see if we can find him. He can hardly have gone far in this weather." Lucy turned and went down the stairs, and Robert followed her.

They exited through the front door, which led on the high street, and set off down the hill toward the center of the village, where the church of St. Mary and the rectory were situated. It was still icy underfoot. Robert waited for Lucy to slip her arm through his before proceeding, and wished he'd brought his cane.

"Do you see any sign of him?" Lucy asked as the ground leveled out.

"No, but I doubt he has gone far. He still hadn't recovered from his cold."

"Robert." Lucy stopped walking and looked behind them. "What?"

"There are no other footprints leading down from the inn to the village. If Mr. Penarth only just went out, surely we would see some evidence of him?"

Robert turned to look and saw only two sets of prints. "Not necessarily. It might have thawed since he set out, or his particular boots don't leave a mark. Let's walk as far as the church and reassess."

"As you wish."

As they approached the church, the snow was thicker and there were still no footprints in it. Robert stood still and listened to the silence around them, his ears and nose hurting from the cold.

"I don't see any sign of him at all."

"Perhaps he had already returned to the inn and we merely missed him?" Lucy suggested. "He could've been in the kitchen or one of the private parlors."

"Then let's go back."

It was harder going uphill with the icy wind battering their faces, but neither of them complained as a sense of urgency consumed them. Robert opened the door for Lucy to step into the taproom and he followed her, stamping the snow from his boots.

"Mr. Penarth?" Lucy called out in her clear voice. "Are you here?"

While Lucy continued her search downstairs, Robert went back to check that his quarry had not returned to his room, but it was still empty.

"Where on earth has he gone?" Robert murmured as he rejoined his wife. "He can't possibly have left on horseback without his luggage, can he?"

"He hated to ride, so I doubt it," Lucy said, her gaze on

the kitchen. "I hear Mrs. Jarvis. Perhaps she can tell us where Mr. Penarth is."

"Lady Kurland! What a nice surprise!" Mrs. Jarvis was sitting at the kitchen table in front of a teapot across from a man in a severe black coat who wore a miserable expression. "Sir Robert. Mr. Jarvis is in Kurland St. Anne's today picking up the mail for the coach if you need to speak to him. Two of our grooms are suffering from colds, so my poor husband had to drop everything and rush out."

"That's quite all right, Mrs. Jarvis," Robert said. "We came to see Mr. Penarth"

"So did this gentleman!" Mrs. Jarvis smiled at her companion, who stood and bowed.

"Good afternoon, Sir Robert, Lady Kurland. I am Mr. Barry, Mr. Penarth's secretary. He asked me to bring certain documents down with me from London for your attention."

"He said he would send the documents to me." Robert frowned. "I certainly wasn't expecting you to put yourself out and bring them in this weather."

"I was more than willing to do so, sir. From what Mr. Penarth disclosed to me, I felt as if the matter might need my personal attention and my complete discretion."

"Indeed." Robert hesitated and looked around the kitchen. "Did you come in a carriage? Has Mr. Penarth already returned to London and left you behind?"

"No, sir." Mr. Barry's brows drew together. "I came on horseback. We intend to travel back together on the mail coach tomorrow morning."

"Then, where is Mr. Penarth?" Robert asked.

"I understand that he went out for a walk. Mrs. Jarvis and I were just sharing a cup of tea while I waited for him to come back."

"Ah." Robert glanced over at Lucy and drew out a chair for her. "Then perhaps we can await Mr. Penarth's return together."

*   *   *

Lucy was unable to sit still and chat while she grew increasingly concerned about Mr. Penarth. After a few minutes, she excused herself and went back up the stairs to Mr. Penarth's bedchamber. She examined the room carefully, but there appeared to be no signs of a struggle. For all intents and purposes the occupant of the room had dressed to go out and simply not returned.

She peeked into the other bedchambers and walked through the three private parlors for hire, but there was no sign of him. She was just about to go back into the kitchen when the door abruptly opened and Mr. Barry came out. He half smiled when he saw her.

"Sorry if I startled you, my lady. As the landlord isn't here, Mrs. Jarvis asked me to go down into the cellar and fetch up a bottle of her best brandy for Sir Robert."

"The trap door is just behind the bar in the taproom." Lucy pointed. "You'll need a lantern."

"Thank you, my lady."

The trap door into the cellar was already open, and Lucy peered down into the darkness. She knew from past experience that the cellars beneath the pub were extensive, as it was previously part of an abandoned abbey. Was it possible that Mr. Penarth had gone down there to fetch his own brandy and not come back out?

"Excuse me, my lady."

She jumped as Mr. Barry appeared at her side with a large lantern. A flare of light flooded the narrow opening, and Lucy gasped.

"What the devil is that?" Mr. Barry muttered before turning to Lucy. "You hold the light steady, my lady, and I'll go down the steps."

"Yes, of course." Lucy took the heavy lantern and shone it downward. "Please be careful."

Mr. Barry inched his way down the steep steps and paused at the bottom beside a dark, huddled shape. Lucy leaned out so that the light shone more clearly.

"It's Mr. Penarth!" he shouted up at Lucy, his face a pale circle in the gloom.

"Is he all right?" Lucy half turned to call out for Robert and Mrs. Jarvis

"No, I think he's broken his bloody neck!"

Chapter 13

"His neck is definitely broken." Dr. Fletcher covered up the body with a sheet and went to wash his hands. It had taken two ostlers to retrieve Mr. Penarth and bring his body up to his old bedchamber. "The steps down into the cellar are very steep, and there is nothing to hold onto to slow a fall onto the stone floor. I've warned Mr. Jarvis to shut that damned door more than once."

Robert grimaced. "I suppose there is no way of knowing whether Mr. Penarth tripped or if he was pushed?"

"I can check for bruising on his back or neck if you like, but that could also be caused by the fall. He does have some discoloration on his right cheek, but that's probably from his descent." Patrick eyed Robert. "He is not familiar with the inn. It's possible that he simply didn't notice that the cellar door was open and fell down by mistake."

"I wish I could believe you."

"You think he was pushed?" Patrick raised an eyebrow.

"Yes, because no one in this damned place really wants to know who killed Northam, and they are all busy trying to obstruct my investigation!" Robert flung up his hands. "I might as well rest my case and allow the murderer to get away with it."

"It's not like you to give up so easily," Patrick observed.

"I am aware of that, but my current alternative is I commit my damned father-in-law to trial at the assizes. I hardly think that will recommend me to my wife."

"But what if the rector did murder Northam? It's not beyond the realms of possibility." Patrick dried his hands as he spoke.

"I bloody well know that, too." Robert headed for the door. "I'll speak to Mr. Barry and see if he wants to discuss bringing Mr. Penarth's body back to London. I doubt he would want to be buried in Kurland St. Mary. He hated the countryside."

"I'll be here for a while making the body presentable, so send him up when you are ready."

"Thank you, Patrick."

"You're welcome, Major."

Robert went down the stairs to the kitchen, where a fluttering Mrs. Jarvis was feeding a very shaken Mr. Barry brandy and tea. He looked up as Robert entered the room.

"I can't believe Mr. Penarth is dead, sir. He was like a father to me. Took me on from the foundling school, said I was a bright lad, and taught me everything I know."

"I am sorry for your loss." Robert took the seat opposite and helped himself to a large brandy. "Our village doctor is upstairs with the body and would like to speak to you about burial arrangements when you have a moment. Our local undertaker, Mr. Snape, is very capable of following any instructions you give him. Did Mr. Penarth have a family who should be informed of his death?"

"Not that I know of, sir. He was an orphan himself, which is why he was such a generous patron to those of us who came through the same pauper schools."

"That is commendable." Robert agreed. "Did he attend church in London?"

"He did, sir. Not every Sunday, but enough for him to be known by the local vicar, and regularly applied to for donations."

"Then I am sure his vicar would be more than happy to

organize a funeral to celebrate his life and accomplishments." Robert paused to refill Mr. Barry's glass, aware that Lucy was keeping Mrs. Jarvis busy at the other end of the kitchen, which he greatly appreciated. "I hate to impinge on your sorrow, Mr. Barry, but were you aware why Mr. Penarth decided to come to Kurland St. Mary?"

"Indeed, sir. He wanted to speak to a Mr. Harrington who is the current rector here, and he heard that Lord Northam was also visiting."

"Was this in regard to the fake shipping scheme?"

"That's correct." Mr. Barry hesitated. "Did Mr. Penarth tell you about that, sir? He hates to lose money, and isn't usually one to mention his failures. He was hoping the rector would stand as a witness for him if the case came to trial."

Robert set his brandy glass on the table. "Mr. Harrington is my father-in-law, and Lord Northam is married to my cousin, so you might say that I have some interest in the matter."

"Good Lord," Mr. Barry blurted out. "I mean, I beg your pardon, sir."

"It's quite all right."

Mr. Barry was obviously the kind of man who tended to babble when he was in shock, something Robert was more than willing to exploit.

"Did Mr. Penarth tell you Lord Northam had died?"

"He mentioned it in his letter when he instructed me to offer you my assistance." Mr. Barry stuck his hand into his inner coat pocket and brought out a sealed packet. His hands were shaking as he passed it over. "I almost forgot. This is for you, sir."

"Thank you. Did Mr. Penarth say how Lord Northam died?"

"Only that he had been stabbed to death in the rector's study." Mr. Barry lowered his voice. "And that it was God's justice."

"Did he have any thoughts about who might have killed Lord Northam?"

"Not in so many words, but I assumed it must have been Mr. Harrington, sir."

"Why is that?"

Mr. Barry frowned. "Because Mr. Harrington had sunk a lot of money into that fraudulent scheme and lost it all. He was probably very angry. I know I would've been."

"That would certainly make sense." Robert pondered his next question. "Do you think Mr. Penarth could have been the murderer?"

"I . . ." Mr. Barry finished his brandy in one huge gulp and then coughed. "I wouldn't like to speak ill of the dead, sir, but he wasn't a man you would want to cross."

"He's killed before?"

Mr. Barry looked appalled. "Not directly, sir, no, not at all. But he certainly had associates to deal with people who forfeited his good regard, or failed to pay back a debt." He shot to his feet. "I should go and speak to the doctor before he leaves."

Robert did nothing to prevent Mr. Barry's hasty if wobbling retreat. He'd gained a lot of interesting information about Mr. Penarth, and would find out more if the need arose. He signaled to Mrs. Jarvis, who was stirring something on the stove with great vigor.

"Has Mr. Jarvis returned yet?"

"No, Sir Robert. I can't wait for him to come home! Such a tragedy! A good man like Mr. Penarth falls to his death. I cannot fathom it." She sniffed hard and blew her nose. "If my husband left that damn cellar door open, he will be *mortified*."

"I don't think you should blame yourselves," Lucy said soothingly. "It was just a terrible accident. I remember the same thing happened to one of the kitchen maids here when I was a child."

"Thank you for that, Lady Kurland, but I won't sleep a

wink tonight worrying about that poor man's last moments." Mrs. Jarvis pressed her hand to her heart.

"May I leave your husband a note?" Robert asked.

"Of course, sir. I'll see he gets it the moment he crosses the threshold."

Robert went into one of the private parlors. In his note, he asked the landlord to keep a close eye on Mr. Barry and to let him know if the secretary ventured out into the village. He really didn't need Mr. Penarth's secretary meddling in anything.

He sealed the folded paper with melted wax and his signet ring and took it into the kitchen, where his wife was still speaking to Mrs. Jarvis.

"I'll send a message to Mr. Snape, my lady." Mrs. Jarvis nodded. "I think Mr. Barry is anxious to return to London as soon as possible."

"Then we will take our leave of you," Lucy said. "But please do not hesitate to send for either my husband or me if the need arises."

She turned to Robert and they left the kitchen together. Just before they reached the outer door, she placed her hand on his arm.

"Is Dr. Fletcher still with the body?"

"Yes, why?" Robert asked.

"Because one has to wonder whether Mr. Penarth had five hundred pounds secreted away in his luggage."

"Ah." Robert paused. "I'll go up and tell Dr. Fletcher not to leave Mr. Barry alone with the body until we can come back and search the room and Mr. Penarth's belongings."

After delivering his message, Robert rejoined Lucy and they were soon on their way home. A slight flurry of snow made it hard to see the road. Robert was grateful both for the sure-footedness of his horse and his wife's calm presence beside him.

He let Lucy down at the side door of the house and continued on to the stables, where one of the stable hands came out to grab the horse's bridle.

"Mr. Coleman thinks it's going to snow all day," Joseph said as Robert got down.

"He might be right." Robert dusted the snow off his greatcoat and hat. "Are all the horses accounted for?"

"Yes, sir."

"Good." Robert was about to walk away when a thought struck him. "Joseph, were you on duty the day of the christening?"

"I was, sir." Joseph scowled and scuffed his booted feet. "What with me being the youngest, I had no choice but to get up early and stay put."

"Did you see Lord Northam ride out?"

"I did, sir."

"Did anyone else go out?"

"I saw Captain Coles, sir, but he was the only other one. It wasn't the best weather for riding."

"Thank you, Joseph. By the way, how is your family?"

"All well, sir—much happier since my father died. There are three of us working now, so Mum is much better off."

"I'm glad to hear it." Robert nodded. "And if you still want that introduction to my regiment, let me know."

"They're in India, sir. That's too far away from my mother." Joseph drew himself up. "As the oldest son, I can't just up and leave her, you know."

"Very commendable," Robert said. "She should be proud of you."

He turned away still smiling and made his way back to the house. It was reassuring that even though Joseph's father had been a rogue and a villain, his son had turned out to be anything but.

On reaching the house, he asked James to make him a pot of coffee and went through into his study. There was a letter on his desk from Rose. He picked it up, slit the seal, and began to read.

*   *   *

After making sure that her guests were all occupied and happy, Lucy made her way to Robert's study carrying the coffee he had requested. When she entered, he was sitting at his desk, his brow furrowed and his spectacles perched on the end of his nose.

"Ah, there you are." He pointed vaguely at the corner of his desk. "Thank you for the coffee. You can set it down there."

Lucy put down the tray and poured him a cup, which she set at his elbow. "Are you reviewing Mr. Penarth's list of shareholders?"

"I'll do that in a moment. I had a letter from Rose."

She waited patiently until he lifted his head to look at her. "What did Rose have to say?"

He sighed and handed the letter over. "To summarize, she did change her will quite significantly. She cut Henrietta's share down to almost nothing, left substantial trust funds for her grandchildren, and bequeathed half of her fortune directly to your father to do with whatever he pleases."

"Oh, dear." Lucy gulped. "If Henrietta and Basil knew about this, they would have been furious."

"One has to suspect that they *did* know, or else why would they have come down here?" Robert asked.

"Henrietta indicated that Rose's solicitor had written to her about some elements of the new will," Lucy said slowly. "She didn't say which ones, but even if it was only about her share being reduced, she wouldn't have liked it."

"Especially when Northam's fraudulent schemes had been exposed and he was counting on Rose to help pay their debts," Robert reminded her.

Lucy smoothed out the pages of the letter. "One has to question whether Northam threatened Rose over this."

"According to her letter, he did, which makes me wonder whether she told your father and he *did* murder Northam."

When the silence became too long to bear, Lucy slowly raised her head. "So we're back to that, are we?"

Her husband didn't flinch from her accusatory gaze. "Yes."

"And do you think my father decided to murder a man for money, or because he loves his wife and feared for her life?"

"That's hardly a fair question, Lucy. Rose says she hasn't told your father how she's changed her will." Robert paused. "But maybe during their last fatal encounter, Northam *did* tell him, and that's why he was murdered."

Lucy carefully placed the letter back on the desk without reading it.

"Can you at least agree that this is a plausible explanation for everything that has happened?" Robert asked.

Lucy raised her chin. "Seeing as I am not the one prosecuting this matter, my opinion hardly counts, does it?"

"Devil take it, Lucy, don't get all high and mighty with me now. I need you to think!" Robert glared at her. "If this was anyone other than your father, I'd wager you'd be agreeing with me."

"Of course I would!" Lucy snapped. "But it is my father, and I cannot see him killing Northam!"

"You *know* what Northam was like. He enjoyed taunting people! He thought he was cleverer than anyone else and nothing was sacred to him." Robert sat back. "The simplest explanation is often the correct one, and in this case, your father looks increasingly like a guilty man."

"What about Max?"

"As you so rightly pointed out, if Max had been going to kill Northam he probably would have done it that night at the inn when Northam humiliated him by mocking his attempt to call him out. I can't see Max arranging to meet Northam the next day in the rectory to murder him. And we already know it was the earl who lured Northam to the rectory to pay off Max's gambling debts."

"Maybe Northam taunted the earl about Max, and *he* murdered him?"

"Lucy, as it stands, the only person who stands to gain financially from Northam's death is your father." Robert grimaced. "I'm sorry, my love, I know it hurts you, but that is the truth."

Lucy made her way up to the nursery and spent a comforting hour having her midday meal with her children. The quiet rhythm of the ticking clock and the creak of her rocking chair as she sat holding Elizabeth helped soothe her troubled mind. After Robert had challenged her to dispute his theory, she'd found she had nothing to say—not only because his facts were on point but also because she'd been perilously close to tears.

Her father might be a selfish and difficult man, but she struggled to see him as a person capable of murder. He'd been a minister in the church and a man of faith for more than thirty years. If he had killed Northam over Rose, surely he would've confessed to the crime? A man of his rank and standing would probably never have to face the full consequences of his actions if he had family and influence, which the Harringtons certainly did.

The door opened, and Robert stepped inside the nursery. He looked tired, his expression strained. Lucy instinctively raised her finger to her lips and then pointed down at their sleeping daughter. Robert nodded, took the seat opposite her, and held out his arms. For a moment Lucy hesitated, then offered him Elizabeth's shawl-covered form.

He took the baby carefully, his expression softening as he looked down at his daughter's face. He brushed a fingertip over her delicate nose and looked over at Lucy.

"What would you have me to do?" he asked quietly.

"About what?"

"Your father."

She turned her attention to the window, noting that the

tree branch scraping against the glass needed to be cut back.

"You will do what you deem right and necessary, Robert. You always do."

"Would you want me to be a different man to the one you married? To ignore the sound principles that have guided my life and yours since the day we met?"

She shrugged, her throat aching. "No, of course not."

"If I could think of another way—"

She held up her hand. "Please don't do this. Your instincts are generally sound, and if you truly believe my father is guilty, then I suggest you get on with proving it." She met his gaze. "But don't expect me to applaud your efforts, or offer any countenance to your actions."

He reached carefully around the baby into the pocket of his coat and drew out a letter.

"This is the list of shareholders in Northam's fake shipping enterprise. Your father's name is there, near the very top. From what I can tell, he invested a substantial amount of capital in the venture, which has compromised his finances considerably."

Lucy took the list. "Thank you for offering further proof of my father's guilt. When do you anticipate hauling him off in irons to the assizes?" She concentrated her gaze on Elizabeth's sleeping form. "Perhaps you should wait until Rose is well enough to withstand the shock before you take the father of her unborn child away."

"Lucy . . ."

She rose to her feet. "I have to go and speak to Cook about dinner."

Chapter 14

Robert gently set his daughter in her crib, smiled at the nursemaid, and made his way downstairs. There was no sign of his wife, which wasn't surprising. If she wanted to distance herself, the house was big enough for her to avoid him for days. He'd known she would be upset at his conclusions, but her complete lack of understanding hurt him more than he'd anticipated. And her point about taking the rector off to Hertford while his wife was bedridden had been a low blow.

"Major Kurland!"

He turned to see Joshua hailing him from the hall below.

"Good afternoon. Is luncheon being served?" Robert went down to join his friend. "I do apologize for my continual absences, but I had to go to the Queen's Head on an urgent matter this morning."

"I just came from the stables," Joshua said. "I heard that Mr. Penarth had a terrible accident. Is that true?"

"Unfortunately, it is. He must have tripped and fallen down the cellar steps. His neck was broken."

"Good Lord." Joshua shook his head. "How dreadful. With the weather taking a turn for the worse again, will you be able to get a message through to his family in London?"

"His secretary, a Mr. Barry, arrived this morning on horseback. He intends to take the body back for burial in London as soon as the weather permits." Robert glanced over at the door to the dining room, where James was setting out an array of dishes. "Will you give my excuses to the rest of my guests and explain that I have to go out again to make sure Mr. Penarth's affairs are set in order?"

"Yes, of course." Joshua bowed. "Unless you would like me to accompany you?"

"You have just come in," Robert reminded him. "I have no intention of making you go out in the snow again."

"I don't mind it at all. I hate to be bored. I've managed to take a walk or ride every day since I arrived."

"That's right." Robert stopped walking. "You rode out on the day of the christening, didn't you?"

"Only down to the village. It was snowing quite heavily."

"Did you see Northam on that particular morning?"

"Why?" Joshua studied him carefully. "Does it matter?"

"It might." Robert sighed. "I'm trying to work out what he did after he left Kurland Hall and ended up dead at the rectory several hours later. According to everyone who lives there, Northam wasn't seen until his body was discovered."

"On my way back to the hall, I saw someone." Joshua frowned. "It might have been Northam. It's hard to tell when everyone is bundled up in cloaks, hats, and mufflers."

"Where were you when that occurred?"

"Near the Queen's Head. I'd walked my horse a little way along the county road to assess the chances of the mail coach getting through the drifts that morning."

"As you and Northam were the only guests who ventured out that day, one has to assume it was him you saw," Robert said. "Do you think he noticed you?"

"No, his attention was fixed on the Queen's Head." Joshua hesitated. "Now that I think about it, his behavior was quite odd."

"How so?"

"He rode past the entrance to the stable yard and doubled back at least twice, but when I went past, there was no sign of him or his horse there."

"You couldn't see him in the stable yard?"

"No, and I was only a minute or so behind him. I doubt anyone had come out to take his horse that quickly."

"It was a particularly cold day," Robert offered. "Perhaps the ostlers were very efficient."

"I suppose that might be true, but I stopped there myself to get something warm to drink before I returned to Kurland Hall, and there was no sign of him in the taproom either."

"He could have been in one of the private parlors, in the kitchen or upstairs visiting a guest."

"I suppose so." Joshua nodded. "He *was* acquainted with Mr. Penarth."

Robert looked up the stairs to see the Stanfords descending and turned back to Joshua. "I'd best be on my way. If anyone inquires as to my absence, please let everyone know the sad news about Mr. Penarth."

"I will, Major." Joshua headed for the dining room door.

Robert asked James to inform Lucy as to his movements and then walked down to the stables. Mr. Coleman spent a few minutes alternately praising Ned's burgeoning horsemanship skills, warning Robert not to overtax the horse, and instructing him to return home quickly if the snow kept falling. Having grown up with Mr. Coleman in charge of the stables, Robert took the advice in good part and was soon on his way back to the inn. If his wife was determined to make things as difficult as possible between them, perhaps he should consider taking up permanent residence there.

Mrs. Jarvis informed him that Mr. Snape had taken Mr. Penarth's body to his premises in the village. He'd been accompanied by Mr. Barry, which left Robert free to go through the dead man's belongings without interference. He started with the trunk he'd watched Mr. Penarth pack only a day before, carefully removing the clothes and searching each item before he set it aside.

It occurred to him that he didn't know whether the five hundred pounds the Earl of Harrington claimed he had handed over to Northam had been in coin or notes. Knowing Northam, he would have demanded golden guineas, which held their value regardless of the currency. Coin would be far heavier to store than notes. Robert checked the weight of the emptied trunk and couldn't believe there was a secret cache of coins within it. He carried on searching, locating a false bottom to the trunk and a metal box below it, complete with key.

The box contained about ten pounds in various coins, a quill pen, a well-thumbed Bible, and a set of keys Robert assumed were connected to Mr. Penarth's business or residence in London. If Mr. Barry continued to be helpful, Robert would ask him to identify their uses. He checked the side panels and found nothing but a shirt button and a small rusted pocketknife with the initials EP.

Discouraged, Robert sat back and surveyed the rest of the room. If Mr. Penarth had wanted to conceal his ill-gotten gains until he was just about to get on the mail coach, might he have hidden them somewhere in the room? Had he intended to carry the coins on his person, or ask Mr. Barry to do so? It was a considerable amount of money. He would ask Mr. Barry that question as well.

Feeling remarkably foolish, Robert began to explore the bedchamber, peering under the four-poster bed, removing each drawer from the tallboy, and checking every wall hanging. He wished Lucy were with him. Her eye for detail would have been most useful.

He grimaced. Even if he begged for her help he had a

suspicion she would not offer it. That thought sat heavy in his heart and made him miss her presence even most acutely.

"Damn the entire Harrington family," Robert muttered. "I wish them all to Hades."

He took one last look around the room, collected his hat and coat, and went down the stairs. After conferring with Mrs. Jarvis he strode out into the village, his gaze on the church spire and the mellow golden stone of the rectory opposite the ancient church. Dr. Fletcher might not want him going anywhere near Rose, but Robert needed to speak to her, and this time he wasn't going to let anyone get in his way.

Lucy waited as her friend Sophia gathered her dog in her arms and headed back toward the house. The sleet had turned to snow, making the arrival of the mail coach on the morrow unlikely. Lucy was beginning to feel as if her guests were destined to stay with her forever. Not that she didn't appreciate them all individually, but with things as they were between her and Robert the effort of appearing unconcerned when all she really wanted was curl up in her bed and enjoy a solitary weep was difficult to maintain.

She couldn't fault his reasoning, but that didn't seem to matter when the whole idea of his sending her father to trial made everything inside her scream in protest. Part of her wanted to attempt to talk some sense into her father again even when she knew he was already offended by her actions, and stubborn enough not to listen.

Sophia called out to her. "This is where I was standing when I saw Lord Northam going toward the stables." She sighed, her breath frosting on the cold air. "I must have been one of the last people to see him alive."

She paused and shaded her eyes. "Now I come to think of it, he can't have been the first person to have gone out that morning. There was at least one other set of tracks in the snow."

"That's because Captain Coles went out ahead of him," Lucy replied.

Sophia frowned. "That can't be right, Lucy, because I saw Captain Coles leaving when I returned to the house."

"Did you mention this to Robert?" Lucy turned to her friend.

"No, because he only asked if anyone had seen Nor-tham heading for the stables." Sophia's brow furrowed. "Maybe Captain Coles had forgotten something and re-turned to the house to fetch it. He did look in rather a hurry. I don't think he even noticed me and Hunter in the scullery."

"I suppose that's possible." It was Lucy's turn to frown. "May I suggest that you tell my husband about this? It might be important in some way that I am as yet unable to understand."

"Of course I will." Sophia nodded. "Now, shall we go back in? My teeth are beginning to chatter."

Lucy led the way to the back of the house and held the door open for Sophia and Hunter to precede her.

"Are you all right, Lucy?" Sophia inquired as they made their way into the dank stone-floored scullery to discard their boots and reclaim their kid slippers and shawls. "You seem rather distracted."

"I'm just concerned about the weather." Lucy managed to find a smile from somewhere. "If the snow continues to fall at such a rate, you will not be able to leave the village tomorrow as you hoped."

"I must admit that I am anxious to return home to see my boys, but I am also aware that you and Robert have been excellent and patient hosts." Sophia wrapped her dog in a towel and rubbed him dry. "You must be wishing us gone!"

"Not at all," Lucy hastened to reply. "Although I sus-pect my aunt Jane also wants to be home."

"With Julia?" Sophia asked. "The last time I saw her and Lord Penzey together they looked so happy, I cannot believe they decided to part. Andrew said Penzey was devastated."

"I don't understand what happened, either," Lucy confided. "My aunt said that Julia is unwell and needs to go abroad to recover."

Sophia lowered her voice. "I did hear a rumor that she had broken off the engagement due to an illness. Perhaps she thought Penzey deserved a bride who wasn't an invalid."

"That would be just like her," Lucy agreed. "But such a decision must have broken her heart."

Sophia set her dog down on the slate floor. "What do you plan to do with Henrietta? She is hardly in a fit state to travel up north by herself."

"I believe Robert intends to accompany her and Lord Northam's body back to their country estate," Lucy said, glad for her friend's adroit change of subject. "He will do all that is proper to ensure that excellent guardians are appointed to oversee her young son." Lucy hurried to wrap herself in her shawl.

"Your husband is a good man," Sophia said.

"Indeed." Lucy opened the door, and Hunter bounded off ahead of them.

Sophia touched her arm. "Are you sure that you are all right? Is there something you wish to confide in me? You know I will keep your secrets."

"I must admit to some worries about my father's involvement with Lord Northam's death." Lucy spoke reluctantly. "Robert seems convinced he's a murderer."

"Good Lord." Sophia stopped walking. "Andrew was right."

"What?"

"Andrew said that any prosecutor worth his salt would take a very dim view of anyone who claimed to discover a murdered person in his own study." Sophia rushed to continue speaking as Lucy stared at her aghast. "Not that I agreed with him in the slightest! I've known you and your father my entire life and, if I may be frank, Lucy, the rector is far too selfish and indolent to *ever* commit a murder."

Lucy fought an absurd desire to laugh at her friend's impeccable logic. "But your husband, who is one of the finest barristers in the country, believes my father could be convicted?"

Sophia met Lucy's gaze. "Not if he was the person representing him. Andrew has already offered his services to Robert and your father if required."

"Let's hope it doesn't come to that," Lucy said. "But please tell your husband that I appreciate his offer with all my heart."

To Robert's relief, a quick discussion with the stable hands yielded the information that his father-in-law was out visiting the sick of his three parishes and would return for his evening meal. He let himself in through the rectory kitchen, startling the cook and kitchen maid, who were enjoying a comfortable chat around the table.

"Sir Robert!"

He held up his hand. "There's no need to get up. I had a message from Mrs. Harrington asking me to come and speak to her. I'll just go and see her. I promise it won't take a minute."

Neither woman made an attempt to stop him, and he proceeded up the stairs. There were voices coming from Rose's room as he knocked on the door. Mrs. Culpepper answered him; her surprised expression mirrored those of the staff downstairs.

"Sir Robert! This is quite unexpected."

"Good afternoon, ma'am." He looked over the top of her head at his aunt, who was sitting up in bed, her embroidery hoop in her hand.

"May I speak to you for a few moments, Aunt? I think it is important."

"Yes, do come in," Rose invited. She smiled at her small guardian. "Perhaps you might make us some tea, Dorothea? It would be most kind of you."

Mrs. Culpepper stepped aside, but not before fixing Robert with a surprisingly determined stare. "Dr. Fletcher insists that Mrs. Harrington needs to rest as much as possible and not become agitated. I do hope you will remember that."

"I promise I will." Robert held the door open for her. "Thank you."

He firmly shut the door behind her and came to sit beside his aunt. He'd already decided that he would keep things brief and to the point. Rose knew him well enough not to be intimidated by his direct manner.

"Thank you for your letter."

"I hope it helped clear things up," Rose replied, setting her embroidery hoop to one side. For a woman who was spending her entire time in bed, she still looked exhausted. "I swear that I haven't told Ambrose what I did with my will, so he has no reason to murder Northam at all."

"What if Basil and Henrietta found out, and they told him?" Robert asked.

"Why would they do that?"

"Why do you think? You can hardly imagine they would be happy to learn that their share of your fortune had been significantly decreased in favor of your new husband."

"But I compensated for that with the trust fund for my grandchildren," Rose protested.

Robert took her hand in his. "Northam was badly in debt. He needed the money, or at least the promise of the money, to get a loan to save his very existence. He would have been furious with you and the rector for stealing what he already considered as his."

Rose raised her chin. "I have a perfect right to leave my fortune to whomsoever I please."

"I am well aware of that," Robert agreed. "Is it possible that Northam came to confront the rector about the matter, and that is how he ended up dead?"

"You mean that Ambrose somehow decided to kill him?"

"Yes, but maybe he was trying to defend himself, and it was an accident—maybe there were extenuating circumstances that I am not yet aware of."

Rose withdrew her hand from his. "I am disappointed in you, Nephew. You sound like a man who is determined to believe Ambrose is guilty."

"Please believe me when I say that is the last thing I want." Robert held her indignant gaze. "Your husband is also my father-in-law, and Lucy would never forgive me if I accused him unjustly."

"Just because Northam ended up dead in Ambrose's study does not mean my husband killed him! He was thoroughly disliked by all who had the misfortune to know him. Why aren't you investigating those people?"

Although aware of Rose's rising agitation, Robert decided he had no option but to persist. "Did you know that the rector had invested in a fraudulent shipping venture?"

Rose went still.

"I recently met a gentleman at the Queen's Head named Mr. Penarth." Robert continued speaking. "He came to Kurland St. Mary to speak to Mr. Harrington and apprehend Lord Northam, who was the prime instigator in a scheme to defraud investors."

Rose sniffed. "Don't be silly. Ambrose would never willingly choose to invest in one of Northam's schemes."

"From what Mr. Harrington told me, he didn't know Northam was involved but was invited in by one of the other partners." Robert hesitated. "He invested a lot of money, Rose, and lost enough to significantly reduce his capital. Can you not see that to a judge and jury such loss of capital might make him seem very eager to get rid of any threat from Northam?"

Rose picked up her embroidery frame and stabbed her needle through the fabric. "I am very tired, Nephew. Perhaps we might continue this conversation at another time?"

Robert exhaled and stood up, his gaze fixed on his aunt's averted face.

"I apologize if I have upset you, but I think in your heart you would rather know the truth than remain in ignorance."

She didn't reply, and after another moment, he bowed and went out the door. Mrs. Culpepper was just coming up the stairs with a tray of tea, and he stepped back to avoid her.

"Are you leaving, Sir Robert?"

He nodded and held the door open for her. "My aunt is very tired. I will come back and see her in a few days."

"As you wish, sir. Good afternoon." She adroitly managed the tray and shut the door in his face.

He stared at the wooden panels, aware that he had managed to upset another of his favorite women. Rose's incredulous expression when he'd stated his suspicions had mirrored that of his wife's. He truly disliked himself and the pain he was currently inflicting on those he loved, but he had a duty to uphold the law even if it meant he ended up as a pariah in his own village.

He walked down to the stables, aware that the snow was now falling steadily and that his journey back to the hall in the gig would take time and intense concentration. He'd failed to find anything in Mr. Penarth's luggage, he'd failed to reassure Rose in any way, and his welcome at home would be nothing to cheer about. He paused at the entrance to the stables, taking in the warmth emanating from the stalls and the smell of manure and hay. Perhaps it would be better if he spoke to Mr. Barry before he went home.

Aware that he was being somewhat craven, yet also keen to make certain Mr. Barry wasn't intending to remove five hundred pounds from Kurland St. Mary, Robert wrapped his scarf tightly around his neck and set off on foot for Mr. Snape the undertaker.

"Lucy?"

Henrietta rose from her seat by the window as Lucy came into the bedchamber. For the first time in days she was fully dressed and her hair was up.

"What is it?"

"I would like you to accompany me to Mr. Snape's." Henrietta pointed at the bed. "I have chosen a set of clothing for my darling Basil to wear in his final resting place, along with some of his favorite trinkets."

Lucy carefully considered her guest, who sounded far calmer and composed than she had been since her husband's unfortunate death.

"You do not need to worry yourself. I can arrange for the items to be taken down to Mr. Snape this afternoon."

"I'd like to do it myself." Henrietta clasped her hands. "I was . . . overwrought when I first saw his body, and did not offer him the attention he deserved. It would please me greatly if I could tend to him for one last time."

There was a note of sincerity in Henrietta's words that Lucy found hard to ignore. If Robert had died, would she not want the same thing? A last chance to see his face, to care for him, and offer a final farewell?

"If you truly wish to go, I will accompany you."

"Thank you," Henrietta said simply. "That is very good of you."

"We will have to take the carriage. It is snowing quite heavily," Lucy said. "When you are ready to go, ask Frederick to accompany you down the stairs. I will meet you in the hall."

Lucy was not averse to allowing Henrietta to stretch her wings a little. Robert's cousin was used to speaking her mind without any concern for those around her, and might be more likely to reveal her true feelings when faced with the reality of her husband's body.

Less than half an hour later, they were on their way in the smaller of the Kurland closed carriages. Henrietta had drawn her black veil down over her face, leaving Lucy alone with her thoughts. She did hope Sophia would tell Robert about Captain Coles, but feared she might have to do it herself. Speaking to her husband about Northam's murder was far too fraught a subject to engage in when he was intent on prosecuting her father.

Mr. Snape lived in a discreet stone house at the end of the high street with a large cold basement suitable for the storing of the dead. Sometimes during the winter months it was impossible to dig a grave in either of the two churchyards and burials had to wait. Mr. Snape was also used to constructing simple wooden caskets to transport the bodies of those who had died and wished to be buried elsewhere.

It was quiet in the village—the shops mainly shut, their windows boarded against the snow. The only bright spot was the bakery, which had stayed open despite the cold to sell the locals their daily bread. Lucy waited for Fred to let down the step and then helped Henrietta navigate the snowy yard that led to the discreet back door of the undertakers.

As she pushed open the door, Lucy heard voices and paused, but Henrietta carried on without her and called out.

"Snape?"

"Yes, my lady?" The undertaker appeared at the inner doorway. He noticed Lucy and bowed. "Lady Kurland, what an honor."

"Good afternoon, Mr. Snape. Lady Henrietta wishes to see her husband's body and dress him for his final journey home."

Mr. Snape glanced back at the door. "That can definitely be arranged, my lady. If you will just allow me to finish up with my other client, I will be with you directly."

Henrietta harrumphed but walked over to the window overlooking the backyard. A string of washing had frozen on the line in stark unwieldy shapes that could have been cut by a knife. The Snape family lived in the upstairs level of the house and had obviously learned to be not only quiet but also unobtrusive.

Lucy edged closer to the inner door, her attention on the conversation within. Whomever Mr. Snape was speaking to had a slight Cockney accent she immediately recognized. Mr. Barry must have come to deal with the transportation of his employer's body back to London.

Henrietta swung around to look at her. "What on earth is Snape doing? Doesn't he know who I am?"

"I believe he is speaking to a man called Mr. Barry," Lucy said.

"Barry?"

"He's a secretary from London."

"Then why on earth is he here in Kurland St. Mary?"

"His employer met with an unfortunate accident in the Queen's Head. He has come to collect the body."

"Not Mr. Penarth," Henrietta breathed. At Lucy's nod, a smile grew on her companion's face. "He's dead?"

"Yes."

"That's . . . wonderful! With him gone, who will continue to pursue his debts? He has no family, only his business partners who lived in fear of him." Henrietta paced the small room. "None of them are strong enough to go after me or my husband's estate."

"Henrietta—" Lucy was just about to reprimand her companion when the back door opened and Robert came in, his gaze quickly moving from her to his cousin.

"Why are you here, Henrietta?"

"I want to make sure that Basil's body is properly prepared before I take him home to be buried. You can hardly begrudge me that, can you?"

"I think you should do what feels right and fitting, Cousin." Robert bowed. "Is Mr. Snape here?"

"He is attending to Mr. Barry." Lucy spoke for the first time.

"Ah, good." Robert looked straight past her to the door. "That's exactly whom I wanted to speak to."

"Why?" Henrietta came toward Robert. "How do you even know him?"

"I met him at the Queen's Head when he came to see Mr. Penarth." Robert hesitated. "Were you aware that Mr. Penarth is dead?"

"I gathered as much from Lucy." Henrietta smiled again. "I wish I could thank whoever got rid of that loathsome little man. Without him hounding my family, my future will be far easier."

"You don't think his associates will seek repayment of their debts from Northam's estate?" Robert asked.

"They might, but with a good lawyer, one can keep them busy in the courts for years. Mr. Penarth sometimes preferred more . . . direct methods of repayment."

"Did he threaten you?"

"Last time I saw him I slapped his face. He was not the kind of man who took such an insult lightly." Henrietta straightened her back. "I am glad he is dead. I wish I had killed him myself. Who did?"

"It was an unfortunate accident," Robert said shortly. "He fell down the cellar steps at the inn."

"Or he was pushed." Henrietta turned to Lucy. "And where was the very reverend Mr. Ambrose Harrington when this supposed accident occurred? I do hope you've accounted for his movements, Robert. If the rector killed once, he is more likely to kill again."

"My father has not killed anyone." Lucy spoke up.

"Is that so?" Henrietta smiled and glanced from her to Robert, who was refusing to meet her gaze. "Methinks your husband does not agree with you."

Mr. Snape emerged from within the house with a subdued Mr. Barry beside him, and stopped when he saw Robert.

"Good afternoon, sir! Are you here about Lord Northam as well?"

"No, I came to speak to Mr. Barry." Robert bowed to the secretary. "If your business with him is concluded, I will walk back with him to the inn."

It only occurred to Lucy that her husband had neglected to address a single direct remark to her after he had left. She also noted he hadn't jumped to defend her father, either. Perhaps matters between them were already far worse than either of them had anticipated.

Chapter 15

"Is there something in particular you wish to speak to me about, Sir Robert?" Mr. Barry asked as they walked up the street together. "Mr. Snape said he will have the coffin finished by tomorrow and that as soon as the roads open, he will hire a carter to bring the body back to London."

Robert, who had been busy mulling over his wife's lack of interest in speaking to him, glanced down at his companion.

"I do apologize, Mr. Barry. I was woolgathering. Do you intend to accompany the body, or will you go back on the mail coach to prepare for its arrival?"

"I intend to leave as soon as I can." Mr. Barry shivered. "I am not used to the countryside, Sir Robert. I find the silence and lack of people quite unnerving."

"I believe Mr. Penarth felt the same way," Robert said. "I do have a question for you. It relates to the vexing business of the fake shipping venture."

"Yes, sir? What about it?"

"I believe Lord Northam came into some funds while in Kurland St. Mary. Is it possible that he gave that money to Mr. Penarth in repayment of at least part of his debt?"

"I'm not aware of any sums of money being handed over, Sir Robert, but I wasn't here for the entirety of my employer's visit." Mr. Barry frowned. "The debt was very large. Mr. Penarth had almost given up on ever seeing a penny of it again."

"If Mr. Penarth *had* received a sum of money, where would he have placed it?"

"In the bottom of his trunk in his strong box, sir."

"Is it possible that he might have hidden it somewhere else and given it to you to bring back for him?"

"He might have done that, but as I didn't get to speak to him in person, it's hard to say." Mr. Barry plodded on for a few more steps and then looked up again. "If you are asking me if I have that money, Sir Robert, I swear I do not. I am more than willing to let you search my belongings to make sure."

"That is very good of you, Mr. Barry," Robert said. "As the local magistrate I fear I might need to accompany you back to the inn and take you up on that very generous offer."

Having attended to the laying out and preparing of many bodies when she carried out her duties at the rectory, Lucy was more than willing to aid Henrietta with Northam. To her surprise, Henrietta seemed genuinely affected by the experience, but Lucy still struggled to have any sympathy for her. It was all well and good for her and Robert to have a private marital disagreement, but when even Henrietta noticed, it was galling.

"I still don't know what happened to that money Basil swore he had secured for our trip to the continent," Henrietta said as she buttoned her husband's shirt. "If he did leave it in our room, one of your household is a thief, Lucy."

"And what if he didn't?" Lucy attempted to ease a cuff link through two pieces of freshly starched linen. "As I said earlier, he could have used it to pay off part of his debt to Mr. Penarth."

"Who is also dead," Henrietta noted as she went to find

the elaborate embroidered waistcoat she had chosen for her husband. "Did you know that your father also owed Mr. Penarth money?"

"If he did, he certainly hasn't mentioned it." Lucy helped Henrietta draw the waistcoat around Northam's cold flesh and button it up.

"Because it would incriminate him further."

"How so?" Lucy looked up. "Your husband lied to his investors, causing my father and others to lose money on a fraudulent shipping company. The fault lies entirely with him."

"There is no need to speak so harshly of the dead, Lucy. Basil can hardly defend himself now." Henrietta dealt with the cravat, setting a single black jet pin to secure it at Northam's throat. "If I have anything to say about it, your father will be found guilty, convicted of murder, and hung for what he did to my husband."

Lucy realized she disliked this measured and reasonable Henrietta even more than the spiteful hysterical one. "My father didn't kill anyone."

"I almost feel sorry for you," Henrietta said. "Your loyalty to your father is admirable, but you must face the facts. Your father hated my husband because he'd foolishly spent more money than he should have on a somewhat dubious scheme, and—"

"Somewhat dubious?" Lucy interjected. "The whole thing was a lie from start to finish!"

"Then your father should have done his due diligence. It's hardly Basil's fault if he falls for every scam, now is it?" Henrietta shook out the gray coat. "And he thinks he is so intelligent!"

"My father didn't know Northam was involved in the scheme. Was that deliberate?" Lucy asked as they dressed Northam in his coat. "Because I doubt he would have willingly invested in anything that bore your husband's stamp on it."

Henrietta offered her a pitying smile. "Mayhap your father should take better advice, then." She stepped back from the table. "There. Basil looks quite handsome again."

After making sure Henrietta didn't have any opportunity to add anything to Northam's pockets, Lucy left the body to Mr. Snape's tender mercies and followed Henrietta out into the carriage. She prayed the snow would soon be gone so that the Northams, both dead and alive, would finally leave Kurland St. Mary and its inhabitants for good.

When she got home, she would leave a note on Robert's desk, asking him to speak to Sophia about Captain Coles, and then retire to the nursery to spend some time with her children. When Robert returned, if he returned, she would leave it entirely up to him as to whether he wished to tell her what was going on.

After making sure that Henrietta was secure in her bed-chamber, Lucy went to change her gown and petticoat. The hems were soaked from the snow and clinging to her legs in a most annoying way. She didn't bother to ring for Betty and methodically emptied out her pocket, which contained a ribbon from Elizabeth's fine hair, a half-eaten toffee she'd stopped Ned from eating off the floor, and the folded list of shareholders she'd forgotten to return to Robert.

She got dressed, sat by the fire, and unfolded the list, her finger running down the list of names and stopping at her father's. She winced as she read the column detailing the size of his investment. No wonder he was in financial trouble. If only he'd restricted himself to using the yearly interest payments rather than dipping into his capital. His private income supported the currently comfortable existence his meager stipend from the Church of England would not.

Why had he agreed to join such a risky scheme? It was not like him at all. Lucy kept reading the names of investors and stopped when she reached another familiar one. She raised her head and stared into the flames. Now she would have to talk to Robert whether she wanted to or not.

After a fortifying breath, she went down the stairs and found James in the kitchen.

"Has Sir Robert returned home yet?"

"No, my lady."

"Will you inquire if he has time to speak to me when he does come in? I'll be in the nursery."

James bowed. "Yes, my lady."

She was halfway back up the stairs when Robert came striding through the hall looking thoroughly disagreeable and rather damp. He looked up and saw her, her frown deepening.

"What is it now?"

"I wanted to ask you about something."

"Does it have to do with this business with Northam?"

"Yes, I—"

He held up his hand. "Can it at least wait until I've changed?"

His impatient tone echoing through the hall made Lucy stiffen. "It can certainly wait until you regain control of your temper. Please let me know when that occurs, and I will consider then whether I wish to talk to *you*."

"Damn and blast it!" He marched over to his study and flung the door open. "I am entirely at your disposal, madam."

She wanted very badly to refuse, but what she had to say was too important for him to ignore. She followed him inside, her hands clasped tightly, and stood in front of his desk.

"Please sit down." He gestured impatiently at a chair.

"I prefer to stand." She took the list and placed it on his desk. "Am I correct that Captain Coles is named after his father?"

"Yes, what of it?"

She jabbed at the piece of paper. "Then perhaps you

should have read the entire list. A Mr. Joshua Coles is also listed as a subscriber to the fund."

Robert took the list, put on his spectacles, and started to read.

"With all due respect, my dear, you might be jumping to conclusions. It's not an uncommon name."

"But it is rather a coincidence, is it not?" Lucy countered. "Captain Coles mentioned that his father was not good with money and that his estate would require a lot of careful handling to recover from recent losses."

"That's true," Robert said slowly.

"And Sophia told me today that she saw Captain Coles leave the house just after Northam left, not before him—unless he had doubled back for something, which I suppose is still possible."

"Hold on a moment." Robert looked up at her. "I spoke to Joshua earlier. He said he thought he saw Northam at the Queen's Head that morning but that when he followed him into the inn, there was no sign of him."

"Then perhaps you need to have another conversation with your friend, the man you chose to be our daughter's godfather, and ask him what really happened." She turned toward the door.

"Where are you off to now?" Robert demanded.

"To the nursery." She looked back at him over her shoulder. "I've done my part. I wouldn't want to be accused of meddling. The rest is entirely up to you."

Robert ran a hand through his damp hair and glared at the door his wife had shut firmly behind her. He'd wanted to sit down and go over everything he had learned that morning with her, but she was still not willing to compromise or cooperate, and that was probably his own damn fault. She never responded well to orders, and he had a habit of reverting to officer type when things weren't progressing as he wished.

He picked up the note she'd left on his desk detailing her conversation with Mrs. Stanford that morning and placed it with the list of shareholders. He'd change his clothes, speak to Mrs. Stanford, and then find Joshua to see what he had to say for himself. He stood up, aware that his bad leg was aching after all his activity in such cold weather, and headed for the stairs. Joshua had better tell him the truth this time. He was in no mood to be trifled with.

"I'm not sure what you are implying, Major."

Joshua's bewildered frown was almost convincing, but Robert had dealt with many liars in his time. Some were definitely better than others.

"Why didn't you tell me that your father was among the investors in Northam's fraudulent shipping scheme?"

"I—" Joshua closed his mouth and then tried again. "I didn't think it had any relevance to your investigation."

"Well, your father certainly isn't here or involved in this matter directly, but you are, and so was Northam, the man who deliberately defrauded your family. One has to wonder what you thought when you arrived here and found Northam and his wife mingling with our guests."

"I wouldn't have come if I'd known Northam would be here." Joshua's voice was clipped, and his normally good-humored expression disappeared. "At first I wondered if it was some cruel joke at my expense."

"A joke I instigated?" Robert asked

"Not you, Major. Lord Northam. He loved to embarrass and ridicule his victims. I almost turned about, made my excuses, and left. It was only when I discovered the Northams had invited themselves and were not welcome that I decided to stay." Joshua met Robert's gaze. "I thought it best if there was someone here to keep an eye on him."

"You thought I was unaware of his reputation and needed protecting?"

"You are related to him by marriage, Major. That brings a certain level of complication to all your interactions with the man and his wife. As far as I knew, you might not have been aware of what he'd been up to recently. You rarely visit London."

"I know exactly what Northam is, and always has been. May I ask how your father was drawn into the fraudulent scheme?"

Joshua sighed. "As far as I can tell, my father regularly corresponded with a group of his classmates from Cambridge about the ancient history of this land. One of those gentlemen recommended the venture."

"Ah." Robert sat back. "Would that gentleman be Mr. Ambrose Harrington?"

"Yes." Joshua looked astounded. "How did you know? My father trusted him implicitly."

Inwardly, Robert winced. "When did you discover that the scheme was a fake?"

"When the ship and cargo failed to arrive, my father wrote to Mr. Harrington expressing his alarm. The rector promised to find out what had happened, and that was the last my father heard from him."

"I didn't ask when your father found out, I asked when you did," Robert pointed out.

"Just after I returned home from my final military assignment on the continent." Joshua grimaced. "As I mentioned, I made the mistake of asking my father about paying for a new commission for me. As you might imagine, he was very reluctant to disclose such a loss, and embarrassed that he had been duped by Northam."

"Was he also angry with Mr. Harrington?" Robert asked.

"He didn't say it directly, but one has to assume he was, although my father is very loyal, perhaps too loyal, to his friends." Joshua hesitated. "I believe he thought Mr. Harrington might have been lied to as well."

Robert nodded. "Did you attempt to speak to Northam about the matter after you arrived here?"

"I certainly intended to, but he proved remarkably difficult to pin down. I suspect he took one look at my face when I saw him and decided to keep clear of me."

"You didn't speak to him on the morning of the christening?"

Joshua blinked at him. "Why? Is someone saying I did?"

Robert didn't reply but drew out the note Lucy had left him and pretended to study it as Joshua shifted uneasily in his seat.

"You told me you were the first person to leave my stables the morning of the christening. Was that true?"

Joshua contemplated his boots for a long moment before slowly raising his head. "I certainly intended to be that person."

"I don't understand."

"I woke up early to go for a ride, looked out of my window, and saw a figure heading for the stables. I wondered if it might be Northam, because I knew he'd already been told that his presence at the christening would not be required. I guessed he had decided to ride out to see friends. I thought it worth my time to make sure he went."

"You intended to follow him," Robert commented.

"I *did* follow him. I told you I saw him at the Queen's Head."

"Did you speak to him?" Robert asked again.

"I . . ." Joshua slowly exhaled. "Yes."

"I trusted you enough to ask you to become my daughter's godfather." Robert studied his friend. "Has it really come to this? That you can't bring yourself to trust me in return?"

"I can assure you that nothing I said to Northam made any difference, and it has no bearing on his death," Joshua eventually spoke. "You have to believe me about that at least."

"How can I when you refuse to tell me what was said?" Robert asked.

"I told him I wanted my father's money back. He laughed and said good luck, that he had none to spare and was leaving for the continent. I must confess that I grabbed hold of him and hauled him up against the wall by his neck. In my rage, I probably threatened to kill him." Joshua shot Robert a defiant look. "Is that what you wanted to hear? Am I now a suspect?"

"Were you in the Queen's Head when this occurred?"

"We weren't inside the actual inn, but the stable yard. As I said, I saw him riding in there and followed. I caught hold of him before he went inside."

"Was he carrying anything?"

Joshua frowned. "Not that I remember."

"How about his saddlebags?"

"I can't recall. I was far too angry. Is it important?"

Robert chose not to answer that question. He was still convinced that at some point Northam had taken his money and either given it to someone or hidden it. From what Joshua was saying he'd either concealed it well enough not to be noticed or disposed of it before he reached the inn.

"Am I a suspect now?" Joshua asked again. "I will happily swear on the Bible that I didn't kill the bastard even though I wanted to."

"I still don't understand why you didn't tell me the truth from the outset," Robert countered with a question of his own.

"Because it seemed blatantly obvious to me that the person who murdered Northam was the rector. He was *late* to the ceremony to baptize his own granddaughter, Major. What more proof do you need than that?"

"In my experience, working out who committed a crime is like putting the pieces of a puzzle together in the right order. Sometimes those pieces don't make much sense on their own, but when linked together they mean something." Robert looked Joshua in the eye. "Your decision to keep your part of this puzzle to yourself impacts every other piece."

"Then I apologize," Joshua said stiffly. "Perhaps I was too intent on protecting my father and my family interests to realize that. It is humiliating to admit that one's father has been duped and that one's whole existence is now dependent on a financial resurrection that is unlikely to succeed."

Robert nodded. Despite his irritation he could understand Joshua's pride. He just wished he'd exhibited it in a different time and place.

"There is one more thing. Can you confirm that you followed Northam to the Kurland stables?"

"Yes, I loitered around until he'd mounted up and left before following at a discreet distance, why?"

"Did you see anyone else in the village when you got there?"

"Apart from Northam?" Joshua frowned. "I might have seen the Harrington twins on horseback and the curate hurrying over to the church to start the early morning service."

"Thank you." Robert inclined his head.

"I am deeply sorry for everything that has happened, Sir Robert." Joshua paused. "I feel as if I have let you down."

"We all make mistakes," Robert conceded somewhat reluctantly. "After your altercation with Northam, did he remain at the inn?"

"I believe so." Joshua grimaced. "I mounted my horse and left in something of a rage as he sauntered merrily on through the door."

"I am surprised you didn't plant him a facer."

"I was tempted, but I didn't want the day of the christening to start with a fight." A faint smile emerged on Joshua's face. "It seemed wrong somehow."

"I suppose I should thank you for your forbearance."

"I don't know about that. If I'd knocked him out cold he probably wouldn't have ended up in the rectory dead now, would he?"

"I suspect Northam would have met his comeuppance at some point." Robert stood, and Joshua followed suit. "Have you spoken to Mr. Harrington about your father's losses?"

"As matters stand. I . . . didn't think it would be fair to do that right now. At least my father isn't facing a murder charge."

"I suspect Mr. Harrington is well aware of his transgressions, but I promise you that should the occasion arise, I will have no compunction in reminding him about your father. He at least owes him some kind of an apology."

Joshua stood to attention as if he were on parade. "Am I free to go then, Major Kurland?"

Robert glanced out the window. "Indeed you are, although I doubt you will get very far in this weather if you decide to run."

He escorted Joshua to the door and followed him out into the silent house. He suspected that several of his guests had been busily engaged packing their belongings hoping to leave the next morning. He doubted anyone would be traveling any time soon. In truth, he'd much rather have the house to himself so that he could start making amends to his wife.

He went up the stairs to the nursery and discovered his son sitting at the table working on his alphabet with his mother. They made a charming picture of concentration together as Ned slowly copied out the letters.

"Father!" Ned saw him, jumped up, and ran over. "I spelled Lizzy's whole name, and she has too many letters!"

"Well done," Robert said, squeezing his shoulder. "We'll make a scholar of you yet." He glanced over at his wife, who was smiling indulgently at her son and not really looking at him at all. "We should search for a tutor for him soon."

"Mr. Fletcher says he has a younger brother named Brendan who might suit us admirably."

"Another Fletcher? I cannot argue with that. I'll tell Dermot to arrange an interview." Robert came and sat at the table beside Ned, who had resumed his seat. "Can you spell your own name in full?"

"'Course I can!" Ned immediately bent over his paper.

"Joshua said he followed Northam to the Queen's Head on the morning of the christening and they had a disagreement over his father's losses," Robert murmured to his wife over their son's head. "He apologized for not mentioning it sooner. He thought it had nothing to do with Northam's demise."

"How convenient." Lucy's pained expression showed everything she felt about that. "Do you believe him?"

"Yes, he seemed genuinely sincere. But one thing he said did stick out to me," Robert continued, hurriedly aware of both his son's limited attention span and his wife's dwindling patience. "He followed Northam. He didn't set out ahead of him and come back to the house."

Lucy met his gaze over Ned's head. "Then who went out ahead of both of them?"

There was a knock at the nursery door, which opened to admit James.

"I'm sorry to bother you, sir, my lady. Mr. Harrington has just arrived and is asking to speak to you both most urgently."

"Finished!" Ned sat back and showed the paper to Robert.

"That is very well done indeed, Ned," Robert commented admiringly, and then looked over at James. "Tell Mr. Harrington that we will be with him very shortly."

Lucy glanced over at her husband as they descended the stairs. The fact that he'd come to tell her about his interview with Captain Coles was both heartening and maddening at the same time. He should have respected her request not to involve her in the issue, but he also knew her well enough to understand that she would resent not being kept informed.

His complete acceptance of Captain Coles's story was probably because they were both military and that Joshua had once been a protégé of Robert's and a trusted officer. Lucy wasn't quite so sure of his innocence. Even though his first altercation with Northam hadn't ended in a fight, it was still possible that Captain Coles had discovered Northam at the rectory and finished what he had started. As a soldier, he was well used to violence and more than capable of killing.

Robert held the door of his study open for her, and she went inside to find her father pacing the room, his hands clasped behind his back.

"Is everything all right, Father?" Lucy asked as he swung around to confront them.

"No, it damn well is not!" He glared at Robert. "How *dare* you come into my house against my strict orders and upset my wife!"

Behind Lucy, Robert went still. "She wrote to me, sir. I had no other option than to speak to her directly. I was barely there for more than ten minutes."

"And in those ten minutes you upset her greatly!"

"I apologize for that," Robert said evenly. "But some things need to be said in person, and I did not want my aunt to hear them from any other source than me."

"You told her I was in debt!"

"With all due respect, sir, you risked your capital on a fraudulent investment scheme and lost it all," Robert replied evenly. "I only told her the truth."

"She did not need to know about such a thing in her present delicate condition!" Lucy's father fumed.

"Why not? Surely she should be aware of her financial situation? If you can't pay your bills and she is running the household, she'll notice soon enough."

Lucy winced at Robert's directness as her father bristled. It was an abrasive tactic that would not work well with her father, who always preferred to avoid a straightforward truth.

"Father, please remember that Robert is working to clear your name and find Lord Northam's murderer," Lucy intervened. "There is no point in getting angry with him when he is just trying to help."

"You should have stopped him going anywhere near the rectory, young lady. If Rose loses this baby or God forbid her life, it will be on both your heads!"

"That's remarkably unfair, sir." Robert's hand came to rest on Lucy's shoulder. "Neither of us wish Rose anything but the best."

"She didn't need to know about the debt," he repeated stubbornly. "It is none of your business or hers how I decide to use my capital."

Lucy glanced up at Robert. She knew her father well enough to understand that once he took offense, it was impossible for him to let the matter go.

"You look very tired, Father," Lucy said gently. "Would you like a drink or something to eat?"

"I'd rather go home, where I will not be subject to your presence, Lucy." He glared at her. "You have disappointed me greatly, but then when has that ever not been the case?"

Robert stepped between Lucy and her father. "My wife is in a very difficult position, sir. She is worried about the charges laid against you and yet still has to listen to me exploring all the evidence, which tends to point directly at you. What would you have her do? Take a side? You ask too much of her, sir, and if you continue to speak to her in such a manner in her own house, I will have to ask you to leave."

Lucy briefly closed her eyes as Robert took her hand and faced her father.

"I am doing my best to save you from the gallows, Mr. Harrington," Robert said quietly. "The least you could do is show some respect for my efforts and those of my wife."

For a moment, her father looked as if he would explode again, but he suddenly sat down in the nearest chair and dropped his face into his hands. Lucy started toward him, but Robert murmured in her ear.

"Go and ask James to send up a bottle of my best brandy, some coffee, and something for your father to eat. I'll deal with him. He won't want you to see him like this."

After Lucy left, her face stricken, Robert took the seat opposite his father-in-law and waited in silence for the rector to compose himself. A tap at the door heralded James with a tray Robert took with a murmur of thanks. He set it down between them and watched as his father-in-law deployed his handkerchief and finally blew his nose.

"May I suggest you eat something, sir?" Robert nudged the tray toward him. "I often find that life seems much less complicated on a full stomach."

The rector didn't comment, but he did apply himself to the slab of beef covered in mustard between two slices of bread along with the coffee. Robert poured them both a brandy and sat back to sip his.

"Thank you."

Robert shrugged. "You are dealing with many complicated and challenging things at the moment, sir. It is no wonder that it sometimes becomes too much for you."

"That is a remarkably kind thing to say when I just upset my eldest daughter and harangued you in your own house."

"You can seek forgiveness from her in your own way. As to the rest of it. I suspect I am the only person you can shout at. My aunt is too beset by her own problems, and your brother will always put his own family first."

"I know that all too well." The rector sipped his brandy. "I am beginning to feel rather like a fly trapped in a web. I cannot see an honorable way out of this mess."

"You could confess," Robert offered. "If you claimed that Northam was the aggressor, I doubt a man with your family standing would receive a harsh sentence from any judge."

"It sometimes feels as if that would be the easiest way," the rector agreed. "But I didn't kill him, and I can't find it within myself to admit to something I didn't do."

"Even if you insist you are innocent, it is looking increasingly likely that you will have to face a trial. Unfortunately, the evidence all points to you. You have a legitimate grievance against Northam, and he was murdered in your study with your letter opener." Robert poured more coffee and brandy. "I understood from Mr. Penarth that he was hoping you would testify against Northam if the matter of the fake shipping venture came to court."

"That is correct. Of course, one has to weigh the option of looking like a gullible fool against the satisfaction such a conviction would bring. I was willing to take the risk."

"If Northam found out and came to Kurland St. Mary to threaten you not to testify, that would be a point in your favor," Robert said slowly. "Have you thought of that?"

"But Northam didn't do that, and Mr. Penarth is dead, isn't he?"

"Unfortunately, yes, but his secretary, Mr. Barry, was aware of Mr. Penarth's intentions, and Mr. Penarth also revealed them to me. I'm sure we would both be willing to testify in your defense."

"But I didn't kill Northam," the rector repeated. "It would've been easier if I had. You can't say that he didn't deserve it."

"Regardless of your plea, I have to tell you that I am required to write a report to the assizes judge in Hertford. If that court chooses to pursue you for murder, I will not be able to stop them."

"Thank you for your honesty, at least." The rector sighed and finished the last of his meal. "Your friend Mr. Stanford sent me a very kind note offering to represent me in court if necessary."

"He is an excellent barrister," Robert agreed. "You could not be in better hands."

"My brother is more concerned that Max is kept out of everything than in my supposed innocence or guilt." The rector's faint smile disappeared. "Even though he offered to pay my court costs, I am remarkably disappointed in him."

"Max's actions were definitely suspicious, but I can't see him killing Northam, can you?" Robert asked, aware that it was the first time he'd had quite such an unorthodox conversation with a murder suspect. "Is there *anyone* you could think of who might have done this?"

The rector shook his head. "Even if it were Max, he would never be sent to trial. David would do anything for his children."

"So I've noticed," Robert said, aware that his father-in-law hadn't actually answered his question. "Then who else?"

"Northam was universally disliked. It could have been anyone."

"But we can only consider who had the opportunity," Robert reminded him gently. "I understand that your friend Mr. Joshua Coles senior lost some money in the venture as well."

There was a long pause before Mr. Harrington was able to look at Robert.

"That was my fault. I encouraged him to invest." The rector swallowed painfully. "He wrote to me in his despair, and I did not have the courage to answer him. Me— a supposed man of God." He dabbed at his eyes again. "How pitiful is that?"

"His son is here," Robert reminded him. "Perhaps you could convey your regrets to him?"

"I already have. I gave Joshua a letter for his father the morning of the christening. He came to see me and expressed his disgust at my actions. I simply heard him out because I had no defense."

Robert considered that interesting piece of information.

Had Joshua lied to him again? He could hardly claim that such information wasn't pertinent to the murder investigation this time.

There was a knock on the door, and James came in with a folded note.

"Excuse me, Sir Robert, but this was just delivered from the rectory."

"Is it for me?" Mr. Harrington held out his hand.

"No, it is for Sir Robert." James passed over the note.

"Thank you." Robert broke the seal and read the almost illegible script. "Rose wants me to bring Henrietta to the rectory to speak to her immediately." He frowned at the rector. "I don't think that is a good idea, do you?"

James cleared his throat. "It was Dr. Fletcher who delivered the note, sir. He's in the kitchen having a warm drink. He said to tell you that he's in favor of the meeting."

"Ask him to join us here when he is ready, will you?" Robert asked.

"Yes, sir."

James withdrew, leaving Robert staring at his father-in-law, who had picked up the note to read.

"Did you know about this?" Robert finished his coffee and eyed the remaining slab of beef. If he was going to be deprived of his dinner, he should probably eat something before going out into the storm again.

"I didn't tell her I was coming here, but she might have guessed." The rector's smile disappeared. "I regret that I lost my temper when she said you had visited her. I even shouted at Mrs. Culpepper for allowing such a thing, which was neither fair nor kind."

Dr. Fletcher came in through the door in his stockinged feet, a glass of whisky in his hand, his expression somber.

"I regret to inform you both that Mrs. Harrington is not well at all. I think she should be allowed to speak to her daughter before anything worse occurs."

Mr. Harrington's face went ashen, and he slumped back in his chair. "Good Lord. This is a nightmare."

Robert went over to his doctor, who wasn't exactly looking at him in an approving manner.

"What's going on?"

"I asked you to leave Mrs. Harrington alone, Major."

"I spent ten minutes with her," Robert responded. "I hardly think I am entirely responsible for her current condition. Maybe her husband losing his temper in front of her was a major contributor as well?"

"You're as bad as each other," Patrick snapped. "If it wasn't for my patient begging me to allow you speak to her, I'd never allow it."

Robert grimaced and touched his arm. "I really do apologize. Now, can you keep an eye on Mr. Harrington while I inform Lady Northam? I'll order the carriage so that you don't have to ride back through the storm."

Within less than a half hour, Robert, his cousin, his father-in-law, his doctor, and his wife were crammed in a carriage heading toward the village. He hadn't asked Lucy to come. She'd just appeared with Henrietta, her very expression a challenge, and he hadn't dared argue with her.

Even Henrietta was uncharacteristically silent, her gaze drawn toward the small frosted window, which offered a stark white view with very little variation. When they arrived at the rectory, Robert helped everyone down and retained his grip on his wife's elbow.

"What is it?" she whispered as they watched everyone precede them into the house.

"I would appreciate it if you could keep an eye on Henrietta."

"Why do you think I came?" Lucy responded. "I am fully aware of what she is capable of, and I will not allow her to upset her mother."

"I believe her mother is already upset." Robert set off down the path. "Patrick seems to think her life might be in danger."

Lucy gasped and brought her gloved hand to her cheek. "Then why is he allowing *this*?"

"Because there might not be another opportunity for her to say what needs to be said to her daughter?" Robert took her hand and brought it to his lips. "Let's pray that Dr. Fletcher is wrong, shall we?"

It was blissfully warm inside the rectory. After removing their outer garments, Robert escorted Lucy up the stairs to the best bedchamber, where Dr. Fletcher, Mr. Harrington, and Henrietta already surrounded Rose. She was propped up against her pillows, her face pale except for the hectic color of her cheeks. Her prayer book sat on the patchwork quilt beneath her left hand.

"Mother." Henrietta inclined her head an icy inch. "How kind of you to finally deign to speak to me."

"I am sorry for your loss, Henrietta," Rose replied just as formally.

"No, you aren't. You never liked my darling Basil. You're probably delighted that he is dead."

Dr. Fletcher cleared his throat and directed a glare at Henrietta. "Lady Northam. May I remind you that Mrs. Harrington is very weak, and if you wish to remain in this room you will at least attempt to be civil."

"For your sake, and for the sake of your children, I am glad that Basil has gone," Rose admitted. "You are a far better manager of the estate than he will ever be, and an excellent mother."

Henrietta opened and closed her mouth before seemingly finding words to speak. "From what I understand about your new will, my prospects are extremely limited."

"I wonder who told you that?" Rose asked. "Was it Northam? His idea of fairness was for him to have everything and the rest of the family could go to the devil. You can hardly say I haven't been more than generous to you, Henrietta. I have a record of all the money I have turned over to you since your marriage for very little thanks, and a lot of condescension and derision. I did it for you,

Daughter, not for Northam, and yet you constantly allowed him to malign me and waste your inheritance on his debts."

As Henrietta seemed temporarily lost for words, Robert asked a question of his own.

"Did your solicitor leak details of your new will to Lord Northam, Aunt?"

Rose turned to Robert. "Apparently, he bribed one of the clerks to copy out any new instructions for my will and send them on to him. That man has since been dismissed."

"But you did change your will," Henrietta spoke up again. "And not in my favor."

"I settled money on your children, Henrietta. It was my attempt to stop your husband from stealing from *you*." Rose's voice cracked, and Dr. Fletcher moved instinctively toward her.

"You also gave away my fortune to your new husband," Henrietta snapped. "Don't forget that! And strangely enough, as soon as that happened Basil is murdered in this *very* rectory." She glanced pointedly at the rector, who was standing protectively beside his wife's bed. "How very *convenient* for you."

"I did not kill Lord Northam," the rector stated.

Henrietta rounded on him. "Of course you did! All the evidence—"

Just as Dr. Fletcher went to intervene, Rose spoke over him.

"Enough of this!" She gripped her prayer book in her hand and struggled to sit upright. "*I* murdered Lord Northam! Now make of that what you will!"

Chapter 16

"I-I . . . beg your pardon, Rose?" The rector was the first to stutter into speech. "Are you feeling quite well?" He glanced wildly over at Dr. Fletcher, who was frowning. "Has my wife imbibed too much laudanum, Doctor? Is she perhaps delusional?"

Robert held up his hand and approached the bed. "Aunt Rose, could you kindly repeat what you just said?"

"You heard me quite clearly." She raised her chin. "I murdered Northam."

"But that is ridiculous!" Robert said. "Why on earth would you do that?"

"Because his very existence is a threat to my daughter and my grandchildren!" She glanced around the silent room. "You all know what he was like."

"But . . ." Robert met Lucy's startled gaze. "When did you make this decision, and what in particular did Northam do to provoke you?"

"He came to the rectory and threatened me." Rose folded her hands together on the quilt. "He said that if I didn't give him money, he would take Henrietta and my grandchildren away and I would never be allowed to see them again."

Henrietta made a dismissive gesture. "For goodness'

sake, Mother, you know how Basil was. He often made silly threats that he couldn't possibly carry out."

"I believed him this time." Rose met her daughter's gaze. "I asked him to meet me here on the morning of the christening, and when he refused to listen to reason, I killed him."

Robert went to speak, but Lucy touched his arm and slowly shook her head as Rose continued.

"Northam not only threatened me, Henrietta, but also my husband and my unborn child. He said he could easily arrange for me to fall down the stairs or for Ambrose to have an accident while out riding." She shivered. "I saw his face. He was enjoying every second of it."

Dr. Fletcher pushed past the rector and took hold of Rose's wrist.

"Her pulse is erratic. I realize that this is not what any of you want to hear right now, but Mrs. Harrington needs to rest before you can question her anymore."

"It doesn't matter now." Rose sank back against her pillows, exhausted. "I've said my piece and I have nothing more to add. I killed Basil Northam, and I don't regret a thing."

Lucy was the first to go down the stairs to the back parlor, which looked cold and unused because of Rose being confined to bed. She knelt and set the meager fire to rights, adding wood and coal until she had a blaze going. Behind her she heard her father in the corridor request tea and brandy to be sent in for his guests as everyone else except Dr. Fletcher filed in.

If her father had known Northam had threatened Rose and his unborn child, would he have been capable of killing to protect them?

"Well," Henrietta burst out. "I never expected my mother to be so under her husband's thumb that she would be willing to admit to a murder just to save him from the gallows."

Lucy dusted off her hands and stood up. Trust Rose's

daughter to get right to the heart of the matter. She sounded quite aggrieved.

"We have no evidence that Rose murdered Lord Northam, Henrietta," Robert said evenly.

"Because it simply isn't true!" Henrietta looked at Lucy. "You must agree with me on that at least!"

"It does seem rather unlikely," Lucy said reluctantly.

Robert shrugged. "If she insists on writing out a confession, I have to accept her word for it."

"Then don't let her!" Henrietta snapped at Robert. "Ask Dr. Fletcher to say she isn't of sound mind or something. Pay him off if necessary."

"She sounded quite lucid to me," Robert said as Lucy's father came back in with the maid and a tray of tea. "Would you care to pour, Lucy?"

Lucy moved away from the fire and set out two cups, one for Henrietta and the other for herself, before lifting the pot. Robert helped himself to a brandy as did her father, who still looked like a man who had received a terrible shock.

Henrietta ignored the tea, marched right up to the rector, and poked him in the chest. "You cannot allow my mother to take the blame for your actions. You *have* to admit your guilt and set her free."

"If I had murdered Northam, I would already have confessed to the crime." Lucy's father's voice trembled. "But I did not, and I simply cannot believe that Rose *did*. Why would she say such a thing?"

"Because she is a fool." Henrietta's eyes filled with tears, and she dashed them away. "Why does she have to ruin *everything*?"

"Rose said that she wanted you and your grandchildren to be safe," Lucy reminded Henrietta as she offered her a handkerchief. "How can you malign her so when she has always had your best interests at heart?"

"My best interests by falsely claiming she murdered my

husband?" Henrietta dabbed at her eyes. "I loved him!" She sank down onto the couch, covered her eyes, and fell back as if she was about to swoon.

Lucy stepped over Henrietta's trailing skirts and ignored her pitiful moaning as she walked over to Robert, who had retreated to the window.

"This is ridiculous," he muttered. "Rose no more killed Northam than you or I did."

"Then what are you going to do about it?" Lucy inquired.

"I hate to agree with a word Henrietta says, but I think I will ask Dr. Fletcher to confirm that Rose is not well enough to make such a confession at the present time."

Lucy glanced back at the widow and grimaced. "I'll wager Henrietta is upset because her mother is attempting to prevent my father from being prosecuted for murder, and for no other reason than that."

"She is remarkably self-centered and vindictive when roused," Robert agreed. "But I can't say I blame her on this one. I never imagined my aunt confessing to a murder myself."

"And we already know that she didn't lure Northam here that morning. That was my uncle David," Lucy reminded him.

"So he said." Robert paused. "You have to admit that it would've been easy for Rose to take a piece of her husband's writing and send it to Northam. It would also have been easy for her to kill him with the letter opener. He would never have expected that."

"Are you seriously suggesting she might have murdered Northam?" Lucy squeaked. "Have you run mad?"

"There's no need to take that tone with me, Lucy." Her husband frowned. "I do have to consider every possibility, but I agree that this is a very unlikely one."

"Why would the Earl of Harrington mislead you?"

"As he's spent quite a lot of time doing exactly that, I

wonder why you ask? For someone who has been remarkably eager to clear her father's name, you suddenly seem loath to even consider other possibilities."

Lucy pressed her lips together and turned away to retrieve her tea. Henrietta appeared to have sunk into a decline on the couch, and Lucy wasn't in the mood to humor her further. She went out into the corridor and saw Dr. Fletcher entering the kitchen. As quickly as she could, she changed direction and went up the stairs, knocking lightly before she went back into Rose's room.

The curtains had been drawn and Rose lay on her back, the drowsy stillness in her eyes an indication that Dr. Fletcher had given her something medicinal to calm her. Lucy knelt beside the bed and took Rose's hand.

"I know you didn't kill him."

"You don't know that." Rose's voice was weak. "I am quite willing to stand up for my family, my dear."

"I appreciate that, and I am deeply thankful for it." Lucy squeezed her fingers. "Your defense of my father is admirable, but I cannot allow you to take the blame for something you didn't do."

"Why not? If I die because of this pregnancy—" She hurried on as Lucy went to protest. "No, let me finish—this whole mess dies with me. Ambrose and Henrietta will both be free. Can't you see that?"

"But I don't want you to die," Lucy whispered. "My father would be devastated."

"But at least he'd still be alive." Rose's voice trailed away into sleep. "I can at least offer him that."

Lucy went back down the stairs, her mind in turmoil. If Rose stuck by her story, would Robert have to take her confession to the court in Hertford, or could he, as the local magistrate, make sure the matter went no further? He'd been reluctant to pursue a conviction against her father, so how on earth would he deal with prosecuting his aunt?

She paused at the bottom of the stairs and looked toward the front door, where Robert, Dr. Fletcher, and her father were having an animated discussion. She didn't have to guess the subject. With a heavy heart she returned to the parlor, where Henrietta had roused herself sufficiently to ignore the tea and help herself to a brandy.

"Did you sneak off to speak to my mother again?" Henrietta asked as she refilled her brandy glass. "I hope you managed to get her to say that she lied and was just trying to protect her murdering husband."

"She was sleeping." Lucy drank the lukewarm tea and grimaced. "If it makes you feel any better, I doubt Robert, Dr. Fletcher, or my father will allow Rose to confess to anything while she is bedridden."

"Well, thank goodness for that." Henrietta jerked her glass toward the door, slopping brandy everywhere. "Our menfolk will save us again."

"What do you want to happen, Henrietta?" Lucy stared into her companion's eyes. "Would you prefer your mother to testify in court?"

"A wife can't testify against her husband." Henrietta sniffed. "Your father doesn't need her to absolve him when he is guilty as charged." She suddenly sat up straight. "And I'm not sure if my mother is that unwell. Perhaps she is in it with him up to her neck."

"You really are quite despicable, Henrietta," Lucy said slowly. "Your mother might die, and all you can think about is yourself."

Henrietta slammed her glass down on the table. "My husband is dead. Why *shouldn't* I be thinking about my family and myself? Somebody has to."

"Robert and your mother will always stand by you— you know that." Lucy picked up the tea tray. "I think it is time for us to return to Kurland Hall, don't you? I'm sure Dr. Fletcher will let us know if your mother's condition worsens."

Lucy was still quietly fuming when they reached her

home, and after escorting Henrietta upstairs, she went down to find Robert in his study. He was sitting behind his desk, his capable hands folded in front of him staring at nothing.

"I asked Cook to serve dinner in an hour," Lucy said as she shut the door behind her.

"Good, I'm famished." Robert picked up one of his pens and twisted it in his fingers. "Does Rose's 'confession' really change anything?"

"No," Lucy admitted as she sat down in front of him. "It merely complicates matters unnecessarily."

"Agreed." Her husband returned to studying his pen.

"Rose told me that it was the best solution for everyone." Lucy hadn't realized how much her voice would shake until she started to speak. "That if she died after confessing to the murder, it would set Henrietta and Father free."

"You went back upstairs to speak to her."

Lucy managed to nod.

"How very like you." Robert got up and came around to place his hand on her shoulder. "I hate to admit it, but if that was why she did it, she was right."

"But I don't want her to die," Lucy gulped, and then much to her mortification she started to cry. "She's been so wonderful with the twins, and with Anna, and me. . . ."

Robert drew her to her feet and wrapped her in his arms. She inhaled the comforting smell of his cologne and damp wool.

"How would my father survive having his second wife die in childbed like his first?"

Lucy barely choked the words out before she dissolved into a storm of weeping. Robert patted her hair and made soothing noises until she was able to compose herself sufficiently to look up at him.

"I do apologize." She hunted for a clean handkerchief and then remembered she had given hers to Henrietta. "This is not helpful."

He handed her his much bigger handkerchief and waited until she blew her nose and composed herself.

"There." She managed a watery smile. "I am quite myself again."

"I am beginning to wish this whole matter to the devil," Robert said savagely. "I hate seeing the people I care about most in such distress over a man who didn't give a damn for anyone except himself." He hesitated. "I'd almost rather let his killer go than cause any more harm."

Lucy frowned. "You don't really mean that."

"At this point, my love, I fear that I do." He tucked an errant strand of hair behind her ear. "I'm beginning to feel as if everyone is deceiving me, and that way lies madness."

He eased away and took her hand. "Shall we visit the nursery before we change for dinner? Half an hour spent with my children might just about restore my faith in humanity."

Lucy smiled and nodded at her dinner guests, but her attention was distracted by Rose's startling confession and her husband's response to it. The Stanfords and the Harringtons had been hoping to leave on the morrow, but so much snow had fallen during the day that travel seemed inadvisable. The earl was somewhat subdued, and it was left to Sophia and Captain Coles to maintain the bulk of the conversation.

It was something of a relief when Lucy was able to take the ladies through to the drawing room for tea while the men enjoyed their port. Henrietta had remained in her room, which had also been a blessing. According to James she'd eaten a hearty dinner, drunk the best part of a bottle of wine, and retired to bed.

"Good riddance," Lucy murmured to herself.

"Did you say something, my dear?" Aunt Jane looked over at her inquiringly.

"Nothing of interest, Aunt." Lucy smiled at her. "Would you like some more tea?"

"No, thank you," Aunt Jane drew her shawl closer around her shoulders. "I do hope the weather improves. I am worried about Julia being alone."

"I thought she was staying with your cousin Eliza," Lucy said.

"She is, but it's not the same as being with your own family, is it? Julia is of a somewhat melancholy disposition and needs constant encouragement to be cheerful—especially at the moment."

Lucy didn't remember her cousin as being melancholy at all but hesitated to disagree with her aunt. "When are she and Eliza setting out on their travels?"

"Soon, I believe." Aunt Jane frowned. "And I am not there to supervise her packing or make sure that our dressmaker provides all the necessities."

"I'm sure you will be home very soon," Lucy reassured her. "Julia is a sensible girl, and she will understand why you cannot be with her quite yet."

"I have written reassuring her that I will be home soon, and my husband assures me that the message has been sent off by horseback." Aunt Jane looked toward the fire. "She is so . . . fragile at the moment. So unlike herself."

The admission was so unexpected that Lucy didn't know quite how to reply and cravenly decided to change the subject.

"How is Max coping?"

Aunt Jane's smile returned. "Quite well, actually. Being stranded in the countryside has meant that he and his father have had an opportunity to mend some fences. They even managed to joke today about how much money Max has saved by not being in London for a week."

"Perhaps after his unpleasant experience with Northam, Max will be a reformed man," Lucy said.

"One would hope so, but I find such lessons rarely stick with the young. I only pray he has learned to avoid heavy gamblers such as Northam."

"So do I." Lucy refilled her aunt's teacup. "I doubt my

uncle will be quite so willing to pay off his debts again if he hasn't."

"Pay off what debts?" Aunt Jane asked, her cup half-way to her lips.

For a second Lucy's mind went blank. How much did her aunt know about what had transpired between Robert and the earl?

"You'd have to ask Max about that." Lucy smiled. "It is hardly my story to tell."

The welcome sound of male voices and a whiff of cigar smoke came drifting in from the hall, and Lucy shot to her feet.

"I'll just go and order a fresh pot of tea from the kitchen."

She hurried toward the door, where Robert was shepherding their guests inside, and caught hold of his arm.

"Is it possible that my aunt doesn't know my uncle paid off Max's debt to Northam?"

"I have no idea. Why do you ask?"

"Because if she didn't know, it is highly likely that she might be asking some rather awkward questions to her husband and son in the near future."

Robert shrugged. "That's hardly our problem. The earl didn't ask for secrecy. I'm far more interested in why he was conveniently traveling with five hundred pounds in currency he could hand over to Northam."

"I hadn't thought of that," Lucy mused.

"And I'd also like to ask Captain Coles why he denied meeting your father when they apparently met in the rectory on the morning of the christening."

"I thought you'd decided to give up?" Lucy asked him.

His faint smile warmed her heart. "It seems I'm a dog with a bone that I cannot let go."

She briefly cupped his cheek. "I'm glad." She gathered her courage and looked him right in the eye. "And if Northam did threaten to kill Rose and her child, I could quite see my father overreacting and trying to protect her."

"Thank you for that." He took her hand and kissed her fingers. "There is still something I am missing, but I feel that if we keep pulling at the threads, then some of this tangle will unwind. I'm going to speak to Joshua first."

"Don't forget that Captain Coles traveled down to Kurland St. Mary with Mr. Penarth. Perhaps there is some connection between them," Lucy suggested.

"Well, Joshua's father lost money in that shipping venture, and I'd wager Mr. Penarth was clever enough to work out exactly whom he was traveling with." Robert looked back over the top of Lucy's head and spied his prey chatting amiably to the Countess of Harrington. "Wish me luck."

"I spoke to Mr. Harrington earlier today." Robert lowered his voice as he came up behind Joshua. "He said he gave you a letter apologizing to your father."

Joshua went still and then slowly swung around to face Robert.

"Nothing to say about that?" Robert asked. "I must admit that I am disappointed in you, Captain. I thought you a man of integrity, and it appears as if you have none."

"I . . . can explain."

"Please, be my guest."

Joshua glanced wildly around the room. "In private if possible."

Robert started toward the door. "Then come into my study."

He sat behind his desk and faced Joshua, who stood to attention. "Well?"

"I know that you won't believe me, but—"

"I can't think why I should when you have consistently lied to my face, but out with it, man."

"I didn't want you to know I'd been at the rectory on the morning of the christening." Joshua sighed. "I knew it would look bad."

"Because you have just as much of a grudge against Lord Northam as the rector and, as a soldier, have a far more intimate knowledge of how to kill someone?"

"Yes, that exactly, but I didn't see Northam at the rectory. If you remember, I left him at the Queen's Head. I only decided to go and speak to the rector after I'd seen the twins and the curate leave the house." He swallowed hard. "It was something of an impulse."

"Go on," Robert prompted him.

"I was already furious after encountering Northam, and having someone I could finally hold to account, someone who was so ashamed and apologetic was . . . cathartic."

"The rector admitted he was at fault and immediately wrote a letter of apology to your father?"

"Yes." Joshua nodded. "Then I left the rectory and came back to Kurland Hall to prepare for the christening."

"Thus abandoning your original plan to keep an eye on Northam in favor of venting your spleen against an elderly rector who was gulled by the same liar who impoverished your father."

Joshua's face flushed a dull red. "That's hardly fair. If it hadn't been for Mr. Harrington, my father would never have invested in that ridiculous scheme."

"Did you ask the rector why he chose to invest?"

"Because, as I said, he knew his brother would cover his losses. He needed to understand his liability in the matter, Major. My father doesn't have a rich family to tow him out of the River Tick."

"Yet you let the real villain, Lord Northam, get away from you in favor of extracting an apology from the rector." Robert paused. "I am beginning to wonder whether you also coerced Mr. Harrington into writing another letter—one that asked Northam to meet him at the rectory so that you could kill him."

"That's outrageous!" Joshua took a step forward, his fists clenched. "You can't possibly believe I would do that!"

Robert stood as well and faced his friend. "The thing is, Captain Coles, I absolutely and positively know you well enough to believe not only that you *could* do that but that you *would*."

He walked around to the door and opened it. "James? Will you and Matthew escort Captain Coles up to his room and ensure that he stays there?"

"You're locking me up? For *what*?"

"On suspicion of murder." Robert stared into his old friend's furious eyes. "As a military man I am certain you will respect my authority as the local magistrate to act in this manner until I have finished investigating Lord Northam's death."

He paused as James and Matthew came to stand on either side of Joshua. "Think of it as a time to reflect on your conduct and decide whether you finally wish to tell me the truth."

"This is quite unnecessary," Joshua fumed as Matthew bowed and politely indicated the stairs.

Robert beckoned James closer and lowered his voice "Make sure to search the captain's room and belongings and remove any weaponry. If you find a considerable sum of money, I'd like to know about that, too."

"Yes, Sir Robert."

Satisfied that his orders would be carried out, Robert returned to the drawing room and made his way over to his wife, who was occupied pouring tea.

"I've confined Captain Coles to his quarters," Robert informed her.

"Do you really think he might be the murderer?" Lucy asked.

"I'm not sure, but I am tired of him lying to me. He suggested that your father was less of a victim than his because the Harrington family would save him." Robert snorted. "I haven't seen much evidence of that, have you? In truth the earl has been so busy ensuring his precious son is kept out of everything that he's quite keen to fix the blame on his own brother."

"I had noticed that myself," Lucy agreed. "I did wonder whether my father hadn't told Uncle David about his financial woes out of a misguided sense of pride or embarrassment."

"That's highly likely knowing the Harringtons." Robert sighed and took the cup of tea she offered him. "Perhaps one of us should ask him—and it won't be me, because he is already annoyed about my interference in Max's affairs."

"I doubt he'd be willing to listen to me, either, and I hate to worry Aunt Jane when she is so concerned about Julia." Lucy glanced worriedly over to the couch where her aunt was deep in conversation with Sophia.

Robert's gaze strayed to the Earl of Harrington and stayed there.

"Excuse me."

"What is it?"

"I've had enough of this. Perhaps it's time to stir up the woodpile again."

He was already on the move. The earl saw him coming and deepened his frown.

"Kurland."

"My lord." Robert inclined his head.

"Hopefully the road will be cleared tomorrow and we can leave you in peace. You have been most . . . hospitable," the earl said stiffly.

"I'm not the kind of man to throw his guests out in the snow or leave them to the tender mercies of the posting inn," Robert replied. "I just wanted you to be aware that Lucy mentioned you paid off Max's debts to your countess earlier this evening, and she seemed surprised."

"Devil take it!" the earl muttered. "I was relying on your discretion about this matter, Kurland."

"You certainly didn't swear me to secrecy," Robert

pointed out. "But I thought it only fair that you knew what had occurred."

"I suppose I should thank you." The earl cleared his throat. "Are you any closer to discovering who killed Northam?"

"I think we both know the answer to that, my lord, don't we?"

"Do we?"

"The rector sank a huge portion of his capital into Northam's nefarious scheme. It's blatantly obvious that he murdered Northam to protect his new wife and unborn child and revenge himself on the man who ruined him."

"I—"

Robert continued, his voice scathing. "I am undecided how to proceed. Should I send him off to await the quarterly assizes in Hertford now, or wait until the birth of his child is closer? What would you advise, sir? Is it better that the child survives if both its parents are destined to die, or should I attempt to erase the entire family with one stroke of my pen?"

The earl just stared at him.

"Perhaps you could discuss this with your son on the journey back to London. I'm sure it would amuse you both greatly." Robert bowed and walked away, his desire to strangle the earl completely at odds with his duties as host.

Lucy touched his arm. "What on earth did you say? He looks like he received a death sentence himself."

"I simply asked him to adjudicate the case for when to detain your father for murder," Robert said shortly. "If that doesn't get through to him, then I'm afraid nothing will."

Chapter 17

Lucy rose from her bed, put her dressing gown back on, and ventured down the stairs. Between Robert's still simmering anger and her own worries, she'd been unable to sleep at all. Even seeing her children at bedtime had only made her think about poor Rose and her unborn baby. She'd decided to go to the kitchen, warm up some milk and honey, and hope that she'd finally grow too tired to resist the desire to sleep.

Her aunt and uncle had retired early, and Lucy had been glad to see them go. Their lack of support for her father had shocked her considerably and somehow lessened them in her eyes. She could at least understand Aunt Jane's pressing concern for her daughter, but her uncle's decision to protect his son at the cost of his only brother was shameful.

She paused in the shadows of the main hall beside a suit of armor that guarded the entrance into the old medieval part of the house and heard voices engaged in a furious, whispered argument. Her intimate knowledge of the house, its layout, and its furnishings made it easy for her to navigate the darkness and draw closer.

"Max, just calm down for a moment and think before you go rushing off and cause more damage."

Lucy recognized the earl's voice.

"How can you say that when you have put Uncle Ambrose at such risk? I'm sick of all this *lying*. I don't want to see him hang, Father. Do you?"

"It won't come to that, Max!"

"All my uncle was trying to do was help us. You got him into this mess—all of it."

"And I will get him out of it. I promise you that if you will only go back to bed I will make things right."

There was a long pause, and Lucy instinctively held her breath.

"As you wish," Max said abruptly. "I'll take your word for it this time, but if Uncle Ambrose does have a trial, I am going to offer myself as a witness in his defense, and be damned to you and your craven, cowardly schemes of appeasement."

Max turned and went back toward the hall passing so close to Lucy that she feared discovery.

"Thank God," the earl muttered as he, too, walked back toward the main staircase. "Will this farce never end?"

Lucy stayed where she was for so long that her feet grew cold enough for her to notice. What had the earl involved her father with, and how had it ended in Northam's murder? She considered that matter as she made her way to Robert's study, which tended to retain its warmth more than the rest of the house.

She lit a candle and sat in Robert's chair, her feet drawn up under her. Max seemed to be implying that the earl's actions had caused his brother to murder Northam.

"The money," Lucy whispered into the darkness. "Oh, dear God."

She crept back up the stairs and into her bedchamber, where her husband was snoring quietly in his sleep.

"Robert, wake up." She set her candle down beside the bed and gently shook his shoulder. "Robert."

"What?" He glared at her. He always hated being woken unexpectedly.

"I need to talk to you." She sat on the side of the bed while he pulled himself upright and regarded her with increasing disfavor.

"Are the children all right?"

"Yes, thank goodness. This is about my father."

"And it can't wait until morning?"

"No, because . . ." She struggled to draw a breath. "I just overheard Max and my uncle arguing."

"And?"

"Max implied that the earl was responsible for my father's current situation and that unless the earl did something, Max was going to tell the truth at the trial."

"And convict your father?"

"*No*, to testify in his defense, which didn't make much sense to me until I thought it through." Lucy reached for his hand. "Do you remember wondering why my uncle 'happened' to have five hundred pounds on him when he came to Kurland St. Mary to give to Northam to pay off Max's debts?"

"Go on." Robert was fully awake now, his blue gaze focused on her face.

"What if he brought the money for my father?" Lucy couldn't bring herself to go on.

"Because the rector had already agreed to kill Northam when the time and opportunity arose?" Robert asked gently. "I suppose it would be one way for your father and his brother to get revenge on Northam."

Lucy nodded, and after a moment her husband continued.

"But luckily for the earl, Northam was unexpectedly here, and he decided to take the opportunity to get rid of him once and for all. He used the lure of the money to get Northam to the rectory, where your father killed him." Robert tightened his grip on her hand. "Is that what you fear?"

"Yes."

Robert was silent for such a long time that Lucy began to imagine he would never speak again.

"I understand why this sounds possible, my love, but it still doesn't sit right with me. Maybe it's even simpler than that. The earl asked your father to be the go-between to pay off Max's debts to Northam. I could quite see that happening, which would be why he brought the money with him."

"But Northam ended up dead, and the money has disappeared," Lucy pointed out.

"Joshua could have murdered Northam as could the earl, as could Max," Robert replied. "They all had reason to dislike him."

"But what if my father decided to use the money his brother gave him to pay off his *own* debts rather than Max's? If Northam were expecting to be paid off, he would not have taken that well. He and my father could've fought and Northam ended up being stabbed during the struggle."

"Also possible." Robert studied her. "You seem determined to prove your father is guilty."

"Because the more I think about it, the worse it gets for him," Lucy confessed.

"But you're forgetting something important. Your father doesn't *need* the money, does he? He's married to Rose and she has left him very well provided for in her will."

"Which Rose says he didn't know, so perhaps he was desperate enough to take the money, kill Northam, and hope his brother would use his influence to have him acquitted?" She flung up her hands. "I can't believe I'm sitting here in the middle of the night trying to find ways to convict my own father of murder."

Robert recaptured her shaking fingers. "You are being very brave, my love." He paused long enough to get her full attention. "Will you allow me to question Captain Coles further before we put this to your father?"

"If you think it will make a difference." Honesty compelled her to add, "But I don't think Captain Coles killed Northam, either."

"I'm hoping that a night of quiet reflection will have encouraged him to be frank with me about everything." Robert pulled the covers of the bed down. "Now, will you get in before you freeze to death? We still have several hours before dawn, and I would like them to be peaceful ones."

Robert knocked on Joshua's door, waited for Frederick to unlock it, and went on through. His friend was sitting by the window just finishing up his breakfast. He went to stand. Robert waved to him to stay where he was and took the seat opposite.

"Good morning, Joshua. I am very much hoping you have decided to make a clean breast of everything this morning?"

"I have, Major." Joshua set his coffee cup back on the tray with a determined thump. "I would just ask you to hear everything I have to say before you jump to any more conclusions."

"Despite the fact that I have been remarkably accurate about your 'discrepancies' so far, I'll do my best." Robert gazed at him expectantly. "Spit it out, man."

"As you know, I traveled down to Kurland St. Mary on the mail coach with Mr. Penarth. It was a long, tedious journey. For the latter part of the trip we were the only two passengers left in the interior of the vehicle, and we spoke at some length. Mr. Penarth recognized my name and brought the conversation around to the matter of the fraudulent shipping venture and my father's considerable losses."

Joshua blew out a breath. "I did not stint in expressing my displeasure at the situation, and Mr. Penarth was quite happy to encourage me. On the last night, just before we reached Kurland St. Mary, Mr. Penarth made a proposal to me. He said he had information that Northam would be attending the christening and that if I really wished to be of service to my father, and to everyone else who had been defrauded and humiliated, he would pay me to kill Northam."

Robert sat back and tried to mask his surprise. "How much did he offer you?"

Joshua shrugged. "Enough to cover my father's losses and for a commission to the rank of major."

"Quite a considerable sum, then."

"I cannot deny it. I said that if the occasion arose I would consider carrying out his wishes." Joshua met Robert's gaze head-on. "I am not ashamed of my offer. I have killed many men for far less, Major, and so have you."

"*Did* the occasion arise?"

"I tried to talk some sense into Northam at the inn, and he taunted me with my father's losses. I threatened his life and walked away." Joshua met Robert's gaze. "As you suggested I turned my attention to an easier target and lambasted the rector instead."

"Did you encounter Northam at the rectory just before the christening began?"

Joshua frowned. "I thought I caught sight of him speaking to someone in the garden just after I arrived, so I left them to it."

"Do you know whom he was talking to?"

"I'm not sure. I could hear only his voice. The other was much quieter, but he wasn't happy." Joshua stopped speaking and sat up straight. "The thing is . . . I did go back later."

"Into the rectory?"

"Yes. I went into the rector's study and I saw him. Sitting at the desk."

"The rector?"

"No, Northam. He was hunched over, his head almost touching the surface. I went as close as I dared and then realized he was dead." Joshua swallowed hard. "I left him there, shut the door, and went back to the church."

"Why didn't you raise the alarm?" Robert asked.

"I didn't want to ruin Elizabeth's christening." Joshua's mouth twisted. "It sounds ridiculous, I know. I suspect I was also somewhat in denial of what I'd seen. I knew Northam would be discovered at some point, and there was nothing to be done for him, anyway. I thought the farther away we all were from the scene, the better."

"If you had sought him out with the intention of killing him, Captain, I can easily understand why you didn't wish to be found." Robert couldn't help but comment on his friend's somewhat disingenuous reply.

"I truly wasn't thinking properly. It was almost as if I actually *had* killed him, because that had been my intention." Joshua looked up at Robert, who assumed he must have looked skeptical. "I told you that you wouldn't believe me."

"I'm still listening," Robert said mildly. "What I don't understand is why you didn't come forward earlier to clear all this up?"

"Because I did something incredibly stupid," Joshua said. "I went to see Mr. Penarth and asked him for my money, claiming I was the killer."

Robert allowed a short silence to fall as he digested that unexpected information. "Did he give it to you?"

"He didn't believe me."

"Why not?"

"I assume because he truly believed Mr. Harrington had killed Northam."

Robert frowned. "What does that have to do with you not coming forward later to tell the truth?"

"Mr. Penarth didn't want me to do that. He said that if I didn't leave things as they were, he would take my father to court and sue for the remainder of the money still owed him."

"Your father also owed Mr. Penarth money?"

"They all did." Joshua threw out his hands. "He worked it beautifully. He pretended to be sorry about their losses and offered them loans *just until they got themselves back into credit*, which of course almost none of them could do because the interest rates were so exorbitant."

"So Mr. Penarth couldn't lose either way. He recouped his losses either from the Northams or through their victims." Robert could quite believe it. "Are you aware if Mr. Harrington also took out a loan?"

"His brother probably wouldn't have allowed it." Joshua's smile wasn't pleasant. "Even the Earl of Harrington might think twice about deceiving his own brother again."

Robert was just about to ask a question when Joshua started speaking.

"Here's where things get even more complicated. The day before he was supposed to leave, I went to see Mr. Penarth. He was just about to go out for a walk, but agreed to stop and speak to me. I . . . begged him not to go after my father, recanted my lie about being Northam's killer, and promised to do anything in my power to make sure Mr. Harrington was convicted."

"And what did he say to that?"

"He thought it all highly amusing. He told me that he had written down my confession and placed it in a secure place, and that I was now in his debt. He said he would call on me whenever he needed any dirty work to be done and that I would do it to keep him quiet."

Joshua's mouth twisted. "He turned to leave, and after a stunned moment I went after him. He ignored my calls to stop until I caught up with him, and I attempted to grab the back of his coat. He half twisted toward me, and I lost my grip, and, God help me, he fell down the cellar steps. I didn't stop to see if he was conscious, because I heard you and Lady Kurland coming in the door."

Joshua buried his face in his hands. "I swear on my mother's life that I didn't know the cellar door was open or intend for him to fall."

Robert looked down at Joshua's bowed head and slowly exhaled.

"Joshua." Robert waited until his companion looked up again, the anguish on his face evident. "Are you willing to put this in writing for me?"

"Yes." Joshua gave a shaky sigh. "In truth, I almost feel better for having unburdened myself. My father will be so disappointed in me."

"Write it down and sign it, and I will do my best to make sure your father knows none of it," Robert promised. "There is one other question I would like you to answer."

"What is it?"

"You said the Earl of Harrington wouldn't have allowed his brother to invest with Mr. Penarth again, but how did the earl find out about the shipping venture in the first place?"

Joshua blinked at him. "Because the Earl of Harrington was one of Mr. Penarth's and Lord Northam's partners in the venture. Didn't you know that?"

Robert went down the stairs, paused in his study, and then went straight out to the stables, where he located Joseph who was halfheartedly sweeping snow from the frozen cobblestones.

"I need you to take this note and go to the Queen's Head."

"Yes, sir." Joseph looked thrilled at the prospect of escaping his current task.

Robert held out the sealed note. "It's for a Mr. Barry. I want you to wait for an answer and bring it straight back to me at the house."

"Yes, Sir Robert." Joseph stowed the letter inside his coat. "Anything else, sir?"

"No, that's all. Thank you." Robert had already turned away when Joseph spoke up again.

"Mr. Coleman said to tell you that he worked out why the horses came back in the wrong order, sir."

"Which horses?"

"The one that Lord Northam rode out on came back with Captain Coles, and the captain's horse got left in the rectory stables until he picked it up the next day." Joseph chuckled heartily. "They must have both been at the rectory at the same time and got muddled up."

"I wish he'd worked that out sooner," Robert muttered as he stomped away. "It would've saved me a lot of unnecessary questioning."

"Beg pardon, sir?"

"Nothing, Joseph," Robert spoke over his shoulder. "Now, be off with you."

"Good morning, Henrietta."

Lucy took the stack of newly laundered clothing from Betty's arms and laid them on the freshly made bed. Robert hadn't come to tell her how his interview with Captain Coles had gone, and there was no sign of him in his study, so she had decided to curb her impatience and keep busy.

"Mr. Snape sent a message to say that Lord Northam's body is ready to be transported home. Robert has hired a hearse and four to take you to Northam Park as soon as the roads are open. He will accompany you."

Henrietta was sitting by the window, her expression unusually blank as she gazed out over the whiteness of the park.

"Betty will help you pack," Lucy added. "She is very good at it."

"I don't need any help." Henrietta turned to face Lucy. "It isn't exactly hard, is it?"

Lucy signaled for Betty to leave the room and then approached Henrietta.

"Would you prefer me to stay? I thought you might need some support when you were dealing with Basil's possessions."

"I'm not taking anything except his signet ring and his watch to pass down to my son. You may burn the rest of it." Henrietta raised her chin. "There is nothing else of value. If there was, I would sell it and hoard the money for myself."

Lucy felt an unexpected twinge of sympathy for Robert's cousin. "You should not worry about young Basil's guardians, Henrietta. Robert will make certain that they are honorable men who also listen and defer to you."

"Don't be so naïve, Lucy. Robert can hardly stand over them and make them behave when he lives here and I'm a hundred miles away."

"He will do his best."

"Of course he will." Henrietta smiled. "Did I ever tell you that Basil caught your husband philandering when you were pregnant with your second child?"

Even though her hands curled into fists, Lucy maintained an expression of great interest.

"My puritanical cousin, Robert, was pursuing a very specific woman by the name of Flora Rosa, a known actress and courtesan."

"I am well aware of that," Lucy replied. "She was hiding in Kurland St. Mary disguised as Polly Smith, our nursemaid, when she was murdered."

Henrietta patted her hand. "If that's what you wish to think, who can blame you?" Her mouth twisted. "I had to put up with a whole parade of Basil's whores and actresses. Eventually you realize that every man does it and just stop caring."

"I can't imagine that," Lucy said slowly. "Not caring."

"Then you're a fool." Henrietta rose to her feet and went over to the bed. "If you'll excuse me, I'll get on with my packing."

"If you wish James to take anything down for you, just

let me know." Lucy stood, too. "It would be useful to see how big a cart we need to follow the hearse."

She went slowly down the stairs, her gaze fastening on the door of Robert's study, which was now ajar. He was sitting at his desk writing furiously and looked up as she came in.

"Ah, Lucy, there you are. Do you think you can persuade our guests to accompany us to the rectory this afternoon?"

"All of them? Even Henrietta?"

"Yes, please."

"I'm sure we can accomplish that, but I'm still not sure why. Does this have anything to do with what Captain Coles told you?"

"As a matter of fact, it does." Robert signed his letter with a flourish and blotted the paper.

"Did he confess to murdering Northam?"

"No, but he did say he accidentally pushed Mr. Penarth down the cellar steps." At Lucy's gasp, he smiled. "I'm not sure if I believe it was an accident at this point, but I hope to get to the bottom of that when we all meet at the rectory for tea."

Lucy started to speak, and he held up his pen.

"I know you want all the details, but could you allow me to set out my case for everyone this afternoon? I'm hoping that a recitation of the facts might just persuade someone to reveal the truth."

"That seems rather unfair."

"I apologize, but I promise you it is necessary."

"I didn't kill either of them," Lucy said stiffly. "And I don't appreciate being shut out of your conclusions."

Robert raised an eyebrow. "Weren't you the one insisting I told you nothing earlier this week?"

"That's a completely different argument," Lucy demurred. "I assume you will bring Captain Coles to this tea party of yours as well?"

"Yes, I definitely want him there."

"Good. Then mayhap you should make sure he doesn't kill again."

"I've already relieved him of all his weapons."

"Did he have the money?"

Robert grimaced. "Unfortunately not."

"Then my father must have it. I suppose that is one of the things you will be asking him today." Lucy paused. "I'm still not sure I am ready to see him convicted of murder."

"If things turn out how I hope they will, my love, your wish will be granted."

"And if not?"

"Then he will face trial."

Robert held her gaze until she nodded, turned away, and left the room.

Her attention was caught by the sight of James and Frederick struggling down the stairs with a large trunk that presumably belonged to one of her soon-to-be departed guests. She stepped forward, hand outstretched.

"Take care! The locks aren't fastened properly!"

Even as she called out her warning the lid of the trunk burst open, sending James staggering to his knees. Frederick made a desperate grab for the handle, but it was too late to stop the trunk from tumbling down the staircase to the hall below.

"What in God's name was that?" Robert appeared at his study door, two letters in his hands and a frown on his face.

"A badly fastened trunk." Lucy rushed over to the jumble of garments cascading down the stairs. "Please don't concern yourself. I'll deal with it."

"Thank you. I've got to go to the stables. Please make sure everyone is present at the rectory by three o'clock."

Robert stepped over the debris and went toward the kitchen, leaving Lucy and the two servants on their knees gathering the clutter.

"I do apologize, my lady," James addressed Lucy. "I didn't realize the locks weren't tightly secured until it was too late."

"It's quite all right, James." She glanced over at the battered trunk. "Do you think it is reusable?"

"I doubt it, my lady." He gestured at the damaged and collapsed left side. "From what I can see, it wasn't in particularly good condition to start with."

"Then perhaps one of you could go up to the attic and find another one of similar size that we can use instead?"

James turned to Frederick. "Can you get Matty to help you? Mrs. Bloomfield has the keys."

Lucy picked up a fashionable silk gown, folded it, and set it to one side. She added two lace petticoats and reached for a cherrywood box that had a broken side. The box was surprisingly heavy to lift onto her knees. She realized why only when she opened the lid and saw buried beneath the discreet cosmetics a large leather drawstring bag. When James's attention was diverted elsewhere, she removed the bag from the box and placed it in her pocket.

Her instinct was to take her discovery to Robert, but as he had insisted that all would be revealed that very afternoon, perhaps she would wait until then.

Chapter 18

Lucy used whatever excuse would work best to ensure that all her guests were curious enough to accept her invitation to the rectory. She hadn't been averse to slightly embroidering the truth if necessary to persuade any waverers, and she was secretly proud of her efforts. She'd left her children happily playing in the nursery and brought Matthew and Frederick just in case Robert needed reinforcements, as the rectory staff were mainly female.

The drawing room at the rectory was not often used, and in Rose's absence it hadn't been heated, which meant it had a dank feel to it. Lucy made sure that both the fires were well banked and the curtains were drawn back to allow the winter sun to shine in to its fullest extent.

Aunt Jane pulled her aside as the Harringtons entered the room.

"What is going on, Lucy? I didn't realize that the entire village was going to be present. I have more packing to do and very little interest in this nonsense."

"It won't take long," Lucy reassured her. "Robert has some important information to share, and he thought it better to do it with everyone in one place rather than risk any misunderstandings."

"Goodness me," Jane murmured as Rose was carried into the room swathed in blankets and sat tenderly in a chair by the fire by Dr. Fletcher. "She doesn't look well at all, does she?"

"No, she does not." Lucy agreed. "It cannot be easy for her to deal with her husband being accused of murder."

"It certainly is regrettable." Aunt Jane sighed. "I will go over and speak to her to assure myself that her precarious health can stand this ridiculous assembly."

Robert came into the room with a reluctant-looking Mr. Barry at his side and strode over to join Lucy.

"Well done, my dear. You managed to get everyone here."

"It took some doing. If you aren't quick about it I suspect some of them are ready to revolt and leave at the earliest opportunity. I also have something very important to tell you—"

He grabbed hold of her elbow, marched her out into the hall, and put both hands on her shoulders.

"Listen, my love. I know this might be hard for you to hear, but if I am proved right, then I swear that I will do everything in my power to help your father recover from this."

"But I don't think it is him!" Lucy burst out. "I think you're looking at this the wrong way, and—"

He pressed a gentle finger to her lips. "It's all right. I understand that you are desperate for it to be anyone but your father."

"But—"

"Please don't upset yourself, my love. I have everything in hand. I'd better start. I have Matthew and Frederick stationed at the doors."

Lucy met his gaze. "Robert, you are making a terrible mistake."

"I understand why you might think that, my dear, but as I said, I will make sure that everything turns out for the best, I promise you."

Lucy glared after him as he walked away. So be it. If he wanted to make a complete and utter fool of himself, who was she to argue with him?

Robert strode to the center of the room and loudly cleared his throat.

"Thank you all for joining me at the rectory this afternoon." He bowed to Lucy's father. "And thank you for allowing me to hold this meeting here, which cannot have been easy for you."

"I seek the truth, Kurland," the rector replied. "That is all I care about."

"As do I." Robert looked around the room, his gaze lingered on Captain Coles, who was white-faced, and on Max, who was already fidgeting and glancing longingly at the clock.

"I wish to start by expressing my displeasure with all of you. Almost every single person in this room connected to me by marriage, birth, or friendship has at some point lied to me. In truth this has been the most difficult murder case I have ever had the misfortune to encounter. None of you have covered yourself in glory. All of you have attempted to obstruct me, and I am done with it."

He waited as Lucy took a seat between Henrietta and Mrs. Stanford.

"Lord Northam had many enemies, and it appears that the fates decreed that several of them ended up here in Kurland St. Mary on the occasion of our daughter Elizabeth's christening. Lady Northam was originally invited to attend but didn't reply, leaving my wife to believe that neither she nor her husband would be present. As it turned out, the Northams, whether they intended to or not, insinuated themselves into what was meant to be a celebration."

Robert's tone hardened. "I politely asked Northam to leave, but he seemed determined to make himself as obnoxious as possible. In truth, I was relieved when he didn't show up at the church so that the baptism could proceed in all its solemn and spiritual dignity.

"Unfortunately, what I didn't know was that at some time that same morning, Northam had already met his end in the study at the rectory. But who would want to murder him on such an auspicious occasion?" Robert allowed his gaze to rest on the rector. "Often in such cases, the most obvious answer is the correct one—that Northam was killed by the owner of the letter opener that stabbed him through the heart. The owner being the rector himself.

"At first, I wasn't inclined to believe that was the truth. I've been privileged to know Mr. Harrington my entire life, and he is now not only my father-in-law but also my dearly loved aunt's husband." He smiled at Rose, who had taken a turn for the better since insisting she was a murderer. "A woman who is currently carrying his child.

"Despite my close ties to Mr. Harrington and the deceased, I was determined to be as impartial as possible." He gestured at Lucy who still looked indignant. "Ask my wife if you don't believe me.

"There were also unexplained disappearances, and reports of various members of the christening party being seen in Northam's company, which led me to believe that what appeared on the surface to be a very simple matter was far more complex than I had realized."

Henrietta snorted. "Trust you to unnecessarily complicate things, Cousin. Mr. Harrington murdered my husband so that he could take control of my mother's fortune and leave it all to his new brat."

"Ambrose didn't know I'd changed my will, Henrietta," Rose spoke up. "No one was supposed to know until I died—except your husband paid someone to reveal private and personal information to him."

"I'm glad he did," Henrietta snapped back. "Except it cost him his life, didn't it?"

Robert gently cleared his throat and brought their attention back to him. "Cousin Henrietta does bring up an interesting point. If Mr. Harrington didn't know about the change in the will, why would he murder Northam? He had a substantial private income and a new wife with a fortune of her own. He hardly needed money—or did he?

"On further investigation I discovered that Mr. Harrington had invested in a fraudulent shipping scheme and had lost a considerable portion of not only his income but also his capital. The arrival of Mr. Penarth at the Queen's Head in pursuit of the Northams and other debtors only reinforced my opinion that this scheme was central to the murder."

"My father was also among the shareholders." Joshua spoke up. "He was encouraged to invest in the company by his friend Mr. Harrington, and also lost a lot of money. To make matters worse he took out a loan to cover his losses from Mr. Penarth with ruinously high interest rates that will take me the rest of my life to pay off."

Robert gestured at Joshua. "Yet another person with a grudge against Lord Northam with the opportunity and the training to carry out a murder." He swung around.

"And then we come to Max here, who owed Northam a considerable sum of money for gaming debts. Max was seen by several people at the Queen's Head confronting Northam and demanding a duel, which Northam turned down in a humiliating fashion."

"We cleared Max, Kurland." The earl spoke up. "Don't you remember that?"

"Ah, yes, our little chat when you attempted to use both your family connection with me and your political influence to silence my investigation into your son." Robert stared hard at the earl.

"Is there a point to this?" the earl demanded. "Or do you just like hearing the sound of your own voice?"

"Hush, David." The countess intervened. "I am very interested in the conclusions Sir Robert is drawing, and you should be, too."

"I can't help but agree with you, my lady." Robert

bowed. "Your husband's continued attempts to mislead me or outright lie to my face have proven remarkably infuriating."

"I value my family, Kurland." The earl looked down his extremely autocratic nose at Robert. "I will do anything to protect them."

"Which seems to include offering your own brother up to the authorities for a crime he might not have committed. Where is your renowned family loyalty for him—especially when he had already agreed to do you a favor."

The rector's head snapped up, and the earl took a step in Robert's direction.

"What the devil do you mean by that, sir?"

Robert addressed his next question to the rector. "Did you agree to act as an intermediary between Northam and your brother to pay off Max's debts?"

"I . . ." Lucy's father looked over at the earl, who scowled at him. "I'm sorry, David, but I think it is time to speak the truth."

"Very well." The earl turned to face Robert. "Yes. That's exactly what I did."

"Which is why you had five hundred pounds with you when you arrived in Kurland St. Mary?" Robert asked.

"I didn't want to deal with that scoundrel directly in case I lost my temper and killed the man."

Robert let the earl's words ring around the room before he spoke again.

"Was there any money in it for the rector?"

"A trifling sum," the earl said gruffly. "To thank him for his willingness to help out."

"Were you aware that your brother was in financial distress?"

"We're not the kind of family who discuss such matters, Kurland." The earl took out his pocket watch. "Now, have you quite finished with this ridiculous charade? My wife and I need to complete our packing before we leave on the morrow."

Robert set his jaw. "To be honest, my lord, the fact that Mr. Harrington even agreed to help you is surprising, since you are the reason why he is in this mess in the first place."

"I don't know what you are talking about," the earl blustered, his face going redder by the second.

Robert turned to the rector. "Who suggested that you invest in the shipping company venture, sir?"

"My brother did, why?" Lucy's father looked uncertainly from Robert to the obviously fuming earl.

"Do you blame him for your losses?"

"Of course not. How was he to know that the tip he passed on would result in me losing money? He's given me excellent advice in the past."

Robert turned to Mr. Barry, who had attempted to hide himself in a corner.

"Mr. Barry? Can you confirm who the original stake-holders of the shipping scheme were?"

"Yes, sir. Mr. Penarth, Lord Northam, Sir Walter Sherborn, and the Earl of Harrington." He held up a document with a wax seal dangling from the edge. "I have the legal documentation here."

The rector slowly stood and faced his brother, his hands clenched into fists. "You were one of the *instigators* of that scheme?"

"There's no need to be upset, Ambrose. It was merely one of many such enterprises that my business manager recommended to me. I had no idea that it was fake." The earl made a dismissive gesture. "When I return home I'll make sure to reprimand him."

"When I wrote to you for advice about what to do, you did nothing! You *said* nothing of your part in this!" The rector, who had a temper to match his brother's, was obviously not willing to let the matter rest. "Did you feel no responsibility, David? No shame? And then you have the *gall* to ask me to act for you on the matter of Northam, a man I have every reason to dislike, but I did it for you because you are my *family*." He snorted. "It appears that your loyalty flows only toward yourself."

Robert stepped between the two men. "Mr. Harrington, did your brother at any point suggest you keep the money owed to Northam for Max's debts?"

"Why would he do that?" the rector asked.

"Or to put it another way, did you at any point consider *keeping* that money for yourself?"

"I did neither of those things." The rector paused. "Wait—are you suggesting that I might have killed Northam at my brother's behest, or for my own financial gain?"

Robert bowed. "Yes, sir. That is exactly what I am suggesting."

"But that's preposterous!"

Robert ignored his outburst. "Do you still have the money your brother gave you?"

"No, I handed it over to Northam the morning of the christening. I swear it."

"You told me that you handed the money directly to Northam, my lord. Which is it?" Robert inquired looking back at the earl.

"Does it matter?" the earl demanded. "Northam got his damned money, and as far as I'm concerned that is the end of it."

"But we didn't find the money with Northam. Either it was stolen from him in the rectory or he gave it to the now-deceased Mr. Penarth." Robert reminded him.

Mr. Barry cleared his throat. "Mr. Penarth didn't have it, Sir Robert. I am certain of that."

Robert looked around the room. "Then what became of it? Surely, if we can answer that question, the truth will be revealed."

He frowned as his wife raised her hand. "What is it, my dear?"

She held out a leather bag. "I believe this is the money everyone is looking for."

"Good Lord." Robert blinked. "Wherever did you—?"

"Give it to me! It's mine!" Henrietta reached across Lucy, grabbed the bag, and hugged it to her chest. "It's all I have left of him."

Lucy faced her. "You told me the money had been stolen from your room."

"Mayhap I lied." Henrietta shrugged. "Did you go through my things? I knew you were up to something when you offered to help me pack."

"You forgot to secure the locks on your trunk. When it was being transported down the stairs, it broke open and distributed the contents all over my hall," Lucy said evenly. "I found the bag when I was folding your clothes. It was purely by chance, although I was beginning to suspect you had been lying to me all along."

Lucy looked back at Robert, who didn't look particularly pleased at her intervention and offered him a sweet smile. "I do beg your pardon, my dear. You didn't offer me the opportunity to tell you this earlier."

"It's of no matter." Robert faced Henrietta. "Did you and Northam plan this together?"

"So I believed." Henrietta glanced over at the Harringtons, who had gathered in a tight circle. "He just wanted to make them suffer and make them pay."

"But how did you end up with the money if Northam never came back to Kurland Hall that morning?" Lucy asked slowly.

"That's an excellent question," Robert agreed.

"I knew my husband well enough not to trust him completely," Henrietta said. "I always try to be one step ahead."

"Which is why you left the house before him and Captain Coles on foot," Lucy said. "When I came to your room later that morning, when you were insisting that Basil had disappeared, you had already been out. That's why you were in your petticoats."

"Yes, I knew Basil planned to pick up the money from the rector, because while he was sleeping I read a note he'd received and concealed from me. When I challenged him about it he told me to meet him at the church, where he would hand over the money. He planned to go on to speak to Mr. Penarth at the Queen's Head. He said he didn't want to have any cash on him just in case Mr. Penarth attacked him. I waited for at least half an hour, but he never appeared."

Everyone was listening intently as Henrietta continued to clutch the leather purse to her chest. "Eventually, just as I was about to leave, I saw Basil walking his horse back toward the rectory. I went through the garden and caught him skulking around looking for a place to hide his bag of coins." Her face twisted. "He wasn't pleased to see me. I knew then that I was right and that he hadn't planned on coming back or sharing the money with me. We argued, and he shoved me to the ground and stormed off into the rectory. I followed him into the study, came up behind him, wrapped my hand around his chest, and stabbed him with the letter opener."

"You killed him because he was planning on absconding with the money and abandoning you and your children?" Lucy asked as gently as she could.

"Of course I killed him, but not just for that." Henrietta met Lucy's gaze and laughed without humor. "He had some ridiculous plan to take the money and go back to London. The fool fancied himself in *love* for God's sake, and—"

"Stop."

Lucy turned to see her aunt Jane push her husband's restraining arm away and march toward Henrietta.

"If you are about to suggest that your disgusting and

degenerate husband had any feelings whatsoever for my daughter, then I will slap you silly."

Lucy met Robert's startled gaze over the top of Henrietta's head.

"He ruined her life." Lady Jane spat the words out, her outrage palpable. "He dishonored and ravished her!"

Lucy inserted herself between her trembling aunt and Henrietta. "Are you saying that Julia was involved with Northam, Aunt?"

"Involved? As in romantically?" Aunt Jane's smile was hard to look at. "He came into our house, ingratiated himself with her, and ruined her for sport."

Henrietta laughed. "Good Lord, countess, how dramatic! I can understand how a silly overprotected girl like Julia might come to care for a man like my husband, but how he came to believe he was in love with *her,* beggars belief!"

There was a sharp crack as Aunt Jane fulfilled her promise and swung back her hand. Her palm connected solidly with Henrietta's cheek. Even as she winced, Lucy dove down to the floor to pick up the money Henrietta had dropped as she instinctively tried to protect herself. Lucy turned and handed it to Robert as his cousin reeled in shock, one hand pressed to her face.

"Shame on you." Aunt Jane's voice shook as she stepped back. "For caring more about your husband's appalling betrayal of his marriage vows than about the child he destroyed."

"But I'll wager you're glad he's dead, aren't you?" Henrietta said.

"If you hadn't killed him I was perfectly prepared to do it myself." Aunt Jane met her gaze unflinchingly, and Henrietta was the first to look away. "But may God have mercy on your soul."

Robert motioned to Dr. Fletcher. "Would you ask Frederick and Matthew to come in and escort Lady Northam to a place where she can be secured?"

Just before she was led out, Henrietta raised her chin and looked slowly around the room. "I'm still glad I killed him. I don't regret a thing."

"There is a cellar here with a stout locked door," Lucy said. "I'll accompany Lady Northam and make sure she has everything she needs."

Robert moved over to the sideboard and helped himself to a glass of the rector's brandy as the other occupants of the room all stared at the door closing behind Henrietta. He was close enough to the Harringtons to overhear their conversation.

"There, there my dear," the earl said heartily. "Everything is going to be all right, now, don't fret."

"I doubt it." The countess pulled out of her husband's grasp. "Sir Robert was right about one thing, David. You did create this mess. If you hadn't gone into that scheme with Northam, he wouldn't have been allowed in our house to speak to your secretary and had the chance to make up to Julia."

"That's rather harsh, my dear," the earl protested. "Perhaps you should have been chaperoning her better."

"Don't you dare suggest I was lax in my attentions to her. I thought she was with her betrothed. I was deceived by everyone!" the countess snapped. "And worse than that, you lied to me about paying off Northam. You *promised* me you would never give that dreadful man a penny."

"I wanted him gone," the earl said. "I thought the best way to achieve that was by paying him off."

"Which is why you involved your son and your brother in a murder investigation. Either one of them could have been prosecuted!" The countess shook her head. "I am extremely angry with you about all of it, David."

At this point Robert walked over to the earl and waited until he had his full attention.

"What is it now, Kurland?"

"I believe this belongs to you." Robert dropped the

heavy leather money pouch into the earl's hand. "I certainly don't want it. Perhaps you might consider helping the brother you almost fed to the wolves."

For once the earl didn't speak, and after another withering glare, Robert turned on his heel and went to offer the rector a glass of his own brandy.

"How are you holding up, sir?" Robert sat beside him on the couch.

"I am still rather . . . bewildered as to how it all turned out." The rector mopped his forehead with his handkerchief. "Did you know this would happen when you asked us all to gather together?"

"I hoped there would be some resolution, yes, but I cannot say I thought it would be this one." Robert studied his glass. "I had begun to believe that the earl hadn't been truthful with me or with you, and I hoped that by exposing those lies, one of you would finally confess."

"It sounds like my sister-in-law would've happily done the honors." The rector shuddered and reached for his wife's hand. "There are many role models of female vengeance, such as the esteemed Clytemnestra in the Greek plays. I never thought to encounter such an antagonist in real life."

"Possibly two," Robert said dryly. "Don't forget that Henrietta actually followed through and murdered her own husband."

"Indeed." The rector looked at his wife. "Are you all right, my dear?"

"I am not as shocked as you might think," Rose confessed. "Henrietta always had a very strong sense of what was right and wrong as long as it related solely to herself. I'm not surprised that she took Northam's betrayal so badly." She sighed. "But she should not have taken the law into her own hands and killed him."

Robert nodded. "I must admit that in this instance, I fear the law would have let us all down. Even if the earl had attempted to take Northam to court over what happened to Julia, she would still have emerged as the one with the ruined reputation."

"And Henrietta would never be able to bring a case against her own husband even if he did abandon her," the rector said as Rose nodded

"Am I correct, sir, that you didn't know that the money the earl gave to you was to keep Northam away from Julia?" Robert asked.

"I thought it was for Max." The rector sighed. "A somewhat extortionate sum to be sure, but I was once a young man about town myself and saw others end up in considerable and insurmountable debt." He paused. "Despite my calling, I am not quite in charity with my brother right now. His desperate attempts to preserve his family have led to more harm than good."

"I can't argue with you on that, sir." Robert rose from his seat and kissed his aunt's cheek. "I think you should go back to bed, Rose. The excitement must be too much for you."

"I have never been so shocked in my life, Robert." Rose touched his shoulder, her expression vulnerable. "What will happen to Henrietta?"

"I'll keep her secure in Kurland St. Mary while I confer with the chief magistrate's court in Hertford. I am unsure how a trial for the wife of a deceased peer would be undertaken." Robert patted her hand. "I promise I will do the best I can for her."

"I know you will, my dearest boy." Tears glinted in Rose's eyes. "I'd better concentrate on recovering my strength, hadn't I? Henrietta's children might need me."

"I'd concentrate on yourself for a while first, Rose," Robert reminded her. "They are safe and secure in the countryside in Northam Park with their father's family. Do you want me to write to them about Henrietta and Northam?"

"If you would." Rose nodded and dabbed at her eyes as her tears finally fell. "I don't feel quite up to the task."

Robert watched as the rector and Dr. Fletcher escorted Rose back to bed. He turned to find the Stanfords coming toward him.

"That was all rather . . . unexpected," Andrew said. "If Lady Northam needs representation, I am still willing to offer my services."

"Thank you." Robert blew out a breath. "I must admit that I wasn't anticipating her willingness to admit to a murder in public."

"She believes she was justified." Mrs. Stanford spoke up. "And, to some extent, I can follow her logic, because Lord Northam was a truly despicable man."

"Whom she loved," Robert added. "And who in her eyes betrayed her."

"Indeed." Andrew glanced down at his wife. "As this appears to be something of a family matter, Sophia and I will walk back to the hall and finish our preparations for leaving on the morrow. Thank you for your hospitality."

"Discreet and polite as always, Andrew." Robert shook his friend's hand. "Next time you visit I can assure you that things will be back to normal."

"One can only hope."

Robert's faint smile died as he saw them off through the front door and returned to the drawing room, where Joshua sat alone by the fire.

"Did you write that letter for me?" Robert asked.

"Yes, Major. I left it on your desk." Joshua glanced up at Robert. "What do you intend to do with me now?"

"Let you go and live your life."

Joshua shot to his feet. "You . . . believe me? That it was an accident?"

"I spoke to Mr. Jarvis. He thinks he left the cellar open when he rushed out that morning, which means there is probable doubt that you deliberately orchestrated the move yourself." Robert met Joshua's gaze. "And, to be honest, Captain, even though Mr. Penarth is dead, for the foreseeable future you will still be busy repairing your family fortune, which surely is penance enough?"

Joshua grabbed Robert's hand with both of his. "Thank you, Major. Thank you so much."

"I've also spoken to Mr. Barry. He promises me that he will erase any mention of you he finds in Mr. Penarth's records."

"I appreciate that, sir." Joshua gave a shuddering sigh. "I swear I will do better in the future."

"I damn well hope so. You are my daughter's godfather after all." Robert gestured at the door. "Perhaps you might walk Mr. Barry back to the inn before you return to Kurland Hall. As he will be in control of Mr. Penarth's assets for the foreseeable future, it might be a good opportunity to ask about restructuring your father's loan."

Joshua was just about to turn away when Robert remembered something else. "Just one more thing. Did you accidentally take Northam's horse at some point?"

"Yes, how did you know?" Joshua blinked. "I was in such a hurry to leave that I mounted the first familiar horse I saw in the rectory stables. I only realized it was the wrong one when I reached Kurland Hall."

"Which is why you offered to go down and pick your own horse up."

"I realized that if anyone noticed, it would place me at the rectory when I'd neglected to mention that I'd been there." Joshua hesitated. "Does this change anything, sir?"

"No, I just like to untangle all the snarls."

"And get all the puzzle pieces in the correct order." Joshua saluted him. "Thank you for everything, Major."

Robert nodded. "At ease, Captain. You're dismissed."

Robert made no further attempt to go and speak to the Harringtons, and instead he went to find his wife, who was in the kitchen instructing the rectory staff on how to deal with the detainee in the cellar. He waited politely until she had finished, added a few more pertinent instructions of his own, and offered her his arm.

"Where are we going?" Lucy asked.

"Just into your father's study. I have no wish to speak in front of your uncle, who in my opinion is the primary reason this entire debacle got out of hand."

"I can't argue with that." Lucy turned to face him as she shut the door. "Do you think Henrietta would have confessed if we hadn't found the money in her belongings?"

"*You* found it, my dear." He met her gaze head-on. "And yes, before you remark upon it I should have listened to you before I started speaking. I was wrong to ignore you, but I was very worried that your father was guilty. I'd almost decided that he'd killed Northam at the behest of the earl. I thought to save you pain."

"Then you are a fool."

"I can't argue with that."

They stared at each other for a tense moment before Lucy offered him an approving nod.

"Bringing everyone together like that was a masterstroke, Robert. Henrietta had to listen to the Harringtons arguing about her husband's murder, and her sense of injustice eventually outweighed her caution." She shook her head. "She's such a good liar that I had no idea how I was going to bring her to the point of admitting what she'd done, but you managed it with the help of Aunt Jane."

"I certainly wasn't expecting that," Robert admitted.

"I couldn't imagine what had pushed Henrietta to finally kill Basil after all those years of supporting him." Lucy said. "I didn't realize she believed she had a rival in Julia. It all made perfect sense, then."

Robert sat on the front edge of the rector's desk. "Her reasoning was purely selfish. If she could convince everyone that your father was a murderer, she would regain control over her mother's fortune, hurt the Harringtons, and get revenge on her husband. She didn't even care about the damage done to Julia, just that Northam had *dared* to suggest he cared for someone other than her."

"I wonder what Julia thinks about that?" Lucy bit her

lip. "Aunt Jane said she would be traveling abroad. That is what usually happens when a woman is carrying an unwanted child."

Robert whistled. "Good Lord. I hadn't thought of that."

"I can't quite bring myself to ask Aunt Jane the truth. I fear her grief would be unmanageable," Lucy confessed.

"Her grief? Good Lord, Lucy, that woman was ready to murder Northam if given the opportunity."

"She can both grieve and hate at the same time," Lucy said softly. "She is a mother fighting for her child."

Robert went over and drew his wife into his arms. "She'll be all right. I am more concerned about the earl, who has managed to alienate his entire family."

"He doesn't deserve your sympathy." Lucy rubbed her cheek against his waistcoat. "I will certainly not be seeking either his approval or his countenance in the future."

"Don't worry, neither will I. His offer of that safe seat in parliament can go to the devil."

"Thank you." She kissed his chin. "I'm sure another opportunity will arise that you can accept with a clear conscience."

Robert doubted that under the present king, but under the circumstances he was willing to go along with her. He was quite happy with his quiet existence in the countryside.

"I told Captain Coles that I do not intend to press charges against him."

"Why ever not?" Her smile turned into a glare.

"Because I truly think it was an accident, and even more important, I cannot prove otherwise."

"And Captain Coles is an old and valued friend whose word means something to you."

"There is that." Robert searched her face. "Are you still angry with me for ignoring you earlier?"

"No, I understand why you thought it necessary. Even

while you were speaking, I was desperately trying to work out exactly *how* Henrietta could have murdered her husband when she helpfully confessed all."

"Her arrogance was her undoing."

Lucy worried at her lip. "What will happen to her?"

"To be honest, I am not sure how to proceed against the wife of a deceased peer," Robert said. "Should she be tried in the House of Lords, or should she be treated as a commoner? I intend to consult with both the Hertford courts and the High Court in London to resolve the matter as soon as possible."

"She can't live in my father's cellar forever," Lucy pointed out. "Rose isn't well enough to deal with her."

"Would you rather she stayed at Kurland Hall?"

His wife made a face. "If she must."

"Then if I haven't heard back from the courts within the next week, I will arrange to have her brought to us. If the authorities decide not to prosecute her, I suspect they'll send her back to her husband's family up north where someone can keep an eye on her." Robert hesitated. "Even though what she has done is awful, she is still my cousin, and I will argue for leniency."

"I suspect Rose will be very grateful for that."

Robert brushed a kiss on his wife's forehead and stepped back. "I am tired of this, my love. I never want to deal with another dead body again. I want our visitors to leave and our house to get back to normal."

"I can't argue with any of that." Lucy smiled back at him. "As far as I am concerned, the sooner they all leave the better!"

Robert took her hand. "Let's go home and see our children, shall we?"

"But what about our guests?" Lucy countered.

"Considering their behavior, they can all make their own damn arrangements to get back to the hall." Robert set off purposefully for the stables. "After we've spent time in the nursery I will take you up to our rooms, where we will dine in solitary splendor, and then I'm taking you to bed."

"Robert!" Lucy pressed a hand to her cheek. "Someone might hear you."

"I don't care if they do." He snatched a quick kiss and increased his pace. "And to be honest, my love, from past experience they are far more likely to hear *you*."

He smiled as she turned crimson and stopped speaking entirely. As he settled her into the gig, he could only hope he'd be able to apologize sufficiently before she found her voice again.